the Memory Key

the Memory Key

LIANA LIU

HARPER TEEN
An Imprint of HarperCollinsPublishers

HarperTeen is an imprint of HarperCollins Publishers.

The Memory Key
Copyright © 2015 by Liana Liu
www.epicreads.com

Library of Congress Cataloging-in-Publication Data
Liu, Liana.
 The Memory Key / Liana Liu. — First edition.
  pages cm
  Summary: "In the not-so-distant future, everyone is implanted with a memory key to stave off a virulent form of Alzeimer's. Lora Mint fears her memories of her deceased mother are fading, but when her memory key is damaged she has perfect recall — of everything — which brings her mother's memory vividly back, but may also drive Lora mad" — Provided by publisher.
  ISBN 978-0-06-230664-7 (hardcover)
  [1. Memory—Fiction. 2. Mothers and daughters—Fiction. 3. Science fiction.] I. Title.
PZ7.L73933Mem 2015   2014005868
[Fic]—dc23   CIP
                                                                     AC

Typography by Ellice M. Lee
15 16 17 18 19 PC/RRDH 10 9 8 7 6 5 4 3 2 1
❖
First Edition

FOR MY PARENTS

1.

MY EARLIEST MEMORY IS OF MY MOTHER.

I run toward her, small feet smacking the floor, and when I'm in her arms, so relieved to be in her arms, she is the softest skin, the sweetest smell, a voice that is my favorite song. I must be around three years old—late, I know, for an earliest memory. But I didn't get my memory key implanted until I turned four.

My best friend Wendy thinks she can remember being born, although Keep Corp claims this is impossible. Their user manual clearly states: "Your first memory will be of a time not before infancy." But Wendy says she has nightmares about the bright and cold and shock and fear. I believe her. She's my best friend and though she likes to exaggerate, she doesn't lie. Besides, her key was implanted early, just after her first birthday.

Wendy is normal in that way. Most parents rush to get their children memory keys because they think it'll give their kids a competitive edge. My mother thought otherwise. It's a preventative measure against Vergets disease, she would say, not a learning aid. She thought such early implantation was unnecessary and possibly detrimental to brain development. I suppose she would know since she was a scientist at Keep Corp until she died—five years ago, in a car accident.

Five years. On the one hand, it's only been that long. On the other hand, it's already been *that long*. I flip-flop between these two ways of thinking, but in either case, the problem remains the same: lately, I've noticed my memories of her seem fainter, vaguer, as though worn down from overuse. I used to be able to see her by just closing my eyes. Now I strain to call her image to me, reminding myself of the facts. Black hair, pale skin, twisty half smile. Even then, the pieces don't necessarily form a picture.

Occasionally I wonder whether I'd remember more, or better, if my mother had had my key implanted sooner. I know I'm being irrational. Memory keys are designed to work just like natural human memory; as natural memories grow dusty and faded, so do memory key memories.

Still, sometimes it feels as if I'm losing her all over again.

I don't mean to sound so tragic.

I'm fine, really. I'm fine.

This is how fine I am: the day after our high school graduation, Wendy and I are drinking milk shakes at the Middleton Mall and we're not talking about loss or grief or memory. No, we're discussing her new boyfriend, a football player named Dan. "He can bench-press three hundred pounds," she says.

I tell her I don't know what that means.

"His arms are huge." She holds her hands apart to show how huge.

"He should probably see a doctor about that," I say.

"Dan has this cute friend . . . ," she says.

I shake my head. Wendy is always setting me up with her new boyfriend's friends, and it always ends one of two ways. Either I like the friend and we all double-date until Wendy and her boyfriend break up. Or I don't like the friend and we all double-date until Wendy and her boyfriend break up.

She looks at me with eyes mournfully wide, lips a squiggle of sadness. Wendy is famously good at using her face to convince people to do what she wants them to do. "We'll all go out this weekend. It'll be so much fun," she says. "Please, Lora?"

"No, thanks," I say, immune to her miserable expression. We've been friends for so long that I know all her tricks.

She glares at me. I glare at her.

She frowns at me. I frown at her.

Then we're suddenly interrupted: "There you are, girls!" The words soar across the room, somehow simultaneously cheerful and reprimanding, while also being clearly directed at us; the voice is *that* impressively expressive.

Wendy and I look up apprehensively, as if we expect to be punished for fighting. But we smile when we see the elderly woman shuffling toward us. She is so frail it seems a miracle that she is able to stand upright unsupported, let alone shout at us with such strength. It takes a long minute for her to walk to our table.

"Good morning, Ms. Pearl!" Wendy and I say together, perfectly together, as we used to do in middle school, even though
middle school is years past. Even though it's not morning, it's
mid-afternoon. But every day our class used to greet her this
way, and the habit is too strong to break.

Ms. Pearl tilts her head to one side, accepting our greeting
as her due. It's been a while since I last saw her. She retired
after we started high school. There was a rumor she was forced
out by parents claiming she taught a partisan view of current
events. I didn't believe any of it: not that Ms. Pearl was biased (I
recall her being critical of everyone and everything, regardless
of political affiliation), and not that the school would force her
out. She was the history teacher there for decades. It had surely
been her time to retire.

"It's so nice to see you!" says Wendy. Then she asks Ms.
Pearl about her shopping, and her summer, and isn't it a hot
day, and so on, and so forth, all charmingly polite. This is Wendy's way.

But Ms. Pearl appears distracted, though that might be the
effect of her outfit. She used to wear trim pantsuits, but today
she is dressed in a faded floral smock and white sneakers. It's
unsettling; it's like we're seeing her in her pajamas.

"Girls, please remind me of your names," she says.

Wendy and I glance at each other. Ms. Pearl never forgot
anyone's name. She was known for remembering students she
had dozens of years earlier, in contrast to our grumpy chemistry
teacher who seemed to forget us the instant we left his classroom.

I suppose these two opposite examples prove the power of mind over memory—mind over memory key—demonstrating that with enough effort, anyone can remember or forget anything.

Except now even Ms. Pearl has succumbed; she waits for us to remind her of our names. As we reintroduce ourselves, a boy in a blue jacket hurries over to our table. "Ms. Pearl, I've been looking for you," he says.

"No, I've been looking for *you*," she says, her tone so dry it crackles, and for a moment she is exactly the teacher I know, chiding an impertinent student.

But the kid takes it agreeably. "You're probably right," he says.

Ms. Pearl nods and turns back to us. "This is my assistant, Raul."

Wendy smoothes her long hair over her shoulders as she says hello. I can tell she is flirting by the way her voice lilts.

"It's nice to meet you." Raul smiles, a smile that takes up the whole of his face. I guess he's around our age. He has wavy brownish hair and dark skin, and he's cute. That's why Wendy is flirting. Though truly, she flirts with everyone: boys, girls, cats, dogs, lampposts. It's automatic.

"It's nice to meet you, too." Wendy beams.

I sip my milk shake.

"These young ladies were my students," says Ms. Pearl.

"When we were in sixth grade," says Wendy. "Six years ago? Seven?"

"A million years ago," I say.

"A million years? That's a long time." Raul looks at me, eyebrows raised.

"Everybody knows time flies," I say.

"Then I suppose we'd better be on our way," says Ms. Pearl. She tells us it was nice to see us, and we tell her the same. Raul tells us it was nice to meet us, and we tell him the same. Then he takes Ms. Pearl's arm and she allows him to lead her away. We watch them move slowly across the marble mall floors.

Wendy says, "Ms. Pearl is really old. Was she always so old?"

"I can't believe she couldn't remember our names."

She chews on the tip of her straw. "Raul is cute."

"Are you ready to go? It's getting late," I say.

"*Everybody knows time flies*," she says mockingly. Then she grins. "You should go out with Raul."

"You're hopeless." I get up from the table and push in my chair.

"No, Lora, I'm hope*ful*." She stands and adjusts the straps of her dress. Wendy is tall and long-limbed, but the rest of her is so small and delicate—dainty nose and rosebud mouth, fine bones and slim hands—that she somehow seems altogether small and delicate, even though she is four inches taller than me.

We link our arms and glide together across the slippery floor. The place is unusually quiet, despite the music thumping down from the speakers in the ceiling. It's because there aren't many other people here. A number of stores have recently closed. We pass a stretch of dark windows, AVAILABLE FOR

LEASE signs plastered on the dingy glass. "When did it get so empty here? It wasn't like this last time, was it?" I say.

Wendy shrugs and asks what I'm going to wear tonight. Her family is having my family over to celebrate our graduation. Her family consists of her, her parents, her brother Tim, several uncles and aunts, and assorted cousins of assorted ages. My family consists of me and my dad. And Aunt Austin, if she doesn't have to work late. But she probably has to work late. She always has to work late.

The exit doors slide open at our approach, and we step into the sunshine. It's hot outside, a drowsy, drowning hot that is almost unbearable.

"Welcome to summer," says Wendy.

"Maybe I'll wear my blue dress." I look across the street. There's a white van at the curb, and that boy Raul is helping an old man into the backseat. I squint. No, it's not Raul, just another kid in another blue jacket identical to Raul's jacket—that's what confused me.

"The dress with the flowers?" asks Wendy.

"Embroidered straps, no flowers."

"Tiny white flowers along the hem," she says.

"Definitely no flowers." I look again across the street and see Ms. Pearl walking toward us. "She's back," I murmur to Wendy, but Wendy is still trying to convince me she knows my wardrobe better than I do.

Then I notice the car.

I notice the car and I stop noticing everything else: the

searing sun, the lustrous white of the van, the insistence in Wendy's voice, the sweat sticky on my face.

So it is not until my skull cracks against the concrete that I realize I'm no longer with Wendy, walking and talking. No, I have raced into the road and grabbed Ms. Pearl away from that oncoming car with such momentum that I've crashed us both down to the burning black asphalt.

There is a rubber screech.

A burst of horn.

Flailing voices.

Ms. Pearl sighs a quivering sound. And then we are surrounded. We are surrounded and separated and lifted upright and asked if we're all right.

"Lora?" Wendy grips my hand. She is sitting beside me on the curb.

"Where'd Ms. Pearl go? Is she okay?" I ask.

"She's fine, totally fine," someone else says. "How do *you* feel?"

I tilt my gaze and find Raul staring at me, his stare so intense it makes me dizzy.

Or maybe I'm just dizzy from hitting my head on hard ground. "I'm fine," I tell him.

"I'll take her to the hospital," says Wendy. "My car is down the block."

"No, really, I'm fine." I lean forward, eager to get off the hot concrete, reluctant to go to the hospital. Wendy reaches out, but Raul is there first. His arm slides around my shoulders.

"Is that all right?" he asks.

"Yes, thanks." I firm my feet and straighten my legs as he holds me up. Then once I'm up, he still holds me. And I'm suddenly aware of the warmth of his palms, the minty-musky smell of his skin.

"That was amazing," he says.

"Well, I stand up all the time," I say.

But Raul is still staring at me in that intense way, which makes me suspect he's gotten the wrong idea, a suspicion proved true when he thanks me for saving Ms. Pearl.

"It was nothing." I step out from his arms.

"It was not nothing," Wendy says.

"Can we go? Let's go," I say.

We say good-bye to Raul. As we walk to the car, I insist to Wendy I'm fine, really fine, until she agrees to take me home, instead of to the hospital.

And I *am* fine, I truly believe I am, until we're speeding along the highway and all at once the images come upon me like a shower of stones, bruising hard, cutting deep; and I cry out in pain, I try to cry out, but I can make no sound, no noise, nothing; so Wendy keeps driving, and the car keeps going, and the images keep falling, and I am battered down and down and down.

2.

"LORA? WE'RE HERE." WENDY IS STARING AT ME WITH WORRIED eyes, and I see her worried eyes and that we are parked in the driveway of my house, but I also see something else, somewhere else. I see a dark-haired little girl sitting next to me on the first day of school. *My name is Wendy*, she says. *What's your name?*

Her face is all cheery smile, but I'm scared of her. I'm scared of everything: this unfamiliar room, the teacher with her powdered face, even this wooden chair I'm sitting on, which seems unnaturally hard. *I want Mama*, I think. My desire is so strong it makes my head ache. The dark-haired little girl is still talking. *Lora, let's be friends, okay? Want to draw?*

"Lora? Are you all right?" she asks.

I want Mama, I think. But then I see Wendy's worried eyes, and I see that we are parked in the driveway of my house, and I know my wanting is useless.

"I'm fine," I say.

Despite my protests, she comes inside with me, into our two-story, one-family house. Wendy lives on the other end of the same neighborhood, a residential area in the southern part of Middleton, a city appropriately named for two reasons: because it's located in the middle of the country, almost exactly; and because it's midsized, smaller than the big cities on the coasts, bigger than the small cities scattered between us and the coastal cities. My entire life I've lived here, in Middleton; here, in this house.

Wendy helps me upstairs to my room. "Should we call your dad?" she asks.

"No, he's got a class now. He'll be home soon enough." I ask Wendy to get some pain medication from the bathroom, then I stretch out on my bed and close my eyes. My head hurts, it hurts, it hurts so much.

Wendy returns with a bottle of drugstore pills and a glass of water. "I'll stay with you until your dad gets back," she says.

"You don't have to." I swallow one tablet with one sip of water. "And what about our dinner?"

"We'll reschedule." She pats my shoulder.

"We can't reschedule, your whole huge family is coming." I swallow another tablet with another sip of water. "I'm fine."

She looks skeptical. "Are you sure?"

"Go home and get ready. I'll see you tonight."

"You better rest till then."

"I promise I'll do nothing more than lie here and ponder my near-death experience and human mortality and the possible meaning of my existence," I say.

Wendy groans, but doesn't argue. She tells me to call if I

need anything, anything at all. Then she finally leaves. Then I'm finally alone.

I make the mistake of glancing at the dried flower pinned on the corkboard above my desk. It's a mistake because once I see it I'm not just looking, I'm leaping, I'm twirling. There's a pink fluff of tutu tight around my waist. The music trills to an end. All us girls march carefully off the stage while the audience cheers. My parents are waiting. Mom holds out a bouquet of pink roses. *Lora, that was wonderful. You were wonderful.*

Then I'm back in my bedroom, in my bed, and smiling. It's been years since I've remembered her so clearly. Closing my eyes, I summon her back.

I'm slouched in my chair at the funeral home. The casket is closed. My father sits on my right side and Aunt Austin sits on my left side. My black dress is too small; it pinches at my arms and waist. My aunt had offered to buy me a new one, but I refused. I didn't want a new one. I stare down at the floor. The carpet is a wine-colored paisley that matches the wine-colored walls. I rub my sore eyes and find that I'm crying.

Then I'm back in my bedroom, in my bed, and crying. I crush my face into my pillow, trying to smother away the grief.

I'm at the department store downtown, standing in the bedding aisle, squishing all the different pillows. I decide they all feel the same and grab the second-cheapest one from the shelf. The cashier is a middle-aged man in a red sweatshirt. He grunts and asks me if it's started snowing yet. *Not yet*, I say.

Then I'm back in my bedroom, in my bed, and frowning.

The pillow-buying episode is so unimportant, so uneventful, so unworthy of being remembered. Yet here I am, recalling every detail. The checkout clerk's name tag read MICKEY. Next to his register was a rainbow display of bubble gum. And it's not just that I can remember all these stupid, insignificant, little details. I can see them. I am seeing them. I am standing at the register. Mickey the cashier grunts.

I sit up in my bed, so fast, too fast, and have to lie immediately back down because of my poor pounding head. But I don't much notice the pain. I've figured out what's wrong with me: it's my memory key.

Vergets disease, the forgetting sickness, is a degenerative disorder that affects the brain and causes severe memory loss. For most of history, the illness was endemic in our country, primarily afflicting older people. But sixty years ago, the disease began spreading, and it was no longer just the elderly who suffered; more and more of the middle-aged were being diagnosed with Vergets, including several members of my family, most on my dad's side but a few on my mom's as well.

The reasons for the epidemic are still unclear. Most scientists blame pollution and genetics. Some believe that lack of exercise and bad diet were contributing factors. A few religious sects declared we were being punished for our heathen ways. A report circulated that an extremist group, the Citizen Army, had poisoned our water supply. Then there are the conspiracy theorists who believe our own government poisoned our water supply. But most scientists blame pollution and genetics.

Whatever the reason, the whole nation was in crisis (other parts of the world, mostly first world countries, were also affected, though not to the same degree). The workforce was shrinking. The economy deteriorating. The population was afraid and who could blame them? How frightening it must have been to watch their loved ones' brains turn into zombie mush. How terrifying it must have been to wonder if their own brain would be the next to turn traitor.

When I was in middle school, I wrote an essay about the man who invented the memory key, P. B. Fishman. He was not one of the many doctors or scientists or researchers toiling tirelessly toward a cure for Vergets disease, funded generously by the government or private foundations. Mr. Fishman was a technician for a manufacturer of computer chips. He worked at home on his dining room table, ten feet away from his wife, who sat in her recliner knitting sweaters that—despite the beauty of the color work and stitches—no one could wear because the sizing was incomprehensible: sleeves long enough for a giant attached to a body made for a child's narrow chest, or vice versa. She no longer remembered her own name.

Mr. Fishman created a silicone computer chip that was responsive to neural activity, and programmed it to detect and record the patterns of neuronal communication associated with memory. The chip then encoded and stored this information—which was what the Vergets-affected brain was unable to do.

When his invention was made public, the investors appeared, Keep Corp was founded, and just two years later, the first generation of memory keys came onto the market. These were specifically made for those already suffering from Vergets; they did not restore older memories, but enabled the patient to create new memories after implantation.

The impact of this new technology was immediately evident. People with Vergets were able to take care of themselves again. Some even went back to work, like my father's grandfather. After five years in an assisted living facility, my great-grandpa Joe moved home and got a job at a hardware store (he had previously been a lawyer, but he couldn't remember that).

Of course there were side effects. The minor ones: headache, nausea. The less minor ones: rare seizures, the complications of only being able to remember the recent past. The major one: the complications of being able to remember the recent past unnaturally well. For unlike human memory, which softens and distorts and blocks, this first line of memory keys preserved everything without discrimination. Patients complained their heads felt busy—but it was a choice between busy brains and bumble brains. My father says his grandpa Joe never regretted getting one of those early keys, even though he suffered from migraines for the rest of his life.

A decade later, Keep Corp unveiled their new, groundbreaking invention. The H-Filter transformed immaculate artificial memory into something that mimicked the imperfections of human memory. Flawed and fading. Shortly thereafter, memory keys started being used as part of a precautionary program; they were implanted in people not yet suffering from Vergets.

At first keys were prescribed only to those who had a family history of the disease, but because the illness was so widespread, this included nearly every adult. My grandparents' generation all had their memory keys implanted during middle age. My parents' generation all had their memory keys implanted before the end of adolescence. My generation all had our memory keys implanted by the age of four.

It's a normal thing now, like vaccinations or seat belts or an apple a day. An essential preventative measure against Vergets disease, is what my mother used to say. Skeptical as she was about early implantation, she wholeheartedly believed in the necessity of the memory key. Mom also owned three biographies of P. B. Fishman, which came in handy when I was writing that essay about him for my middle school history class. That was before she died. Those books are now boxed up in the attic with the rest of her belongings. Dad kept everything: her jewelry and sweaters, her collection of romance novels. Even her socks. Even her oldest, holey socks.

Only her notebooks and papers are gone. After the car accident, two solemn, suited men came for those things. My father protested until they showed him Mom's contract, which stated all work done while she was employed by Keep Corp belonged to Keep Corp. Then he gave way, as he always did in those days.

The two solemn, suited men were kind. They apologized for the intrusion, offered their condolences, and presented us with a giant fruit basket.

The problem with my key must be its H-Filter, the part that is supposed to keep artificial memory as distant as natural memory. I know I should go see a technician to get it fixed. Keep Corp headquarters are located just north of Middleton, only forty minutes away by car.

But medical procedures make me nervous, they always have.

Don't worry. You won't feel a thing, says the doctor.

I stare at him, disbelieving, while Mama squeezes my hand. Her fingers are cool, her palm is firm. I scream as the needle sinks through my skin.

I felt a thing, I say accusingly. My mother laughs. The doctor apologizes and gives me a lollipop, a green one that sweetly stings my tongue.

Then I'm back in my room, head throbbing, mouth thick with the taste of green lollipop. I grab my water glass from the nightstand to drink away the sugary flavor, drink away the sound of my mother's laughter.

But the cup is empty. So I set one foot on the floor, and the other. Careful out the hallway, careful down the stairs. In the kitchen I refill my water glass. Sip. Sip. Sip. It seems if I focus completely on what I'm doing, I can keep myself in the present. Thank goodness.

The front door creaks open. "Lora?" calls my father.

"I'm here! What are you doing home already?"

"Wendy called me." He comes into the kitchen. His gray hair is rumpled as it always is at the end of the day, and his eyeglasses sit askew on his nose. He looks exactly like what he is: the absentminded professor. My mother called him that, she called him *my* absentminded professor, Dr. Kenneth Mint.

"I knew I couldn't trust Wendy," I say, making myself smile. "It's really just a tiny bump on the head."

"Let me see." He stands behind me, inspecting. "I don't see anything."

"Told you so. Don't you have office hours now?" I ask. My dad teaches contemporary literature at Middleton University. Their summer session just started.

"Canceled for a family emergency. Lora, are you sure you're all right?"

"Positive," I say.

"That's my girl, rescuing little old ladies."

"I'm sure Wendy exaggerated," I say.

"I'm sure she didn't. We still on for dinner?"

"Of course."

"Good, I'll tell Austin," he says, and I'm surprised, but pleased. Aunt Austin is a congresswoman, so she is very, very busy, and usually out of town. But Dad calls and she confirms she'll be there, though she might be late if her meeting runs late, and if that happens, she apologizes in advance.

My father goes into the den to watch the evening news, and

I go sit with him. They're doing a segment about the proposed economic bill. According to one commentator, the obstinacy of the conservatives is getting in the way of the legislative work that needs to be done; the bill must pass. According to another commentator, the obstinacy of the liberals is getting in the way of the legislative work that needs to be done; the bill must *not* pass.

"It's always this same story." Dad sighs. He takes off his glasses and rubs his eyes with the backs of his hands.

The show goes to commercial. A man with white hair and white teeth is at the beach with a little girl. They build a sand castle. The little girl giggles. She's television-adorable with her brown braids and round eyes, but there is something vaguely menacing about her tiny pointy teeth. Before I can point this out to my father, the old man and little girl disappear, replaced by the octagonal Keep Corp logo and the caption THESE MOMENTS ARE FOR KEEPS.

My breath tangles up in my throat. I get the absurd idea the commercial is chiding me about my damaged memory key. But of course I'm being ridiculous. It was just a commercial, a commercial coincidence.

"That's a new one," says Dad. His voice is stiff, and when I glance at him I know he's thinking about *her*.

"That's a dumb one," I say. "These moments are for keeps? More like these moments are for creeps."

He laughs obligingly. "Oh, Lora. What would I do without you?"

The weatherman comes on, his tan as golden as his hair. He tells us it'll be hot and humid for the next few days, with possible storms coming in over the weekend. Then the picture flickers, then the screen empties.

"I'll get it," I say. I run down to the basement and reset the breakers in the fuse box. The past few months, we've been having power problems. Dad called the electric company and they told him it was a statewide issue and they'd send a technician as soon as possible. That was weeks ago. I return to the den to check that the TV is back on.

"Thanks, Lora," says my father.

"Welcome, Dad." I tell him I'm going upstairs to get ready, and I go—carefully again: careful up the stairs, careful down the hallway, careful into my room. Yes, it seems if I focus completely on what I'm doing, I can keep myself in the present.

I pull my blue dress from the closet. On it goes. I smile for the mirror. I look fine, but only fine, and fine is not enough because Wendy's brother will be there tonight. Not that I care about him, not really. I flip through my other clothes, but everything seems wrong: too fancy, too casual, too tight, too loose, too long, too short.

Finally, in the farthest, darkest corner, my hand slides on something soft. I pull whatever it is into the light and find peach silk with tiny printed flowers, cap sleeves, and a fluttering hem. The dress is not my dress, but it's not unfamiliar. It belonged to my mother.

The memories avalanche. At a cousin's wedding, she twirls

on the dance floor, the peach dress floating above her knees . . .
I'm sitting on the floor with my babysitter, and my mother in
the peach dress stoops to kiss me good-bye . . . It's her birthday
and Dad and I are dressed up and waiting. He's wearing a tie
and smells of his spicy aftershave. She comes down the stairs,
blushing in her peach dress, her hair curling soft around her
shoulders, lips pinked with lipstick. She is beautiful.

Why is her dress in my closet? As soon as the question
forms in my mind, the memory answers. I am twelve years old.
I'm in my bed, waiting for her to kiss me good night. *Mom?* I
call out. *Mom!* Finally, she comes. Over her arm is the peach
dress, scrunched and limp around her elbow.

What's that? I ask. *Are you going out?*

This is for you. I don't need it anymore.

I laugh. *That won't fit me. It's way too big.*

It'll fit you one day. And if not, you can keep it to remember me.

Okay, I say happily.

She kisses my cheek. *I love you, Lora*, she tells me. *Don't ever
forget.*

I blink. I'm back in the present. I take off the blue cotton
and slide on the peach silk. The dress fits me as if it were mine.
And I'm pretty in it. Even I can see that, and I rarely think I'm
pretty. My hair seems darker and shinier. I have a waist. I don't
look like her, no, I'll never be as beautiful as my mother was.
But in her dress, I am pretty.

Still, I'm unsettled by my memory of that night. It's not
grief; it's not only grief. There was something odd about what

she said, and the way she said it. There was something odd about the fact she gave me her dress. It still fit her. She still wore it.

Then I realize that night was the last night I saw her.

That night was the night before the accident.

I don't need it anymore, she had said.

I love you, Lora, don't ever forget, she had said.

And the next morning, she was gone.

3.

MY FATHER IS CALLING FOR ME. I GO DOWNSTAIRS AND FIND
him at the front door, tying his shoes, scrambling around for
his keys. He looks at me. He looks at my dress. My mother's
peach dress. He turns away. "Let's go," he says.

I follow him outside and we get into the car. I can't tell if
he is sad or angry or annoyed. Maybe I shouldn't have worn the
dress. I want to apologize, but I'm not sure how to do it without
mentioning Mom and making it worse. It's been five years, but
he still doesn't like to talk about her.

It's a relief when we arrive.

"Finally!" Wendy says as she opens the door. "I'm so glad
you could make it. How are you? How's your head? Do you like
potato salad? Everyone's out in the yard. We got a new grill
and they're trying to figure out how to get it to work. Can you
believe it?"

"Thank you for having us," says Dad.

"Your dress!" Wendy touches the silky fabric. "Is it new?
I love it."

"Thanks." I glance at my father but he is already halfway down the hall.

"Are you mad at me?" whispers Wendy.

"Why would I be mad at you?" I am genuinely puzzled.

"Because I called your dad and told him what happened."

"I'm not mad," I say. "I know you meant well."

"I did mean well!" Wendy slips her arm through my arm, grinning, and when I blink she transforms into that little girl again. She is showing me around her house on our very first playdate. *What do you want to do? Want to see my drawings? Or we can run outside. I have roller skates, do you?*

"Come on, Lora," says grown-up Wendy. "Aren't you hungry?"

My voice is lost somewhere in the past, so I nod, and we go out to the backyard. It's crowded with Wendy's family: her parents and her brother, plus aunts, uncles, and cousins. The adults are sitting around the table. The kids are roaming around the grass. I look for my dad. He appears wholly involved in conversation with two uncles.

"Lora! We heard about your heroics today," says Mrs. Laskey. Wendy's mother is not as tall as Wendy, but just as slender, and looks so young that strangers occasionally mistake mother and daughter for sisters. Mrs. Laskey, of course, loves it when this happens. Wendy, of course, hates it.

"It was nothing." I jab my elbow into Wendy's arm. She jabs me back.

"Are you kidding?" Tim materializes out of nowhere and

sits next to me. "You saved Ms. Pearl, my favorite teacher ever. In seventh grade she told me that girls would like me better if I stopped shooting spitballs into their hair. Best advice I've ever gotten."

Wendy giggles and so does Mrs. Laskey, but I am statue-still, praying that the past stays past. Because I don't want to remember when I had that huge crush on Tim. I don't want to remember how I pined and pined, though I knew it was hopeless. Of course it was hopeless: Tim was older and funny and charming and popular and cute, so cute with his messy black hair and sleepy eyes and enormous laugh. And I was just that pesky girl who ran around with his kid sister.

I don't want to remember that, or what happened after that, so I concentrate on the hardness of my chair under my thighs. "How's college life?" I ask him, casual as can be.

"Terrible." He sighs. "On top of schoolwork and studying, last semester I was working at the lab twenty hours a week. All these responsibilities really get in the way of my social life."

"Don't listen to him, he just loves complaining," says Wendy. "Whenever I visit he's playing computer games with all his nerd friends."

Tim turns to his mother. "She's making it up," he says. "I promise you, Mom, I would never have nerd friends."

Mrs. Laskey beams at her bickering children. It's always loud and jolly at Wendy's house, which I appreciate, and appreciate even more right now—all these distractions seem to be holding back the memories. Perhaps my mind is too busy to go wandering into the past when there is so much to look at and listen to and laugh about and eat.

And there is *so* much to eat. Dinner is a feast of grilled meat and fish and vegetables and potato salad and fruit salad and green salad and zucchini pie. My aunt calls to say she's going to be late, sorry, and we should start without her, so we do. We pile our food high on paper plates, and when one plate starts sagging we simply add another. The adults drink wine; Wendy and I are allowed one small glass each, and Tim is allowed one large glass.

When everyone is stuffed full Mrs. Laskey says, "Save room for dessert!" and everyone groans because it's too late, no one has saved any room for dessert. The unanimous decision is made to take a break. Wendy and I lie in the grass while her little cousins tumble around us. The adults chatter on, sitting around the table and drinking. I'm sleepy from my small glass of wine.

"I can't believe we've graduated," says Wendy.

"Me neither," I say. "Now what will become of us?"

"Fame, fortune, and happiness."

"How can you be sure?"

"It's pretty obvious," says Wendy.

Mrs. Laskey asks us to fix the dessert, so we go into the house. In the long hallway that connects the living room to the kitchen, we meet my aunt.

"My dear girls, I'm so sorry I'm so late," she says. It's clear she came straight from her meeting; she's still in her suit with her shirt buttoned tight to her throat. Her bobbed black hair is sleek to her chin. Aunt Austin looks like a serious woman, and she is a serious woman, but when she smiles her face changes so much it's hard to recognize her as that serious woman. She smiles now.

"We're just happy you're here. We know how busy you are," says Wendy.

"Yes." Aunt Austin nods, but she is looking at me. Or, more precisely, she is looking at my peach dress. Or, most precisely, she is looking at my mother's peach dress.

"How did your meeting go? Was it about the economic bill?" I ask.

She lifts her gaze to meet mine. I blink. I am six years old and I've just spilled my cranberry juice on her white rug. Aunt Austin scowls, her expression first directed at the ruby-red stain, then at me, and I'm sure I've ruined everything, and I'll never be invited over again. My teary eyes are a blink from bursting. I blink. I'm in the hallway at Wendy's house. But Aunt Austin's expression is still the same.

"That's Jeanette's dress," she says.

"I'm sorry," I say, apologizing for the juice, apologizing for the dress.

Aunt Austin turns around and walks toward the backyard. I follow Wendy into the kitchen, feeling thoroughly rebuked. But also slightly irritated: it's my mother's dress, I'm allowed to wear my mother's dress.

Wendy asks me to wash the raspberries and blueberries and blackberries.

"That was weird, right?" I say.

"What was weird?" she asks as she whisks the heavy cream.

"Aunt Austin," I say, swirling fruit through water.

"I think she's so great," Wendy says. Wendy thinks everyone is so great. It's the quality I find most admirable and most annoying about her.

"Maybe I'm being overly sensitive," I say. But I don't think I'm being overly sensitive. First my father stops talking to me because of the peach dress, then my aunt does the same. They're the ones being overly sensitive.

"So that's your mom's dress?"

"Yeah." I drain the berries and gently roll them into a clean bowl.

"I think it's nice you're wearing it. It fits you perfectly," she says. "Will you boil water for the coffee?"

"Sure." I put the kettle on.

"It's really pretty," says Wendy.

"What's really pretty?"

"Your dress."

"Well. Thank you." I sense she wants me to talk about my feelings, and my mother, and my feelings about my mother, but I'm not in the mood.

"Oh, no!"

"What?"

"I got whipped cream all over my shirt." Wendy turns to show me.

"How'd that happen?" I giggle. She really did get whipped cream all over her shirt. And arms. And face.

"I'd better rinse it before it stains," she says as she runs from the room, shouting back that I should finish everything up. So I lift the chocolate cake out of the bakery box and put it on a plate. I set the plate on a tray and add the bowls of fruit and cream. A knife. Some extra serving spoons. The kettle starts screaming. I turn off the flame.

"What's taking so long?" asks someone behind me.

I spin around. It's freshman year. I'm standing on the steps in front of school, searching for whoever it was who'd called my name. Then I see him. And I'm nervous, and I don't know why. Tim is my best friend's brother, that's all. I've known him forever, that's all. But when he grins at me, I notice his mouth, the pink of his lips, and the slight slant of one front tooth; I notice his mouth as if it were new to his face, and I have to fold my fingers together to keep them down in their proper place.

"What do you want?" I say, too rushed, too rough. We're back in the kitchen but my pulse is still too quick.

"Mom sent me to see what was taking so long," says Tim.

"Well, we could have used some help in here." I do not dare look at him. I do not dare look at his mouth. I pluck up a blackberry, drop it into my own mouth, and press it apart with my tongue. The seeds stick in my teeth. My head throbs.

"Everything okay?" He touches my arm, the bare skin of my forearm.

"I'm fine." I move away and his hand falls back to his side.

"It's great to see you. It's been ages, huh," he says.

"Has it?" I say, though I know very well that it has. Even though Tim goes to college only a dozen miles away, at Middleton University, where my dad teaches, I've barely seen him these past two years. Partly because I've been avoiding him, mostly because it's been so easy to avoid him. Tim doesn't often come home during the semesters, and last summer he didn't come home at all because he was interning at a medical technology hospital on the east coast.

"You look good," he says.

"Will you fix the coffee? The water's ready."

"Sure." Tim saunters over to the cabinets. He asks what I'm doing this summer.

"I'm working at the library, same as always." I glance over. His back is to me now, and as he reaches for the tin of coffee grinds, his shirt lifts, revealing an inch of plaid boxers and pale skin. I turn quickly away.

"I better take all this dessert outside," I say.

"Good idea. Those people want their cake, they're getting cranky," he says.

The tray is heavy, so I move slowly. When I get to the door I tap on the glass, and one of the little cousins comes to slide it open. He stares at the chocolate cake. "Can I get some of that?" he asks, eyes wide and hopeful.

"Yes, but not yet." I step carefully around him, bring the tray to the table, and set it gently down. Only then do I realize that the adults are arguing. Not everyone: Dad is staring at the grass and Wendy's parents are clearing away the leftovers. But Aunt Austin and a couple of the other uncles and aunts are shouting and gesticulating and interrupting each other.

I go over to my father. "What's going on?" I whisper.

He sighs. "They're talking politics. What else?"

"Have those people lost their minds?" hollers one of Wendy's aunts, the one with twin daughters. "What about supporting our troops? What about national security? And what about all these crazy radical groups running around?"

"You actually think corporate tax cuts will help matters?" snaps an uncle to a different aunt.

"Look," says Aunt Austin to another uncle, the tall bald one. "I understand what you're saying, but if you don't think we should compromise, and the other side is—let me assure you—just as unwilling to compromise, what happens then?"

The bald uncle says, "Compromise is what got us in this mess to begin with. The system is broken and drastic action needs to be taken. You think the economic bill is going to fix anything?"

"You know what the economic bill isn't going to fix? The fact I've been unemployed for the past year," says the uncle with the fancy black facial hair.

"Maybe you'd have a job by now if you started looking for one," mutters his wife. "And shaved that ridiculous mustache."

She speaks quietly, but loudly enough so that everyone can hear.

Aunt Austin's face flattens as she tries to hide her amusement. "I'm sorry to hear of your troubles," she says to the mustachioed uncle. "If you send your résumé to my office, I can pass it along to a friend of mine, a corporate headhunter." She hands him her card, smiling her congresswoman smile: bright eyes, lips a smooth curve.

"Cake?" Mrs. Laskey says cheerfully. "Who wants cake?"

Everyone cheers. Everyone agrees on cake.

I go sit in the chair next to my aunt and tell her I'm sorry about the fuss.

"That? That was nothing," she says. "Every day I deal with worse, much worse, between the constituents and the lobbyists, not to mention my congressional colleagues. Believe me, I don't mind a little dinner party debate."

"I'm glad," I say.

"Do you want some cake, my dear?" she asks. Apparently I've been forgiven for the dress offense, though it's impossible to know for sure because her congresswoman smile is still stuck to her mouth.

"Sure," I say. "And thanks for coming tonight. I'm really glad you're here."

My aunt reaches over and selects a particularly large and attractive slice of cake—one with a frosting flower—and sets it in front of me. Then she smiles, truly smiles. "Of course, Lora. I wouldn't have missed it for all the economic bills in the world."

* * *

The party breaks up after dessert, which is probably for the best because most of the aunts and uncles will no longer look at each other, let alone talk to each other, despite Mrs. Laskey's chirpy attempts to restart an inoffensive—i.e., nonpolitical— conversation. Also, my head is throbbing again.

When we get home, I say a bleary good night to my father and stumble upstairs to bed. I'm almost asleep when I realize I'm making a rumpled mess of the peach silk. I force myself up, remove the dress, hang it in the closet, and put on my pajamas. Then I go downstairs for a drink of water.

The kitchen light is on. I blink, trying to adjust my eyes to the brightness. My mother is sitting at the counter, one arm across her chest, the other arm folded up so her fingers can gently tap against her cheek. She looks worried. Before I can go to her, there is a knock on the back door. She gets up to answer it. I step backward into the shadowy hall. The door opens. Two strangers stand on the step, a man and a woman, their faces half in shadow.

You have to come with us, says the man.

I know. My mother's voice is soft but steady.

Let's go then, says the woman. A blue-sleeved arm reaches out and takes hold of my mother's elbow. They pull her outside.

I leap forward and wrench open the back door. "Mom!" I shout, peering into the blackness of the backyard. "Mom!"

There's no one there. Of course there's no one there. My mother, those two strangers, they were only a memory. I close the door. Lock it. Pour myself a glass of water. Drink most of it down. Turn off the light. Go back to bed.

But I don't sleep. Because I can't sleep. Though my body feels almost feverish with exhaustion, my mind is restless. I go over it a hundred times, trying to make sense of what I saw that night. I go over it a hundred times, and it still makes no sense.

All I know is that I was wrong before, when I thought the last time I saw her was when she kissed me good night and gave me the peach dress. This was the last time, truly: in the middle of the night, I stood in the hallway and watched as my mother was taken from our home by two strangers.

4.

THE PHONE IS RINGING. I ANSWER, BUT NOBODY IS THERE. THE phone is still ringing. I answer again, and still, nobody is there. Hello, hello? The phone is still ringing. I sit up, abruptly awake, twisted up in the bedsheets. The real phone is really ringing.

"Hello?" I cough.

"Are you still sleeping? It's noon!" says Wendy.

"I had a bad night," I say.

"A bad night? Why? Are you okay?"

"It's nothing. I'm fine now."

"Tim and I are going to the lake. Come with us?"

"Well . . ." I tell her I can't because I have to clean my room and help my father organize the attic and something or other. My excuses are lame, and I can tell Wendy thinks so too. I'm not sure why I don't tell the truth, why I don't tell her what I've remembered and that I can't go to the lake until I figure out what it means. Maybe I'm afraid she'll say I must have imagined it or that I better get to the doctor. Maybe I'm afraid she will sigh in her sincerely sympathetic way and inform me, as she's done before, that I'm still traumatized by the loss of my mother.

"Have fun! I'll call you later," I say, and hang up the phone.

My head hurts. I take a pain pill, and one more. Then I get into the shower and wash my hair, careful around the tender place at the back of my skull, rinse off, towel off, and return to my room. In my closet, the peach dress flutters on its hanger. I touch the soft fabric. It glides through my fingers like a promise.

The phone rings again. I don't answer; I don't want to make any more fake excuses to Wendy. But when the machine comes on, it's not her. I stand silently as I listen, as though the caller might hear if I make any sound whatsoever.

"This message is for Lora Mint. My name is Debra and I'm calling from Keep Corp to let you know our systems have registered a problem with your memory key. Please call us back immediately at CALL-KEEP, extension twenty-two. Thank you and have a nice day."

Debra has a shrilly trilling voice. I imagine her as a little girl with big eyes—the girl from that Keep Corp commercial— wagging a disapproving finger, her pointy teeth bared. The line clicks off. I exhale.

I'm surprised: I didn't know Keep Corp was able to track each individual memory key in this way. I'm unnerved: it's sort of disturbing that Keep Corp is able to track each individual memory key in this way. So the secret I thought was mine alone is actually a secret I'm sharing with a huge corporation.

Nonetheless, I can't let them repair my key. Not yet. I delete the message.

Then I go to the library because there are certain facts I need to check. I go because it's too hot to stay home, because I'm too antsy to stay home, because at home I feel the memories leaning close, breathing into my ear. I get on my bicycle and go. It's downhill all the way downtown; still I arrive sweaty.

Cynthia waves to me from behind the reference desk. She's my favorite librarian, the cheerful librarian, with an elaborate hairdo of ringlets and curls that's a different color every year. Last year was orange. This year it's red. Red is a real improvement.

"Lora! Is it summer already?" she says in an exclamatory whisper. As a professional, she can express even the loudest emotions quietly.

"Doesn't it feel like summer?" I say.

"I can't tell with all this air-conditioning." She shudders dramatically.

I ask about her family. Cynthia has a grown-up daughter who now lives on the east coast, a husband who loves bowling, and a little dog named Gouda. She talks more about Gouda than she talks about her grown-up daughter and bowling husband—combined.

"Everyone's fine. My daughter moved home a few months ago."

"That's great," I say.

"Yes," she says, but her smile sags. "Actually, Kira got laid off and couldn't find a new job out there, so she came back to Middleton. She's already had several interviews, and another scheduled for this week, so I'm sure something will work out."

"I'm sure." I nod enthusiastically, so enthusiastically my head starts throbbing and I have to stop mid-nod. "How's Gouda?" I ask.

"She's such a smart dog. The other day, I was looking everywhere for one of my sandals. Under the couch. Under the table. Then Gouda comes and drops something at my feet. And you know what it was?" Cynthia beams with pride.

"Your sandal?"

"It was my sandal! A little chewed up, but nothing noticeable once I had it back on my foot. My Gouda is a treasure."

"She sure is," I say.

"You come back to work next week, right? I can't wait. No one can organize the periodicals like you can," she says. This is a big compliment around here. I blush as I thank her.

At the back of the library, the computers are arranged in three rows, and it's not too crowded, but I go to the farthest end for extra privacy. There's no one next to me, but two seats down a boy looks over as I settle into my chair. Then he keeps looking. I stare at my screen.

"Hey," he says.

I stare at my screen.

"It's Lora, right?"

I turn reluctantly around. I do know him. But how do I know him?

"I'm Raul. We met yesterday?"

"Ms. Pearl's assistant." I blink and remember: Ms. Pearl is in a floral smock. Her face is pale. Her skin creased. Raul comes and takes Ms. Pearl's arm. He wears a blue jacket and black pants.

It's strange how my broken key works; the connection to the past is not always immediate, but once I have the memory in my mind, I'm right there. Here. Raul's arm is firm around my back as he lifts me from the ground. My head throbs. He smells of mint and musk.

"You're not wearing your jacket," I tell library Raul, who is in a red T-shirt faded pink. And I'm immediately embarrassed. Of course he's not wearing his jacket; it's a zillion degrees out. Then again, it was a zillion degrees yesterday too.

"That's my uniform." He explains that he works at the facility where Ms. Pearl lives.

"She lives in a nursing home now?" I don't know why I'm surprised. She *is* very old.

"Not a nursing home. A retirement home," he says.

"Right, a retirement home." Still, I'm surprised and kind of upset. Ms. Pearl seemed invincible when she was our teacher. "Why does she have to live there?"

"Her memory is failing."

"Does she have Vergets disease? What about her memory key?"

"She doesn't have Vergets, but she doesn't have a key, either," says Raul. "It's just ordinary old age."

"She doesn't have a key?" I'm surprised again. Everyone has a memory key.

"You know how some people are weird about medical technology," he says. "Like those religious groups who say it's unnatural, that it's affecting our humanity or whatever. Turning us into machines."

"Is that what *you* think?" I don't bother keeping the skepticism from my voice. I know it's illogical, but it feels as if he's insulting my mother. At the time of her death she was one of the most senior scientists in the memory key division of Keep Corp.

"No, not at all," he says quickly.

"And Ms. Pearl isn't religious, is she?"

"I don't think so."

"Then why doesn't she have a key?" I frown. My mother was committed to her work. Every year, she would drag my dad to the big fund-raising dinner even though he hated those fancy events. But she insisted they support the cause: the dinner raised money to make memory key technology accessible to all in need. Mom said that in the past, not everyone could afford a key, especially if they didn't have health insurance.

Raul smiles apologetically. But I want him to argue with me, not smile at me, not talk in such reasonable tones. He says: "I'm not sure why Ms. Pearl doesn't have one. I should ask her."

"Do you have a memory key?" I ask.

"Of course," he says.

"Okay." I know I've no reason to be mad at him, not even

on my mom's behalf.

"Okay," he says, smiling again. He has a nice smile: crinkly eyes, dimpled cheeks. Wendy was right; Raul *is* cute. I realize I'm smiling back. I realize we are smiling at each other.

And as soon as I realize it, I get awkward. I tell Raul I have to get to work, and I turn to my computer, straighten my spine, settle my fingers on the keyboard, fix my eyes on the screen, and try not to think about how hideously awkward I am. Because I really do have to get to work.

I type in my mother's name. There are five million results, many of which refer to other Jeanette Mints. I refine the search by narrowing it to articles published in the past ten years.

The first article is about a Jeanette Mint who is, apparently, a model and musician of international fame (though I've never heard of her); the second article is my mother's obituary. I read it closely, even though there isn't anything here I don't already know, even though it makes me feel sort of sick.

Jeanette Mint, a senior scientist at Keep Corp, was killed in a car accident . . . Her research helped refine the data functionality of the memory key . . . She is survived by her husband, Dr. Kenneth Mint, Professor of Literature at Middleton University; her daughter, Lora; and her sister, Congresswoman Austin Lee . . . In lieu of flowers, the family requests that donations be sent to the Memory Key Fund.

The next article is about the car accident. I had always avoided learning the details, but now I want to know everything. According to this account, at approximately six thirty on a stormy morning, Jeanette Mint, scientist at Keep Corp, was

on her way to work when she lost control of her car while driving across the bridge at the city's northern border. Her vehicle
crashed through the guardrail and went over the side of the
bridge. Witnesses notified the authorities, but the search was
impeded by the poor visibility. After two hours of searching,
Ms. Mint's body was recovered a mile down the river.

There is no mention of the two people who came to our
house the night before, no indication of anything unusual
about her daily routine, no question that the accident was more
than just a horribly tragic accident caused by bad weather.

I read the article again. Then again. Then again and again,
until I am gagging on the words. Until I'm just gagging. I clap
my hand over my mouth. I'm hunched in my chair, staring at
the gleaming box. The casket is closed, so I can't see her there
myself, so I can't believe it, so I don't believe it. It is only when
I see my father's expression, his whole face drawn down with
grief, his red eyes spilling tears, that I begin to understand it's
true. I have never before seen my father cry, and seeing it now
makes me cry.

"Are you all right?" asks a voice from somewhere close.
There is the pressure of a hand on my shoulder. The sensa-
tion brings me back to the present, where I find myself at the
library, in front of a computer, with Raul next to me.

"I'm fine." I rub my eyes. My head is throbbing.

"You sure?" His forehead wrinkles in concern.

"I'm sure."

His warm palm slides down my cold arm and I shiver.

"Goose bumps," he says. "Let's go outside and get some fresh air. I could use some fresh air, how about you?"

We sit on the steps in front of the library with cans of soda from the vending machine, and Raul tells me about his research project. In the fall, he's starting the marine biology program at Middleton University, where one of the professors will be taking a few students on a trip to the Green Islands next year. Raul is working on a paper about the cetaceans of the region, in hopes of being selected for the trip.

"Cetaceans?" I ask.

"Marine mammals. Like whales and porpoises."

"And dolphins?"

"Yes, dolphins." He smiles.

I tell him I'm also going to Middleton University in the fall. "But I don't know what I want to study yet," I say.

"That's normal." Raul smiles again. Or maybe he's still smiling. Either way, he really does have an excellent smile, the kind of smile that forces you to smile back. I smile back. It's nice to be sitting out here with him, chatting in the sunshine, drinking our fizzy drinks.

"Do you like working at the nursing home?" I ask him.

"It's a *retirement* home—sorry—it's just that if I don't correct you, I'll start calling it a nursing home, and they really hate that." He says he does like working there, though it sometimes gets depressing. He asks what I'm doing this summer and I tell him about my job at the library.

"Well, good. I'm here all the time," he says, and explains he can't get much work done at home with his two little brothers around. "And they're always around."

"How old—" I say, but then I'm interrupted by someone shouting my name.

"Lora? Lora!" Wendy is standing on the sidewalk. "What are you doing here?"

"You didn't go to the lake?" I say.

"Tim had to work. His boss called just as we were leaving."

"That's too bad," says Raul.

"You remember Raul, right? From yesterday?" I say to her.

"Of course I remember." She comes to sit with us on the steps, careful because she is wearing a short dress. She pulls the lacy fabric down to cover her knees, then extends her long, long legs.

"Which lake were you going to?" Raul asks, and they talk awhile about the various local lakes. His interest in marine biology apparently extends to aquatic recreation. Wendy tells him she's working on a series of lake paintings. He tells her about his research trip hopes. He smiles his nice smile at her. She smiles back. I sip my soda. I fiddle with the tab on the can until it breaks off.

Wendy tells her windsurfing story while Raul laughs in all the right places. I'm used to the way she takes over conversations, and I don't mind it, not usually. But as she goes on and on and on, I start getting restless. I think about the car accident in which my mother died. Then I try not to think about it.

When there finally comes a pause in their conversation, I say, "I have to go," simple as that. And I stand up and go, simple as that. Even though I hear Raul telling me to wait, hold on, come back. Even though I hear Wendy asking me what's the hurry, is something wrong? I unlock my bicycle from the rack, get on, and pedal fast.

My father will be home soon. And I want to be there when he arrives.

5.

I WAIT IN THE DEN. I HAD CONSIDERED WAITING IN THE KITCHEN, but decided I'd first let my dad arrive home, drink a drink, wash his face, and change out of his suit. I'd let him get comfortable. Then, when he comes in to watch the evening news, I will be right here and ready. Such conniving is necessary because he doesn't like talking about her, and I know if he gets a second to reflect, he'll leave out anything he thinks would upset me.

The front door thuds. The locks rattle. A moment later, there is a rush of water flowing from the kitchen sink, then the taps squawk shut. The refrigerator hums and a can pops open. The stairs creak. A minute passes. I shift on the couch. There is a slight ache at the base of my skull. I consider going to my room for the pain pills, but decide not to; he will be coming soon.

Finally, the stairs creak again.

"Hey, Dad," I say as he comes into the room.

He yelps in surprise. "I didn't know you were home. What

are you doing so quietly in here?" he says as he plunks into his usual chair.

"Can I ask you something?" I lean forward so that I'm looking directly at him. "Did anything strange happen the night before Mom died?"

His expression does not change. This is not unexpected: after years of teaching my father has perfected his poker face so as not to give anything away when his students say the right thing or the wrong thing or the offensive thing. But his posture shifts. I notice only because I'm watching for it. His shoulders, formerly slouched against the cushions, are rigid. "What do you mean?"

"Exactly what I said. Did anything strange happen that night?"

"Why do you ask?"

"The night before she died she gave me her peach dress. Isn't that weird?"

"Did she? How interesting. Why do *you* think she gave the dress to you that night?" He is in full professor mode now, nodding thoughtfully, turning my questions for him into his questions for me. Mom always teased him when he employed this strategy with her, but I'm less amused. I just want a straight answer.

"Don't you think that's odd?" I say with a little more force.

"Do you?" he asks.

"Don't *you*?" I ask.

"Perhaps," he says, and I know he knows something

because he will not meet my gaze. What isn't he telling me? It occurs to me he *must* have known something was wrong; even the absentminded professor can't be that absentminded. For if my mother was out with two strangers, then she wasn't in the bed she shared with him.

"What happened that night?" I ask, and I'm startled to find I'm shouting.

He also seems startled. "Calm down, Lora."

"I'm calm!" I yell. "Just answer me!"

"I know it's hard. I miss her every day, and I know you do too."

"Dad . . ."

The telephone rings. My father hurries to the kitchen. I sit still, staring at nothing. I had hoped he would explain away my strange memory, but all he has done is confirm my suspicion that there was something more to what happened that night, more than what he told me, perhaps more than he told anyone. My head is hurting again.

"Lora! Will you please come here!"

I walk slowly down the hall to where my dad is propped against the kitchen counter, the phone receiver tucked between his ear and shoulder. "Is there something wrong with your memory key?" he asks me.

"What?"

"It's Keep Corp calling. Their system has registered a malfunction with your key. Have you noticed a problem?"

"No, it's fine." I turn so he can't see my face.

"She says it's fine," he says into the phone.

I get a cup from the cabinet, pour myself some orange juice, and drink it down.

"Lora, they want you to go see a med-tech, just in case."

"There's nothing wrong. I don't need to go," I say.

"Ten o'clock tomorrow?" he asks.

"I don't need to go!"

"Yes, ten o'clock tomorrow morning, thank you," my father says into the phone as he scribbles a note down on the notepad. He hangs up.

"Dad, I told you I'm fine." My head hurts.

"You'll need the car. I can probably get a ride from Edgar," he muses to himself.

"I don't need to go." My head hurts.

"They said you have to go, so you have to go." He hands me the paper with the appointment information scrawled on it. Reluctantly, I take it. I know he's right. Or rather, he would be right under normal circumstances.

"You take your car. I'll get Wendy to drive me," I say.

"Are you sure?"

"Sure . . . Dad, that night before the accident—"

"I did not notice anything strange," he says calmly. "Now, I've had a very long day and the news is on. Please let me watch in peace."

I go to my bedroom and shut the door. My head hurts, and it hurts more as I consider the possible scenarios. Either my father didn't wake up when my mother got up, or he did. Either he didn't know she left the house with two strangers, or he did. Either he told me the truth, or he lied.

After dinner, I bike over to Wendy's house, and of course it's Tim who answers the door. "Well, if it isn't my favorite Lora," he says, jolly as ever, but there is a gleam in his eyes that makes me want to look away, even though I know it's just a trick of moonlight and starlight and shadow.

"I'm the only Lora you know," I say, not looking away because looking away would mean I've learned nothing from the past. This time he'll have to look away first.

But he doesn't. "Wrong," he says, his gaze steady. "There was a Lora in my Micro-Tech class last semester. She was sort of stuck-up. I like you much better. But now that I think about it, maybe her name was Brittany." And still he doesn't look away. He grins. He grins and becomes the Tim of three years ago: slightly skinnier, hair shorter, but with that same mischievous grin.

I'm here to meet Wendy so we can study for our math exam, but Tim informs me she went to the store. *She'll be back in a minute. Come in, I'll entertain you till then.*

Great! I say in a bright voice that sounds nothing like my actual voice. I know what I'm feeling is puppy love—silly and unrequited—still I feel it all the same. I haven't told anyone about my crush, not even Wendy. Especially not Wendy.

We sit on the couch. It's only the beginning of the school year, but it's Tim's senior year so I ask what he's doing when he graduates, and he tells me he wants to study medical technology at the university. Then he asks me about my classes and I describe the project I'm working on: a series of dioramas illustrating the births of selected historical personages.

So I'm not only showing the circumstances into which these people were born, but also the medical practices and religious customs of their times, I explain. *As a bonus, Wendy thinks it's totally disgusting.*

He laughs and I'm thrilled to have made him laugh. And although he is too good-looking and too popular and too much older (two years older) and I have no hope, I hope anyway.

I blink.

"Come on in," says Tim.

"Thanks." I've returned to the present where I'm merely chatting with my best friend's brother. So why does my heart feel violent inside my chest?

"Wendy's in her room." Tim scrubs his hand across his head, messing his messy hair even messier. He is still grinning. I look away and go upstairs.

Wendy is sitting on her bed, sketchbook propped on her knees.

"Perfect," I say. "Can you do me a favor?"

She glances up from her work. And glares.

"What's wrong?" I ask.

"What's wrong? I asked you to come to the lake, and you said you couldn't because you had to help your dad, but then I found you hanging out with Raul, and when I sat down you left. You just left. Maybe I should be asking *you* what's wrong." Her lips twist down in sadness, her eyebrows straighten in anger, and the combination is perfectly tragic. This time it works on me because I know she's right.

"I'm sorry. I can explain."

"All right, then. Explain."

I take a deep breath. Then I tell her about my damaged memory key and remembering my mother and the two strangers who came to our house in the middle of the night. I tell her about how Keep Corp wants to fix my key. "I'm sorry I was being weird. I'm a little freaked out about this."

She nods. "It's okay. I'm sorry I was mad at you," she says. Only Wendy would apologize for being justifiably upset.

"I should have told you. I just couldn't believe it," I say. It's a relief to have confided in her. It's a relief she doesn't think I'm delusional. It's such a relief that I laugh a little. She laughs, too. Wendy knows; she always knows.

"So how can I help?" She scoots over to make room for me on her bed.

I tell her my dad made an appointment for me to see a med-tech tomorrow morning, and I'm worried I won't remember anything after they fix my key. "I thought maybe I could describe those strangers to you, and you could make a sketch of their faces," I say.

"Like a police sketch?"

"Exactly," I say. "And I was also hoping you could give me a ride to Keep Corp, if you're not busy. I'd rather not go by myself."

"Of course," says Wendy. "But what if you don't?"

"Don't what?"

"Don't go to your appointment."

"My dad would be so mad," I say.

"I'm not saying you never go. I'm just saying you wait a day or two. It's so incredible that you can remember everything! If we were still in school, you'd ace every test with just the slightest bit of studying." Wendy sighs with dramatic longing.

I giggle. I hadn't even thought about that. Though I doubt it would work since I don't seem to have much control over when or what I remember. But I tell her she's right. "I guess I don't *have* to go tomorrow."

"Good. But we'll still draw the sketches, right?"

"Right." I lean against the headboard and close my eyes. But all I find is a hazy image of two people in blue coats. I squint, trying to focus the picture into clarity, but it remains a useless blur. I open my eyes.

Wendy looks expectantly at me.

"It's not working," I say.

"Try again," she says calmly.

I try again. And again. And again.

"I can't do it. I can't remember," I moan.

"What if you start with something you *can* remember?" says Wendy.

I close my eyes again. This time, instead of trying to visualize those two strangers, I imagine myself walking down the hallway, toward the light in the kitchen. I imagine my mother getting up from her chair to answer the door.

And I'm there, suddenly there, bare feet on cold tile, tugging at my pajama pants twisted uncomfortably up my leg, as the man and woman come into the room. Although their faces are half in shadow, I can make out her high forehead and narrow lips. I can make out his thick eyebrows and the bold curve of his nose.

I describe.

Wendy draws.

I describe.

Wendy draws.

It takes a while to get each portrait right. But then they're exactly right. Wendy is really talented. "They're perfect," I tell her. "Do you recognize them?"

She shakes her head. We gaze at the penciled faces. Then I sigh, then she sighs, then I sigh again. "Are you okay? You look kind of pale," she says.

"I'm just tired," I say. And my head is aching.

Wendy perks up. "I forgot to tell you! I gave Raul your phone number." She beams. She is so pleased with herself.

"Why'd you do that?"

"He asked for it."

"He didn't."

"He did, I swear." Wendy solemnly places hand over heart. "He said something about how you two were talking about the library and something and he meant to ask you something, and so something. Then he asked me for your number. You know what that means, right?"

"Yeah, it means nothing." My head is really aching.

"Lora, he's cute and nice. Don't be grumpy."

"I'm not being grumpy," I say. Although she's right: I'm being grumpy. Although she's right: Raul is cute and nice. But I thought Wendy was the one he was interested in. Wendy is the one guys are always interested in.

"Just give him a chance," she says.

"Can we focus on what's important? How are we going to figure out who these people are?" I tap the spiral binding of her sketchbook.

"Let's photocopy the pictures and post them around town. Maybe someone will recognize them," says Wendy.

"If someone recognizes them, he'll probably tell them, not us, then they'll come looking for us." I slouch down in her bed, resting my cheek on the pillow. My head is really aching, aching, aching.

"Then we can ask them what they were doing with your mom."

"But . . . What if they were involved in the accident?" I say, and I say it tentatively, as if this isn't what I'd been thinking all along, though of course it's what I'd been thinking all along. But to say it aloud makes the possibility feel real, terrifyingly real, in a way it hadn't before.

Wendy is quiet for a moment. Then she says, "Should we tell your dad?"

"I tried. He won't talk about it."

"Should we go to the police?"

"I don't know," I say. "I'm worried they won't take us seriously."

"Then we'll wait. We'll wait until we have more information." She nods with conviction, as though it is certain fact that we will soon have more information.

I nod too, and hope she's right.

6.

IN THE MORNING, I CALL KEEP CORP TO CANCEL MY APPOINT-
ment with their medical technician. I tell the receptionist I
have the flu and I'll reschedule when I'm better. "The summer
flu, that's rough," he says. "Drink lots of fluids, okay?"

I hang up the phone feeling victorious.

Then I go meet Wendy. We bike over to the library. Wendy
grumbles something about my obsession with research. I
grumble something about her obsession with disproportion-
ately large biceps. I remind her we have no other leads, not
really.

"Not yet," she corrects me.

"Not yet," I correct myself.

We go in and say hello to Cynthia the librarian. She shows
us a photograph of her dog, Gouda, wearing a yellow ruffled
bikini and a matching pair of yellow sunglasses. After express-
ing our admiration, we walk to the back of the library. Today
it's crowded, all computers occupied. I look for Raul, but he's
not there. I'm not sure whether I'm disappointed or relieved.

"What do you *really* think of that dog bikini?" I ask Wendy.

"I think it's *really* cute," she says. "I'd wear it. Not in yellow, though. I look awful in yellow. Blue would be better. The matching sunglasses are nonnegotiable."

"Obviously," I say.

We lean against the wall, waiting for our turn. Cynthia once told me that since the recession started, the number of daily visitors to the library has doubled, especially in the summer because there's air-conditioning and places to sit and things to do, and it's all free. I tell Wendy this.

"I see the appeal. My parents have this new rule where we're not allowed to turn the air on unless two or more people are home and they all agree it's needed," she says.

"At my house, whenever we turn on the air conditioner a fuse blows. So my dad bought me a new fan. It's got a remote control."

"A remote control? How *fan*-cy," she says. We giggle. Someone shushes us and Wendy shushes back. I poke her and say she'd better not get me in trouble at my place of work. Then we giggle some more.

Finally, two kids get up from their computers and we take their places. We agree that Wendy will read the search results published after the accident, and I'll read the results published before. I'm grateful. I can't handle any more obituaries.

So my lot of articles are all about Keep Corp. Apparently, my mother was frequently called upon to answer questions about keys, as well as the company's other products. Although

the memory key is their signature item—Keep Corp is the first
and still the only manufacturer of keys—they remain the industry leader by continually finding new ways of using medical
technology to solve problems of human biology. Some inven-
tions flopped, like the organ defragmenter. Some have found
moderate success, like the heart-reg. None approach the super-
star status of the memory key.

The more I read, the more I'm impressed by Mom's elo-
quence. It's no wonder the journalists contacted her: she was
able to take complicated topics and describe them simply. With
each article, her voice grows clearer in my mind.

Now do you understand? she asks.

My mother is sitting so close to me that I'm breathing the
lavender-soap scent of her while she helps me with my science
homework, explaining force and friction, her hands moving
gracefully to demonstrate.

Yes, I think I get it, I tell her.

Then I'm back in the library, reading an article about the
data backup function of the newest memory keys. The writer
interviewed a number of people with concerns about privacy.
Local activist Jon Harmon seemed especially riled up. He's
quoted as saying, "First we let Keep Corp into our brains, now
we let them take what's in our brains and store it on a computer. That information doesn't only have personal value. It's
worth billions to market research companies and the consumer
data industry. If we're not careful, we'll commodify our souls
in exchange for the convenience of a memory key. There needs

to be more regulation of the industry."

What he says makes sense, but I'm appalled to find myself agreeing—it feels like blasphemy. So it's a relief to read my mother's reply: "Keep Corp would never share or sell client data. It's not even technically possible. Memory data is encrypted using the unique brain chemistry of each individual. Thus, all memories—whether stored on your key or on our secure servers—can only be read by the memory maker."

Not even technically possible. I nod, reassured by her words. However, the next sentence is also troubling, but for an entirely different reason.

"The remote backup function is for your protection," said my mother. "In case, and this is the worst-case scenario, you should somehow damage your key to the point where your memories are affected."

It's as if she is lecturing me about my own damaged key.

I have to force myself to continue reading. The article ends with one last comment from my mom: "At Keep Corp our number one priority is to protect people from the horror of Vergets disease."

She was very convincing. Even the journalist, impartial as he was supposed to be, seemed convinced. After all, he gave her the last word. I scroll up to the byline. Carlos Cruz. The name is familiar. I click back through the other articles I've read. Several of them, the ones from the *Middleton Tribune*, were also written by Mr. Cruz. I make a note of this in my notebook. Then I elbow Wendy. "Find anything interesting?"

"Not especially," she says. "Mostly articles about the accident, a couple obituaries—you already read that stuff, right? Here's an interview with your aunt that mentions your mother, but only briefly."

"What does it say?" I nudge my chair over.

It's a profile of Aunt Austin, discussing her role in Congress. The piece is largely positive, praising her for working with politicians on both sides of the party line. There are only a few tricky moments, such as when the journalist writes that she has been criticized for her strong ties to certain companies, Keep Corp in particular.

In response my aunt said: "My sister, Jeanette Mint, was a scientist at Keep Corp. While she was alive, I always supported the work she did, and so I continue to honor her legacy now that she is gone."

"Keep Corp again," I say. "It seems like everything's about Keep Corp."

"Well, we should talk to Tim then," says Wendy.

"Why Tim?"

"Because he works there."

It turns out that for the past year, Tim has been an intern in the heart-reg department at Keep Corp, and I had no idea. "It's not that surprising," says Wendy. "Keep Corp headquarters is nearby. Most of the university's med-tech students intern there. I don't know why you're making such a big deal about it."

"You're right. I don't know either," I say.

Wendy taps her fingers on the sticky orange tabletop. We're sitting in a booth at our favorite downtown diner, taking our lunch break. The waiter brings our sandwiches, grilled cheese and tomato for us both. It's what we always order here.

I take my first bite. The oozy salty cheese is sweetened by the tomato and the bread is crunchy perfect. The sandwich is, as it always is, so greasily good. Except . . . I blink and the taste changes. The cheese congeals, the tomato is flavorless, the bread soggy. I'm angry because we'd planned on seeing that new movie together, then Wendy went to see it last night with her latest boyfriend. I'm angry but she doesn't notice. I'm angry and she's chattering about the poems her boyfriend wrote for her, how he's such a talented writer, how sweet he is, how kind, and, most importantly, how cute. My jaw hurts. I'm chewing so hard.

It's only a memory.

I know it's only a memory, yet it feels so true, so real. So right-now.

I take a sip of cold water. The ice cubes jangle against the plastic cup.

"But seriously," says Wendy. "We should talk to Tim. He could help us."

"Why?" My voice is mean. Even though the movie came out years ago, even though she eventually realized I was upset and apologized, even though I forgave her. "Tim doesn't work in the division my mom worked in. It's a huge corporation, you know. And he's just an intern."

"It can't hurt," she says.

"No." I don't want Tim involved. I'm regretting that even Wendy is involved.

But then I remind myself of how helpful she's already been, sketching those portraits, helping me read through old articles. It's ridiculous that I'm angry because two years ago she went to a movie without me. I stifle my resentment, I try. I ask what they're doing today at the day camp where she works.

"We're building stuff out of wooden sticks. It's the worst. There's so much poking, I'm always terrified some kid's going to lose an eye."

I force a smile. It's not that I'm still mad at her. It's just that I still *feel* mad. Unfortunately, one state of being seems indistinguishable from the other.

After lunch, Wendy goes to work, and I go back to the library. This time I search for information on malfunctioning memory keys, specifically cases where the H-Filter is damaged. The only article I find is about a fifty-four-year-old man who was knocked unconscious when he fell from a ladder. A minute later, he awoke in a rage. He tried to attack his wife. She got away only because his leg was injured from his fall. The man was taken to the hospital and had to be physically restrained for his own safety.

Later they found that the H-Filter in his key had been destroyed when he hit his head, resulting in an inundation of memory. Apparently, he and his wife had a tumultuous marriage and the moment he revived, he remembered it all: the arguments, the betrayals, the disappointments.

A spokesperson for Keep Corp—not my mother—called it a one-in-a-million situation, a freak tragedy that occurred only because the patient had such a turbulent marriage *and* because he sustained extreme and unusual damage to his memory key. The article concluded with the information that once the man's key was replaced, he returned to normal, and although his wife did not press charges against him, they have since separated.

My head is aching again.

I decide I've had enough for today. I pack up my pen and notebook and hurry out of the library. I unlock my bike and begin pedaling home. Fast. Very fast. As if my memory is something I can escape. I try staring down at the black road. I try staring up at the cloud-streaked sky. But no matter where I look, my mind stays wound around that man's awful story. I think about how angry I was at Wendy when we were at the diner. I think about how confused and upset I got around Tim.

Then I think of her. My mother. The tilt of her head, the tones of her voice, the touch of her hands—all things I never thought I'd see or hear or feel again. And what happiness it is to see and hear and feel these things again.

Until the memory ends. Until the grief comes.

It's an old acquaintance, this grief; a pit of misery I thought I'd climbed out from. But now I'm back again, slipped deep into the blackness. What will it make me do? Will I hurt someone? Will I hurt myself?

As soon as I get home, I pour myself a glass of water and swallow down two pain pills. Then I go upstairs to my room. I pick up the phone to call Keep Corp so that I can make a new appointment.

I pick up the phone. But I don't dial.

Because despite the anger and confusion and hurt, despite the sadness, despite the fact my head feels like it's about to burst, I'm not ready to give this up, these memories of my mother, this little I've regained after five years with nothing. I'm not ready to give her up.

Besides, there is the mystery of those two strangers at our house the night before she died. And what if beneath the clouding grief, it's there? The memory that will at last explain what happened, and how it could have happened, and why her. And why me.

I spent years obsessing over these questions, even though I knew there were no answers. No good ones.

But maybe I was wrong.

I put the phone back down.

7.

DURING DINNER, MY FATHER ASKS HOW IT WENT AT KEEP CORP this morning. My mouth is filled with potato, so I point at my lips and make a show of chewing. The show lasts even after I swallow, it lasts until I say: "Fine. It went fine."

"See? That wasn't so difficult, was it?"

"Easier than you'd imagine." I clamp a smile onto my face.

"What are you doing tomorrow? Austin invited us for lunch."

I had planned to do more research at the library, or possibly track down the journalist who wrote all those articles about Keep Corp, but I can't make up an excuse quickly enough, and I already feel bad for lying about my med-tech appointment, so I tell him I'm not busy.

Dad nods. He seems distracted, but it's hard to tell. His absentmindedness, a family joke when my mother was alive, intensified after she died. It usually annoys me, but at this moment I'm glad he's too preoccupied to be suspicious.

Though I do wonder if he's thinking about the questions I asked him yesterday.

After we finish eating, after we wash the dishes and put the leftovers away, my father goes into his office and shuts the door. I sit on the sofa with a book from the library. But now I'm the distracted one, thinking about my father, worrying about my father. I read the first page of my book three times. The fourth time, I'm interrupted by my ringing cell phone. I check the caller ID, but the number is unknown. I answer cautiously.

"Lora? It's Raul. I hope you don't mind, Wendy gave me your number. Maybe she told you, I don't know. Anyway, this is Raul." He talks fast, his sentences jumbled. His obvious nervousness almost makes me not nervous. Almost.

"How are you?" I ask.

"Good, and you?" he asks.

"Good," I say.

"Good," he says.

There is a pause, a pause awkward as only a telephone pause can be, but then Raul asks if I want to hang out tomorrow, and I say yes, and we make plans to meet in the evening. After hanging up, I try reading again. I stare at the first page for a long time. Finally, I give up and put the book away.

The last time I went out with a guy and it wasn't a low-stakes double date with one of Wendy's boyfriends' friends, it was with this kid from school, Gregory Lange. We went to the movies. As we waited for the show to start, he alternated between describing the plots of his favorite video games and asking questions about Wendy. What music did she like? What was her favorite food? How serious were things with her boyfriend?

I shrugged in answer. By then I'd realized this was more of an informational interview than a date. I felt humiliated, of course. Yet I was also kind of glad—when I agreed to the movie I hadn't known Greg was so totally dull. Therefore, it was an unpleasant surprise when halfway through the film he launched his face onto mine.

I blink and I'm there in the theater: his worming tongue, his sour breath, his lips greasy from popcorn. For a second, I'm too startled to do anything. Then I spit out his tongue and slouch toward the opposite end of my seat. I stare at the screen without seeing what I'm seeing.

I blink again and I'm back in the den. My head is throbbing and there's a bitter taste in my mouth. I run to the bathroom to brush my teeth. I tell myself Raul is not Greg; Raul is nothing at all like Tim—no, that's not what I meant.

I frown at my mirror reflection, and she frowns at me. What I meant was Raul is nothing at all like Gregory Lange. I rinse the toothpaste from my mouth. My head is really throbbing.

After breakfast the next day, my father hurries me into the car and we drive out to Grand Village, where my aunt lives in an ultramodern condominium building. We leave an hour before we're supposed to arrive, even though Grand Village is only half an hour away. Even though it's Saturday, so there won't be any traffic. Dad is slightly intimidated by Aunt Austin, and I might find that funny if I weren't slightly intimidated by her as well.

She's nothing like my mother. No—that's not true. Like Aunt Austin, Mom was smart and ambitious. But when she wasn't working, Mom relaxed. She didn't bother much with housekeeping or other kinds of domesticity, although she did keep a little vegetable garden in the backyard, which thrived despite bouts of negligence. My aunt, on the other hand, is a perfectionist both at work and at home.

My mother said when they were kids, her sister would get so mad when she teased her, even though Austin was older so it should have been the other way around. They fought a lot when they were little, but as adults they got along much better. My mother really admired her sister; she said so all the time. Although she did agree with Dad and me when we said Aunt Austin could be a little . . . overwhelming.

But after Mom died, my aunt helped us a lot. She cooked hearty, healthy meals to store in our freezer. She took me shopping and bought me my first bra. When I was learning how to drive, she went with me to practice, even though it was clear she was terrified by my driving: she'd get out of the car pale and disheveled, but because I appreciated all she was doing for us, especially since she was so busy with her work, I never joked about it. Not in front of her, anyway.

When we arrive at my aunt's apartment building thirty minutes before we're expected, I laugh at my father for rushing, but he merely suggests we go for a walk in the park, around Grand Lake.

It's a beautiful day. A tousling breeze moves through the

trees. People are lounging on the pebbly sand, children hop around in the shallow water. Dad pats my shoulder. "Remember when we came here for a picnic?"

"I remember." The memory approaches. But for the first time I try pushing it away: I grit my teeth and straighten my shoulders and clench my fists—and am so pleased to discover that I *can* stop it.

I'm so pleased that I imagine it back: Mom kneeling on our gingham blanket, sorting through the basket of food, while Dad and I untangle the tail of my new kite, a violet-colored butterfly, the delicate paper crinkling against our fingers.

When we finally have it fixed up, my father instructs me: *Which way is the wind blowing? Yes, that's right. Now face that way. Hold it up, nose up. No, nose of the* kite *up. Don't throw it. Just let go.*

There's not enough wind, says Mom, but at that exact moment a gust of air flies the butterfly up and up. She laughs gleefully, glad to be proven wrong.

"You had a kite," says my dad. "It was a red bird?"

"A purple butterfly with yellow dots. You gave it to me for my birthday."

"What an impressive memory you have."

"An impressive memory key," I say, voice irony-flat.

"That was a good time." My father sighs. He is gazing up at the sky. He loved her so much, I know. Since she died, he's dated occasionally, but those casual relationships always drifted away because he was mostly indifferent to the woman, or that's how it seemed to me. He loved her so much. I should tell him what I remember. I should tell him about those strangers in the kitchen.

"Dad?" I say.

"Yes, Lora?"

"Isn't it time to go?" I say. Is all I say. Maybe because I don't want to ruin the mood. After all, she is gone. She is gone, she is gone, she is dead. And it's a beautiful day. And I don't want to ruin the mood.

"It sure is," he says. Then he glances at me. "Something wrong?"

"I'm just scared we'll get in trouble if we're late," I say.

"Me too, Lora. Me, too."

At my aunt's building, we say hello to the uniformed man behind the front desk. He asks for our names. Then he asks for identification. Then he spends a minute glancing between the photo on my father's license and my father's face. Then he calls upstairs to tell my aunt we're here. Finally, he directs us to the elevators. It used to be that the doorman would just wave us past.

"They've increased security," I say.

"It's good. Public figures like Austin need protection. There are a lot of crackpots out there, and a lot of anger these days," says Dad.

We walk down the hallway, feet squishing in the thick rug. When we come to the right door, my father tells me I can ring the bell, smiling as if this is a treat he has saved especially for me. As if I'm seven, not seventeen. I dutifully press the button. Bells chime.

"Right on time," says Aunt Austin as she swings open the door. She is wearing a black shift dress that is as no-nonsense as her workday suits. "Come in, come in. Are you hungry?"

In the dining room, the table is set and covered with food, far too much food for just three people. There's a rice noodle salad and cold chicken and sweet-sauced mushrooms and a meat and vegetable braise. These dishes resemble the foods my mother used to make, but Aunt Austin's versions are more complicated, with more ingredients and garnishes. Mom never had the patience to spend hours in the kitchen. To her, food was fuel. Dad always did more of the cooking.

Once we're seated, my aunt lifts her glass of sparkling water. "A toast," she says. "Congratulations to our darling Lora. I know your successes in high school will only be exceeded by your success at university, and in life."

"Thanks." I'm embarrassed by her mention of my "successes," when I was only a good student, nothing exceptional. But this is how my aunt always talks.

"Now please, eat!" she says, so we do. The food is delicious, of course. Everything Aunt Austin does she does well. I tell her how good it all tastes.

"I do love to cook. I only wish I had more time to do it," she says.

My father proposes an intricate theory about the economic

bill, and I smirk. Like a kid cramming for a test, he had spent most of the morning with the *Middleton Tribune*. When I tried talking to him during breakfast, his answer was a grunt and the crackle of newsprint; when I frowned at him, annoyed by his nonresponse, he was protected by his shield of paper. All I could see was the fluff of his hair and the headlines: CITIZEN ARMY BOMB PLOT SUSPECT QUESTIONED; UNEMPLOYMENT RATE REACHES NEW HIGH; 600 ARRESTED AT ANTIWAR MARCH.

As the two of them discuss the economy, I think about the increased security downstairs, and consider the possibility that those two strangers were politically motivated, and their target was my aunt. When their conversation shifts to the bitterness between the two parties—as conversations about current events inevitably become about the bitterness between the two parties—I interject: "Is it really that bad? Does everyone get so personally involved?"

"Lora, you've pinpointed the problem exactly, it's that everyone gets so personally involved. But it shouldn't be personal. It should be about what's best for our country," says my aunt.

"Do you have enemies?" I ask.

"I certainly have enemies." She sounds almost proud.

"That doesn't scare you?"

"Sometimes. But I know it's because I'm doing important work. I've had to make sacrifices, some really difficult sacrifices, and I can't let my fear endanger all I'm trying to accomplish." A look of misery flits so quickly across her face that I wonder if

I imagined it, especially since misery is an emotion that seems incompatible with my aunt's disciplined personality.

"You *are* doing important work." Dad nods. "The main problem is, that's what the other side thinks too. So what do you do then?"

"You do what must be done," she says.

We are in the car, on our way back to Middleton, when my father repeats what my aunt said. "You do what must be done," he intones, mimicking the solemnity of her voice, his eyes wide and earnest. Then he chuckles. "Austin's great, but she's such a politician. She can't ever turn it off."

I laugh. It's true. And it's true it's difficult to have a personal conversation with someone who speaks primarily in platitudes, so I ask my dad the questions I hadn't asked my aunt: "What did she mean when she talked about the sacrifices she made? What sacrifices?"

"Gosh, I've no idea," he says.

"You think it's because she never got married and had kids?"

"But she *has* been married."

"What?" I fall forward in surprise, till my seat belt snaps me back.

"She's been married," he says again, louder this time.

"I heard you. I just don't believe you."

"It's true."

"Then how come I didn't know about it?"

"It was a long time ago. Before you were born."

I scowl at him. "Why didn't you ever tell me?"

"I never think about it, so it never occurred to me. It really was such a long time ago," my father says apologetically. Then he tells me what he can remember (Dad jokes: "My memory key is the same kind the dinosaurs used").

After law school, Aunt Austin got a job as a speechwriter for the governor. While working there, she met a young man named Jonnie. They had much in common: similar values and beliefs, similar lifestyles, and many of the same friends. They fell in love. Got married. But as time passed, Jonnie became disillusioned with the political system while my aunt rose through its ranks. They began fighting and eventually decided to separate.

"You think she regrets it?" I ask.

"Your aunt is a mystery to me." Dad pulls into our driveway and shuts off the engine. We sit in silence for a moment. Then he clears his throat.

"Lora, how about we go to a movie tonight? It's been so long since we've been to the movies, and soon you'll be gone, leaving your poor old father all alone," he says. His tone is jolly, but it makes me feel no less bad.

"I'm sorry," I say. "I wish I could, but I have plans with a friend."

"Which friend?"

"Besides, I'm not leaving you all alone. Campus is so close and you're there all the time. We'll see each other every day,"

I say. When I told my father I wanted to live in the dorms and not at home, he accepted it as though he expected it. However, that didn't keep me from worrying I was abandoning him. That same worry pinches me now.

Dad shrugs. "Yes, but who is this *friend* you have plans with tonight?"

"You don't know him." I open my car door and get out.

"*Him?* So it's a date?" He opens his car door and gets out.

"It's not. I don't know. Maybe. Kind of."

"Yes, indeed, it's a date," he says, chuckling. "Do we need to have *the talk*?"

"No! Please, no!" I cover my ears and rush up to the house. When I was thirteen, my father attempted to have *the talk* with me. I hadn't realized what was happening—I was only half listening because I thought he was philosophizing about humanity or something—until he mumbled the words "safe sex." Then I looked up and saw his face was red, and my face started turning that same red. I interrupted to say they taught us this in school so he could stop right there. Nonetheless, he continued.

I've managed to forget most of that conversation, and I'd prefer it to stay forgotten, so I brace myself against the memory like I did before, at the park. And it works like it did before—the memory remains distant.

My father is not so compliant.

"When two people are in love," he says as he unlocks the front door.

"No! Stop it! Stop it!" I shout as I run inside, laughing, and he chases after me, talking. It's moments like these I realize that despite it all, we did okay.

Dad and I, we're okay.

8.

WHEN I GET TO THE COFFEE SHOP FOR MY MAYBE-KIND-OF DATE, I'm all wriggly nerves in my carefully selected, now regretted outfit—why did I ever think this green shirt was flattering? Plus I'm late, but when I apologize for being late, Raul only smiles and says, "You're not late, I'm early."

Although this is a blatant untruth, it makes me feel a little less wriggly.

We small-talk over our days: I tell him about visiting Aunt Austin, he tells me about the peanut-butter-banana-pickle-jelly sandwich he made and ate for lunch. "Driving back from Grand Gardens, I felt so sick," he says.

"Peanut-butter-banana-pickle-jelly? Of course you felt sick. You deserved it." I giggle, but he doesn't. I worry I've offended him so I quickly change the subject: "Grand Gardens—is that your retirement home? Is it near Grand Village?"

When he nods I tell him that's where my aunt lives. I ask after Ms. Pearl.

"She's good. Did you know she has *two* gentlemen friends?"

"Really? That's amazing!"

"Yeah. Neither seems to mind that she has another fellow. In fact, the two of them are also friends. Though it might be because both of their memories are shot."

"They don't have keys either? Aren't they worried about Vergets disease? Is no one worried about Vergets?" I speak much too loudly; I feel people glancing in our direction. But it had to be said. It's what my mother would have said.

"Well, Earl used to have a key, but had to get it removed because his body rejected it. He'd had it for decades, then one day he was struck by this incredible pain, the worst pain in his life, he told me. They had to cut the key out of his brain. Now he has this gnarly scar on the back of his head."

The back of my own head twitches. I ignore it. "That's awful."

"Yeah. Now he can't remember much of anything because he'd been so reliant on his key. It's really sad," says Raul.

"I can't believe how many people at your retirement home don't have keys."

"Well, that's probably why they're there."

"Oh. Right," I say.

"There's even one resident who had his key purposefully removed, even though there was nothing wrong with it."

"That's weird. Why'd he do that?"

"He said he didn't want to remember. His family—wife and kids—was killed when that extremist group, the Citizen Army, hijacked the plane they were on. He never got over it. I mean, how could anyone get over that?"

And I say nothing more, partly because the waiter comes with our food, partly because there is nothing more to say.

Raul pays the bill—he insists. He smiles his nice smile and tells me that I can get it next time. I agree, feeling a flattered flutter at his talk of *next time*. We walk outside to where my bicycle is chained to a lamppost. As I unlock my bike, Raul tells me about his activist group that makes soup for the homeless. He invites me to come to their next meeting.

"Sounds fun," I say.

"Great." He stands close to me. He leans closer.

"Thanks again," I say.

"You're welcome again." His head tilts forward and his fingers take hold of my shoulder. Then he leans even closer.

And before I realize what I'm doing, I've stepped away and said good-bye and jumped on my bike, and now I'm pedaling farther and farther away, feeling guilty and embarrassed. And relieved.

It's not that I don't like Raul.

It's not that I would mind if he kissed me.

So what's my problem?

I don't know. My problem is that I don't know.

The night air is cool on my hot face. When I'm stopped by a red light, I look up at the unusual billboard on the side of a building, unusual because it's a photograph with no print, no indication of what's being advertised; there's just an attractive man and woman standing arm in attractive arm. I squint through the darkness and see that on the next corner, there's another billboard featuring that same couple.

When the light turns green, I ride over to where the attractive man is sliding a diamond ring on the attractive woman's finger. Still no print. At the next corner, the attractive couple cradles an attractive baby. At the next corner, the couple, older now, but still attractive, stand next to an attractive teenager in a graduation gown. At the next corner, the couple, much older now, but only slightly less attractive, sit with their arms around each other on an attractive porch. Still no print.

But at the next corner, the billboard contains only print. In big letters it announces: THIS TRIP DOWN MEMORY LANE WAS BROUGHT TO YOU BY KEEP CORP.

Has Keep Corp launched a new marketing campaign, or have I just never paid much attention to their ads before?

I grip my handlebars tight, then tighter, and pedal home as fast as I can.

When I come into the house, Dad is still up. He asks about my night and I make up cheerful answers to his questions until I can find an excuse to escape to my bedroom. My chest is heaving, my head is throbbing, but most of all, worst of all, I'm sad. Just all-of-a-sudden and hopelessly sad.

Lora, it's okay.

I'm blinking tears as Mama comes to sit next to me on my bed, where I'm curled up after a terrible day at school. She strokes my hair, her hand soft and slow against my head. She tells me it's all right, that I'll be all right, her voice as soft and slow as her hand. I take deep breaths until I'm calmer. I take deep breaths until I'm calm.

Then I pick up the phone.

"What are you doing tomorrow?" I ask Wendy when she answers.

"I came by earlier, and your dad said you were out. Where were you?"

"Sorry, I was with Raul. What are you doing tomorrow?"

"You were with Raul? Tell me everything!"

"There's nothing to tell," I say quickly. I shouldn't have mentioned him. Now she'll only want to talk about him. "I don't like him like that. He just wants me to join his soup kitchen, anyway."

"What? Never mind. He loves you. I know he—"

"What are you doing tomorrow? I want to find Carlos Cruz."

"Who's that? Is he cute?" she asks.

I sigh. I tell her he's that writer for the *Middleton Tribune*, the one who quoted my mother in several articles.

"Tim and I are supposed to go to the lake, but there's a chance he'll get called into work again. If that happens I'll be able to help you—if you want," she says.

"Yes, I want," I say. "Thanks."

"Good night, sweet dreams . . . *about Raul*." She hangs up quickly, before I can respond. But I am only giggling. Wendy is so Wendy.

I go to the bathroom, brush my teeth, and wash my face. The soap I use is new. I'd gone to the drugstore this afternoon to buy Dad a tub of his favorite chocolate ice cream, but got distracted by the display of soaps wrapped in floral paper, wrapped up pretty as presents. Standing there in the aisle, I held a lavender bar to my face and inhaled it through its lavender paper. It was the soap my mother used to use.

I bought one bar and it wasn't until I was halfway home that I realized I'd forgotten the ice cream and had to go back.

Now I rinse my face and slide on pajamas and fall into bed, and when I close my eyes all I smell is lavender, the herbal grassy sweetness, half perfume, half medicinal, and I imagine that she's sitting next to me, pulling the blanket over my shoulders, smoothing my wayward hair from my face.

And she's there. Here.

Mama says good night. She says sweet dreams. Then she's about to go, so before she can go I hook my fingers into the scratchy wool of her sweater and tug her close, closer, and ask her to tell me a story. I don't let go until she agrees. *Just one*, she says. *Then right to sleep, okay?*

My mother tells me the story of the man who invented the memory key, and it's a tale as good as any fairy tale—the clever technician, the forgetful wife—until she comes to the ending that seems to me like no real ending: *So Keep Corp made keys widely available, saving everyone from Vergets disease*, she says.

But what about that man? I ask. *What about his wife? What happened to them?*

Mom pauses before answering. *They lived happily ever after*, she says at last.

I sigh with relief as she leans over to kiss me, her lips cool against my forehead. She smells like flowers, I tell her so, and she smiles and kisses me again. *Good night*, she says. *Good night, Lora.*

Then she leaves. Then she's gone.

But before I can be struck by the loss, I imagine her back. Cool lips. Calm voice. Scratchy wool sweater. I imagine her back and make the memory happen all over again. It's easy now that I know how.

Mama says good night. She says sweet dreams. And I don't let her go.

9.

WHEN I WAKE UP, I FEEL WORSE THAN I'VE EVER FELT BEFORE.
Worse even than at Nick Jordan's birthday party, where I drank
four cups of jungle punch and spent the rest of the night throwing up in the bathroom. As soon as the thought occurs to me, I
pray I won't revisit that moment. This is bad enough.

I stagger downstairs and swallow three pain pills and a
mouthful of water before going into the den to collapse on
the couch. The blood pounds a hot hammer in my head. The
throbbing sparks all around my brain.

"Back to sleep? You just woke up." Dad looms over me.

"It's my vacation, I'll sleep if I want to." I close my eyes and
wait, hoping he'll go away. He goes away. Then my cell phone
starts ringing. The sound rips up my eardrums. I wait, hoping
it'll go away. It goes away. My arm is numb, but I cannot find
the energy to turn my body over. I wait, hoping it'll go away. It
goes away.

Then finally it's the pain that goes away. I sit up. Very carefully, I ease myself to standing. I shake out my deadened limbs

and go upstairs to phone Wendy.

"I called you," she says. "You didn't answer."

"Sorry, um, I wasn't feeling well."

Her voice softens. "Is it your memory key?"

"I had a bad night of sleep, that's all. Are you going to the lake?"

"Tim has to work. It's Sunday and he has to work, poor guy. But now I can help you track down that dashing and handsome journalist. Want to come over?"

I tell her yes. I eat a small bowl of cereal, take a quick shower, and by the time I'm ready to leave the house I'm good as new. But I swallow down another pain pill, just in case. And I bring the medicine bottle with me, just in case.

It takes five minutes to bike to Wendy's house, and it takes five seconds to find Carlos Cruz—his phone number is listed online. Wendy volunteers to call. She tells him we're journalism students working on an article about memory keys, and simple as that he invites us over.

"Good news," she announces. "His voice is really sexy."

"Stop it," I say.

Mr. Cruz lives in the northwest part of Middleton, in a neighborhood that used to be considered dangerous but is now considered artsy. Once we're on our way, I turn down the volume on the car radio.

"What are you doing?" says Wendy. "I love that song."

"What are we going to say to this guy?"

"Dibs if he's single, okay? I know you don't mind, since you have Raul."

"Wendy . . ." I hate how she is not taking this seriously. But she never takes anything seriously.

I blink. We're in the bathroom during a middle school dance. I'm scrubbing at the orange soda stain on my white dress, the paper towel crumbling as I scrub and scrub, and I can't seem to erase either color or smell, that citrus syrup smell, but when I tell Wendy she only says: *No complaining, you can't even see it, barely even. Come on, let's go back outside. If you won't, I'll go without you!*

I blink. We're walking out of the classroom after a history exam, everyone chattering as they push out the door, knocking elbows, trampling feet, backpacks bumping in their rush to escape. Except for me. I'm worrying over the last question, and the first question, and the questions in between. I'm berating myself for not studying as much as I should have. Wendy grips my arm and asks: *What's wrong? Is something wrong?* But before I can answer she giggles and says: *Never mind. Guess who called me last night? You'll never guess.*

I blink. We're in my bedroom and I'm crying, swollen-eyed, achy-faced, breaking-heart crying. Wendy pats a soothing rhythm into my back, fingers playing the piano on my spine. But when she speaks she sounds more bemused than consoling. She sighs. *I can't believe you like Tim. You know better, Lora, you really should know better. Tim is . . . he's just so immature.*

"Come on, I need some driving music," Wendy says. She

is grinning at the windshield, at the road; she is grinning at the world, and doesn't notice that I am sitting, seething, next to her. My hands ball up into fists, my fists are shaking with frustration, and Wendy doesn't notice. She never notices.

"Would you please take this seriously?" I say. "I know it's hard for you to do that when it's not all about you, but could you try? For once?"

She stops grinning. "Are you kidding? Why would you say that?"

"Because it's true," I tell her, and as angry as I am, I'm also surprised: I've never said anything like this to Wendy before. Even if I've thought it.

"Aren't I going with you to see this guy? Didn't I call him and lie to him for you? I can't believe you said that. Just because I made a joke doesn't mean I'm not taking things seriously. I'm trying to help. I'm trying to keep you from moping around, like you've been doing."

"I haven't been moping around."

"You really hurt my feelings." Wendy folds her lips together. She looks as if she might cry. But I refuse to be convinced by her forlorn expression; I know better than to be convinced by any of her expressions.

The car speeds down the highway, trees a blur of green on either side of the road. The back of my head is throbbing again. We spend a mile in silence, and another.

After the third silent mile, I start feeling remorseful. She's right: it was mean of me to say those things when she has been helping me. And if what I said is also true—that she has trouble taking my problems seriously—it's only a little bit true. Wendy is a good friend, my best friend.

It was my memory key's fault, feeding me years of resentment in one bite.

"Wendy," I say.

She doesn't respond.

"You're right. You've helped me so much."

She doesn't respond.

"I'm sorry. It's just my key messing with my head."

Finally, she nods. She mutters, "Turn up the music, okay?"

I turn up the music. We don't talk for the rest of the ride, but when we arrive at the correct address, Wendy parks the car, looks at me, and says: "So what should we say to this guy?"

As it happens, Carlos Cruz *is* dashing and handsome. And his voice *is* really sexy.

"Please come in," he says in his really sexy voice. He sits us down on a tattered couch surrounded by dusty stacks of paper. I repress a sneeze. The cluttered room is in direct contrast to the man who lives there. Mr. Cruz is tall and lean, his dark hair clipped short. He is wearing a shirt so brightly white it looks brand-new, and an equally crisp pair of pants.

He asks if we'd like something to drink, and as soon as he goes into the kitchen, Wendy pokes my arm. She widens her eyes and tilts her head to wordlessly express her message: he's *so* hot. I swat away her poking finger and look at her sternly.

"This is business," I whisper.

"Pardon?" Carlos Cruz returns with three glasses balanced in his two hands.

"Thanks so much for talking to us, Mr. Cruz," says Wendy.

"Please, call me Carlos. It's my pleasure." He smiles as he hands us our drinks.

"We really appreciate it." I take a small, nervous sip of water.

"No, I really appreciate it. It's a relief to know that in this age of technology, your generation is still interested in print journalism. Media, you know, is the fourth pillar of democracy—the mirror that shows us the truth about our world, keeping our politicians responsive, our government accountable, and our society functioning. Our work is important; we must never forget this," he says.

"I completely agree." Wendy gazes admiringly at him. I am less impressed. Sure, he's handsome. Sure, he's charming. Sure, his voice is magnificently deep.

But he also knows all these things, and covers himself up so completely with his good looks and good talk, it's all you can see of him.

As if he is aware of my skepticism, his expression darkens. "Of course it's not just fun and games. It can be a thankless job. You're juggling your sources, your editors, the bureaucrats, the corporations, and the public. Half these people want to kill your story. Half of that half wants to kill *you*. And it's not always the half you'd expect.

"I can't tell you how many times I've gotten a scoop from a reliable source and my bosses refused to go public. You must never forget that to the people you work for this is a business, or else you'll get crushed by their agenda. If you're going to make it in this world, journalism has to be your passion." Carlos Cruz sighs and leans back in his chair, evidently exhausted by his passion for journalism.

"Wow!" says Wendy. "I had no idea."

"Yeah," I say, less enthusiastically.

"I'm sorry for going on and on like that. Obviously I've got a bit of a chip on my shoulder. How embarrassing," Carlos says. But he smiles in a way that makes it clear he is actually neither embarrassed nor sorry. "Now what can I help you with? You're writing about memory keys?"

I nod. "I have a friend who works at a retirement home and I was surprised to learn that several of the residents don't have keys. So we're writing a piece about the different attitudes different generations have toward medical technology."

"Is this on or off the record?" he asks.

Wendy and I glance at each other.

"Whichever you prefer," she says.

"Are you going to record our conversation?" he asks.

"Um . . . I forgot our tape recorder," I say.

"We're kind of new at this," says Wendy.

Carlos smiles indulgently. "Everybody's got to start somewhere. Let's talk off the record. We're all journalists here."

Wendy's face is very red. I suspect my face is even redder.

"I like your story angle," he tells us. "Memory key use does drop off among the elderly. You must remember that keys have only been in production for the last fifty years or so but still . . . You're writing for your school newspaper—yes?—I expect your peers will find your article quite illuminating. Besides, it *is* odd that keys aren't more popular among the older generation since they were the ones who lived through the worst of the Vergets epidemic."

"It could be they're just paranoid," I say.

"Sure, that could be it." He looks directly at me. His mouth twitches and he shows me his white teeth. It's a sort-of grin, but there is something disbelieving in his expression. I become very aware of the fact that we are two girls in a stranger's home. I glance at Wendy, but she is gazing raptly at Carlos.

"Do you think Keep Corp would talk to us about this?" she asks.

"Maybe you could get some public relations nonsense from them. That would probably be sufficient for your purposes," he says, his eyes so steady on me that I feel smothered by his gaze. "Wouldn't it?"

"But I've read your articles. I know you've gotten some good information from them," Wendy persists. "Could you put us in touch with someone?"

"Those days are over." His face abruptly changes, features drawing closed. For a moment he is no longer handsome, he's just some middle-aged man. "These past couple of years, Keep Corp has tightened up, information-wise. All employees have to sign nondisclosure agreements—well, they always had to sign them, but the new contracts are even more restrictive. Now the only people who'll talk are from the PR department."

"What changed?" asks Wendy.

"I suspect it has to do with their new line of keys. There have been whispers about a big innovation, a development that ranks right up there with P. B. Fishman's work. You're familiar with P. B. Fishman?"

We nod. We're familiar with P. B. Fishman—inventor of the memory key, national hero, and subject of my bedtime stories and middle school essays.

"A couple years ago, when the most recent line of keys came out, the industry gossip was vicious and the press was mostly negative. The public went hysterical. Keep Corp almost had to pull the line. I'm guessing they don't want a repeat of that situation, so they've plugged the boat tight this time and it seems to be working. No leaks," he says.

"But there's always someone willing to talk," I say. "Isn't there?"

He shakes his head. "Not since your mother died."

I stare at Carlos Cruz, and he stares right back at me.

"What do you mean?" I ask lightly, try to ask lightly, but my words thud out.

"You," he says. "You're Jeanette's daughter."

"How did you . . . ?"

"I was at the funeral. I'm good with faces," he says. "It helps with the job. Not to mention—there's a resemblance."

"So all this time, you've been playing around with us?" snaps Wendy.

"You were the ones pretending to be journalism students." He sighs. "No hard feelings, all right? Jeanette and I were close friends."

But I am full of hard feelings. "If you were so close, how come I didn't know about you?" I say, wanting to insult him.

"You were a child. You think she'd tell you everything?" he says, and I'm the insulted one.

"Lora, let's go." Wendy stands up.

"Don't," says Carlos. "You came here for a reason. You wanted to ask me questions. Go ahead. I'll tell you whatever you want to know."

"Why would you do that?" My voice is rough, my tone is rude.

But he answers gently: "Jeanette was a good friend to me. Let me return the favor." Carlos stares out the open window, where faded blue curtains swing gently with the breeze. Against my will, I am softened by his sadness. He is so clearly sad.

"All right," I say. "How'd you meet my mother?"

He tells us they were students together at Middleton University. After graduation, they lost touch until several years later, when Carlos was a cub reporter working on a story about Keep Corp's new heart-reg device. He heard through a friend that Jeanette Lee, now Jeanette Mint, worked at Keep Corp, so he called her to see if she had any information for him. She gave him a nice quote about the rival company's product—nothing that would offend Keep Corp, while still adding interest to his article—and after that they met regularly to talk shop.

"What did Keep Corp think about that?" I ask.

"At first I always referred to her as an anonymous source, though she never said anything negative about the company. We both thought it best. But they tracked her down somehow, and told her if she was going to talk to the press she'd have to go through PR training. So she did."

"They weren't angry?" says Wendy.

"If they were, she never mentioned it. Jeanette was happy there. She loved her work. She was a loyal employee," he says. "Now let me ask you something—what are you after? These questions about Keep Corp, what's it about?"

Wendy looks at me and I look at her. I raise an eyebrow. She shrugs ever so slightly. I speak carefully: "I think there's something strange about what happened to my mother."

"You think the car accident was not an accident," he says.

"Is that what you think?" I say.

"No, I thought that's what *you* meant," he says, but I don't believe him. He had spoken too fast, as though the suspicion had long been waiting on his tongue, ready to leap forth at the first opportunity.

I sit up straighter and nod at Wendy. She takes out her sketches of the two strangers. "Do you know these people?" she asks.

He studies their faces for a long time before shaking his head. "Who are they?"

"I read your article about people angry at Keep Corp over privacy issues. Do you think their anger could have been directed at my mom, since she was a public face of the company? There's a guy you interviewed who sounds kind of fanatical. Jon Harmon?"

"Jonnie? No, no, Jonnie's a good guy. Passionate, not fanatical, though I admit it's a thin line. But he wouldn't have done anything to Jeanette. In fact, she's the one who connected me with him."

"Why did she do that?" I say.

"Especially if she were such a loyal employee," Wendy adds.

"Jonnie is smart and fair. Jeanette knew the other side had to be given a voice, so she wanted someone good to do it, someone who wouldn't take cheap shots or try to stir up groundless hysteria," says Carlos.

"Sounds like my mother," I say with an almost-but-not-quite smile. "How did she know Jon Harmon?"

"You don't know?" He lifts an eyebrow.

"I was just a child," I say, grimacing. "You think she told me everything?"

Carlos smirks. "Jonnie was married to Jeanette's sister. The congresswoman."

"Austin Lee?" I say, tongue stiff with shock. Wendy grips my arm.

"Yes. Jonnie Harmon and Austin Lee used to be married." Handsome Carlos Cruz smiles handsomely.

10.

"HE'S SO MYSTERIOUS," WENDY SAYS WHEN WE'RE IN THE CAR again. "Like a tortured hero in a movie. Don't you think so?"

"Carlos is too old for you."

"I know, I know. Besides, he's in love with your mother."

"That's ridiculous."

"A tragically doomed love. I wonder if they—" she says, then stops.

But I know what she was going to say because she's my best friend and I know how her brain works. Her brain works like an old black-and-white film where the lovers can never be, so they muster bravely on, exchanging meaningful looks from across the room. I hate the thought. I hate Wendy for thinking it. I hate myself for thinking that she's thinking it, for wasting time on an idea so absurd.

"I don't like him," I say. "He's weird. And his house was filthy."

"He's probably too tortured to spend much time cleaning."

"There was a moldy smell," I say.

"I didn't notice a smell."

"I think he was lying about not recognizing the people in your sketches. Did you notice how long he stared at their pictures?"

"You think he knows them?"

"I don't know, but I don't trust him. First he said he can't get any information out of Keep Corp. Then he said he's heard about a new line of keys. If security is as tight as he claims, where's he getting his information?"

"Well, it's his job to know stuff like that."

"Exactly! I'm sure he's still charming or bribing something out of someone."

"I didn't know your aunt was ever married. What happened?"

I tell Wendy what Dad told me, about them being young and in love, then growing apart and going in different political directions. "I wish I knew more," I say.

"Maybe Jonnie can fill us in."

"You think we should talk to him?"

"Aren't you dying to meet your aunt's ex-husband? Your ex-uncle?"

"I don't think he's my ex-uncle since they divorced before I was born," I say. Though of course I'm curious about Jon Harmon. Even if I worry it would be disloyal of me to seek out Aunt Austin's former spouse.

"Details, details," scoffs Wendy.

"Okay, let's do it," I say. Then I turn the radio up loud,

and for the rest of the ride home we scream along to the music with the windows all the way down, and the breeze whipping through the car, twisting our hair into knots.

As soon as we get back to Wendy's house, we look up Jon Harmon, but the internet keeps disconnecting and we can't figure out if it's a problem with the electricity, or the modem, or the computer, or what. We unplug then re-plug all the cords and wait for everything to come back on.

When we finally get online, we find a dozen Jon Harmons in Middleton alone. Plus ten listings for *Harmon, J.*

"And we don't even know if he still lives around here," I say.

"Carlos writes for the *Middleton Tribune*, right? So he must interview Middleton residents. It's only logical." Wendy prints out the list of Jon Harmon phone numbers.

"It's totally *illogical*," I say. "Don't you know anything about newspapers?"

"Of course. I'm a journalism student, remember?" She grins as she picks up the phone. She dials. "Mr. Harmon? I'm a student at Middleton University. I'm interested in starting a group to promote campus activism and someone suggested I call you for advice." She pauses to listen.

"No? Sorry to bother you," she says, and crosses out the top number.

"You're so good at this," I tell her. "It's almost scary."

"Thanks." She tears the list in two and hands me one.

I retreat into the corner of the room with my cell phone.

There's no answer when I call the first number. I leave a message, a modified version of Wendy's speech. A man picks up at the second number. I give the speech and am informed I have the wrong Jon Harmon. Same thing happens when I call the third, fourth, and fifth numbers. No answer at the sixth, so I leave another message.

Wendy and I put down our phones at the same time. She shakes her head. I shake my head. We throw ourselves across her bed and lie there, sighing.

I close my eyes.

My mother is in the kitchen, going to answer the back door. Two strangers stand there, a man and a woman. A blue-sleeved arm reaches out and takes hold of my mother's elbow.

"Wait, I know! Let's ask Carlos for Jon's number," says Wendy.

"I don't want to ask him for anything." My eyes are still closed. I know I'm here, stretched out on Wendy's mattress, but I'm also in the kitchen, watching my mother disappear through the door. I examine her face: her pale lips pressed together, the droop of her eyelids. I'm missing something. What am I missing?

"You know what would make us feel better? A snack."

The mattress bounces as Wendy jumps off. She grabs my limp hands and hauls me up from the bed and down to the kitchen. There she takes out an orange block of cheese, a knife, a box of crackers, and two small plates. She glances at me. "You okay? You look tired."

"I'm fine." I reach for the knife, but she gets it first. It's better that she does it, anyway—she's always reprimanding me for cutting things the wrong size and shape. As an artist, she has strong feelings about size and shape.

"Should we call the J. Harmon numbers next?" She slices the cheese into thin squares that match the crackers exactly.

"Not today. I've had enough for today," I say.

The front door slams. Tim stalks into the kitchen. His face is flushed. His dark hair is crooked around his ears. "I hate my job," he says.

"You don't mean that. You love your job." Wendy waves the knife at him.

"Lora," he says. "Hi." He smiles.

I set my gaze down on the table. "Why do you hate your job?" I ask.

"My supervisor is a maniac." He grabs a fistful of cheesed crackers from Wendy's plate. She smacks his arm and reaches to retrieve her food. But he's already taking long strides out of the kitchen, and a second later he's gone, along with most of her snack.

Wendy scowls. She slices some more cheese, wielding the knife with a viciousness that is slightly alarming. But then she grins. "Here's our chance," she says. "Tim just said he hates his job. Let's ask *him* about Keep Corp."

"He didn't mean it. You even said he didn't mean it."

She shrugs. "He'll help us. He's my brother."

"Yeah, but . . ." I have no good excuse. I settle for a bad one.

"Not now. I've got to get home for dinner," I say.

Wendy shrugs again, her mouth too full of cracker to argue.

I go upstairs to retrieve my things from her room. I slide my notebook into my backpack and zip the bag closed. When I look up, Tim is standing in the doorway. He has changed out of his work clothes and into a T-shirt and a pair of shorts. His hair is still crooked around his ears.

"You're leaving? But I just got here," he says.

"Yeah, I have to go," I say.

But I make no move toward the door. Because Tim is standing at the door. He takes a step into the room, then another, then another, until he's close enough that I can smell the laundry-soap clean of his shirt. Close enough that I can see the flecks of lighter brown in his dark brown eyes. Close enough that it would require only the tilting up of my chin and the tilting down of his chin for our lips to touch.

I step backward and bump into Wendy's bed.

"Are you nervous?" he asks.

"What do you mean?" I say, totally nervous.

"Nervous about leaving home. Starting college. It's a big change," he says.

I blush, I glare, I remember that night. Because of course I remember the conversation we had that night. But I never thought he also remembered.

"You're going to love it," Tim says. "College is much better than high school."

"I have to go," I say. But I don't move.

"Lora, I've always felt bad about . . ."

"Bad about what?" I say sharply.

"I didn't know . . ."

"Didn't know what?" I say sharply.

He doesn't answer.

"Didn't know what?" I say again, softer this time. I want to be angry at him but it's impossible to be angry at him when he is gazing at me the way he is gazing at me, his eyes steady, his face hopeful. Something inside me unfolds.

"I'm sorry if I hurt you," he says. "It was just bad timing, you know, I was going away, and you were still in high school, and my sister's friend, and . . ." He looks away.

That something inside me folds up again, and I find the anger I'd been looking for. "Forget it. It's in the past. Water under the bridge. Water over the dam. What's done is done." I tick off these clichés, lies burning my tongue.

Then I step around him, race out of the bedroom, down the stairs, and through the hallway. I shout a good-bye to Wendy without waiting for an answer. And finally I'm outside, and finally I can breathe.

I unlock my bike with shaky hands, blinking hard as I get on the seat, blinking hard as the memory approaches, and I grit my teeth and shove it away; I grit my teeth but I can't shove it away; all I can do is keep pedaling and pedaling, until I've pedaled my way into the past, to that night two years earlier.

It's late, almost midnight, almost past my curfew, and I'm leaving Wendy's house just as he comes home. Tim.

We meet on the front steps. I know he was at a graduation party because Wendy told me that's where he was. She asked if we should go crash. I said no. I had spent a long time wanting Tim, but had finally begun caving under the weight of his indifference. So I let go a little, and found myself living easier. Then I let go a little more. Wendy is dating a singer in a rock band and she set me up with the drummer. And for once I actually like the guy.

Hey. Tim sways toward me and places a hand on my shoulder. I can tell he's been drinking, I can smell the alcohol-sour on him, but even so my heart thrums as his palm heats my skin.

How was the party? I ask.

Same old people, same old party. Where are you going?

Home sweet home.

Don't go. Stay with me awhile. Talk with me awhile.

I remind myself I'm over him. I try to picture the drummer's shy smile in my head. But all I can see is Tim.

We sit on the porch swing. It rocks gently from our weight. The moon is a sliver in the sky, but the stars are bright. *Are you nervous?* I ask.

Nervous about what?

About graduating. Leaving home. Starting college. It's a big change, I say.

Yeah, I'm a little nervous. Kind of makes me miss being a kid. Remember how we used to play in the sprinklers? Then we broke one and my dad got so mad?

I remember. I remember you making fun of me all the time. I hated you.

You did? He leans forward to stare intently at me.

Remember that time you stuck gum in my hair?

That was an accident! I'm sorry. He is still staring intently at me, gaze steady, eyes gleaming. I look away, blushing, hoping it's too dark for him to see. *You don't hate me anymore, do you?*

Of course not. I probably didn't really hate you back then, either, I say, and even if he can't see my blush in the dark, he can surely hear it in my voice.

Good, he says. Then slowly, slowly, slowly, as if he's moving underwater, his face drifts toward mine. I'm holding my breath, as if I'm underwater too. His lips settle on my lips. He tastes of salt, and a slight beer-bitterness. My head is spinning. I am so happy. I am so scared.

Then a truck roars down the street and we jolt apart. We both laugh, and I know the moment is over. But I don't want it to be over.

That was nice, he says but leans back against the swing, apparently uninterested in repeating that nice thing. I'm confused, then embarrassed, then a little angry.

I should go. It's past my curfew, I say.

Tim walks me to my bicycle, and pats my arm before I go. That's all. Then I'm pedaling home.

Now I'm pedaling home. And I almost fly off my bike, startled first by the howling chorus of car horns, second by the fact I'm in the middle of the intersection, riding the wrong way at the wrong time.

The horns keep howling and I keep going because I can't

turn back, it's too late to turn back, but as soon as I make it across I roll onto the sidewalk and stop. There I catch my breath. I could have been hurt, I could have been killed. My head is throbbing.

Carefully, I bike the rest of the way home. I concentrate on the traffic and the traffic lights, the street and the street signs; I concentrate on my hands on the handlebars and my pedaling feet; I concentrate only on the present.

I concentrate as I come into the house, as I call out to my father and receive no answer. I concentrate as I swallow two pain pills, and two more. I concentrate as I go into my bedroom and shut the door. But then I rub my mouth with my fingers. I can still feel Tim's lips on mine, even though it was two years ago. Even though the kiss hadn't meant anything.

The next time I saw him, Tim acted as if that night never happened. So *I* acted as if it never happened. Until I got home. Then I cried. And cried. A week later, he started dating a girl from his class, some pretty, popular girl who was also going to the university in the fall. I was heartbroken. No, I am heartbroken. No, I'm not heartbroken now. It's my stupid key that's got me confused. I'm not heartbroken because I don't care anymore, I don't care at all.

I pick up my phone and dial. "What are you doing tomorrow? Want to go see a movie or something?" I ask when he answers.

"Yeah, let's go see a movie," says Raul.

"Great," I say.

"Great," he says. Then he asks me about my day, and I ask him about his day, and we talk for a couple more minutes until Raul tells me he has to go. "But thanks for calling. I'm glad you did."

"I'm glad you're glad," I say, and I'm embarrassed, thinking about how abruptly I left him the night before. It's nice of him to want to hang out again. He's so nice. I tell myself I'm lucky. I tell Raul I'm looking forward to the movie.

As I hang up the phone, the floor creaks outside my bedroom. I turn toward the sound. A shadow moves across the wall. A familiar shadow. My pounding heart pulls me forward, to the hallway. And there she is, outside her office door. She startles when she sees me. *Lora, honey, I didn't know you were home.*

Study hall was canceled today.

My mother comes over. She kisses my forehead. She looks tired. The skin under her eyes is dark and swollen. *Are you hungry?* she asks. *Let's have a snack.*

Then she's gone. Because she was never actually here. I leave the empty hallway and return to my room. Standing by the window, I gaze out at the front lawn, the memory shifting uneasily inside me. Because, I realize, there's more to it.

I blink as the unfamiliar car pulls up in front of our house. I'm standing by the window, home early because the new study hall teacher got sick. Rumor is he threw up in the teachers' lounge. Apparently, he ate the steamed carrots in the cafeteria. No one else is affected because everyone else knows better than to eat the steamed carrots in the cafeteria.

The unfamiliar car parks in our driveway. It's a silver sedan, shining like brand-new. I peer down, wondering who that could be. A minute passes before the passenger door opens. My mother gets out and says good-bye to the driver. Squinting, I try to see who she's talking to. As the car pulls away, I get a glimpse of a man with short, dark hair. Then I hear my mother in the hallway, and run to say hello to her.

And that's the whole of the memory.

A few minutes later, as my mother led me into the kitchen for a snack, I had asked whose car that was, who had driven her home? She tilted her head, as if she were the one asking me a question, before telling me it was a friend from work. She was having trouble with her car, so he very kindly gave her a ride. "Oh, good," I said, and thought nothing more of it. Until now.

For now when I examine that moment with seventeen-year-old eyes, I notice my mother's flushed face and the strange set of her lips. She looks as if she's hiding some prickly thing inside her mouth.

I'm wondering where my father is when the door bangs shut, signaling his arrival. I go downstairs. Dad is in the kitchen, taking groceries out of paper shopping bags and putting them in the cabinets, slamming bottles and boxes against the shelves.

"Hey, what's going on?" I ask.

"Keep Corp called about rescheduling your appointment," he says.

"Oh."

"Oh? Is that all you have to say?"

"I'm sorry. I wasn't feeling well that morning. I was going to reschedule." I'm trying to stay calm, but it is impossible in the face of his anger. He is so rarely angry, and when he is, his rage is never directed toward me.

But now it is.

"You lied to me."

"I didn't want you to worry."

He shakes his head. "Lora, you lied to me."

"I'm sorry. It's not a big deal."

"Exactly! Why would you lie about such a minor thing?"

"I'm sorry." I stare at the countertop.

"Here's what you're going to do. Tomorrow you'll go to Keep Corp to get your memory key checked out. You'll bring home a note from the technician, confirming you were there. Are we clear?"

"I'm working at the library tomorrow," I say. "It's my first day back."

"I don't care. Go during your lunch break. Or get someone to cover your shift. You're going. Promise me," he says. "Promise me now."

I promise.

My father hands me the phone.

I call Keep Corp and make the appointment.

Then it's done.

11.

THAT NIGHT I SLEEP BADLY. NOT BECAUSE OF THE PROMISE I
made to my father. Not because I'm anxious about going to
Keep Corp. I sleep badly because I'm not going. I sleep badly
because I've decided to break my promise.

After Dad leaves for work in the morning, I call to cancel
my appointment. This time, the receptionist is disapproving.
"Miss Mint, you really need to get this taken care of," she says.
"If your memory key is malfunctioning, as our system indi-
cates, it could lead to serious problems. You're putting your
health in jeopardy with this delay."

"Well, um . . ." I almost ask her about that article—the one
about the man who damaged his key falling from a ladder, and
attacked his wife. But I don't. Instead I apologize and tell her
I'll reschedule very soon.

Then I make a second telephone call.

"Hello?" His voice is cheery, as if he'd just been laughing
a moment before answering. How can a person be so cheery at
nine in the morning? But this is business, so I am all business.

"I was hoping you could help me with something," I say politely.

"For you? Anything," says Tim.

All day it's busy at the library, and it feels good to be busy, to focus my attention on the task at hand. I scan books, sort books, find books. I help people with the computers. People need lots of help with the computers.

It's not until late in the afternoon that my head starts aching, and only a little, and the pain clears after I take a single pain pill, so I dismiss the Keep Corp receptionist's concerns about my health. When my shift ends, I say good-bye to Cynthia the librarian and she tells me how wonderful it is to have me back and I tell her how wonderful it is to be back.

Then I go outside, and there he is: sprawled over the front steps of the building as if he owned those front steps, face tilted up at the sun as if he owned that sun. I march over and sit a proper distance away, my back stiff and my hands folded together.

"Hello," I say.

Tim squints. "Hi, Lora."

"How was work?" I ask politely.

"Could have been worse." He flaps a sheet of paper toward me. I thank him and take it. "Finally, a job perk," he says.

"What's that?" I say as I read over what he gave me. The document is on Keep Corp letterhead and declares that Lora Mint saw a medical technician on this date at noon. It looks absolutely official.

"I got to do you a favor." He grins.

"I really appreciate it," I say, but I don't smile back.

"So what's this all about?" Tim is still grinning. He doesn't seem to notice that it's pointless to flirt with me. Or if he does notice, he's not bothered by it.

"Nothing." I fold the paper into a small rectangle and slide it into my pocket.

"You're not going to tell me after everything I did to get that for you?"

"Was it hard to get?" I ask with concern.

Tim smirks, shrugs. "Actually? Not at all."

Then I can't help laughing. "Now I'm definitely not telling you."

"Do you want a ride home?" he says.

"No, thanks, I have my bike."

"We'll put it in the back." Tim leaps down the steps, toward the bicycle rack.

I follow, shouting, "Get your hands off my handlebars!"

But I decide I might as well go with him; it's not worth the effort to argue. Everything will be fine as long as he doesn't ask any more questions about why I need that letter from Keep Corp.

And he doesn't. We talk about college the entire way home. Tim tells me about his favorite classes, which professors to avoid, the best places to eat near campus, and the worst. I ask about his dorm, about his friends. I tell him I'm worried.

"About what?" he says.

"About leaving my father," I say, surprising myself. This is the first time I've voiced this thought aloud, and I can't believe I'm saying it to Tim, of all people, and I can't believe I'm saying it now, after Dad and I just had that big fight. But it's true: anger and frustration aside, I'm still worried.

Tim parks his car in front of my house. "Yeah, that sucks," he says.

I nod. I'm glad he didn't say something about how it'll all work out, how everything will be okay. I'm glad he didn't say something we both know isn't true. That's what most people do when you show them your grief.

Tim reaches over and takes my hand. He doesn't hold it, he just covers it with his palm, and it is a gesture only about comfort—it asks nothing else, it says nothing else. We sit there a minute in easy silence. Then he asks what I'm doing tonight. "There's a free concert downtown. Want to go?"

"I'm going to the movies," I say, startled. Our hands come apart. I'm not sure who moves their fingers first.

"I like the movies," he says, and I say nothing.

This silence is not easy; it pushes us away from each other.

"What, are you going on a date or something?" Tim finally says.

"Or something." I don't look at him. I'm afraid if I look at him, I might find myself in a different time, a time when I would have canceled any plan to go anywhere with Tim. I open the door and get out of the car.

"Thanks for the ride," I tell him.

"Hey, Lora," he calls out after me.

"What?" I lift my bike from the backseat.

"Have fun tonight. Don't do anything I wouldn't do," he says.

"I never would," I say, very seriously, and walk myself and my bicycle away.

When my father comes home, I'm waiting in the kitchen with the letter on Keep Corp letterhead. I hand the paper to him wordlessly, and wordlessly he takes it. I watch while he reads. "All right?" I say.

"Lora, you understand why I was angry, don't you?"

"I'm sorry for lying to you." My face is somehow straight and my voice is somehow steady. I don't know how.

"I appreciate the apology." He taps a perfunctory kiss on my cheek and goes upstairs to change out of his work clothes.

I stay there. I stay because I can't move; the guilt and shame have completely cramped my muscles. I feel awful about it, all of it, large and small. For lying to him. For continuing to lie to him.

And for suspecting that he is lying to me.

12.

AT EXACTLY EIGHT O'CLOCK THE DOORBELL RINGS, AND I'M down the stairs, through the hall, my hand on the knob before my father can get up from the sofa in the den. I yell to him that I've got it, then I open the door.

"I'd invite you in to meet my dad," I say. "Except no one wants that."

"Really?" Raul smiles bemusedly.

So of course I make it worse: "No, I mean, not that my dad wouldn't like you, or vice versa, my dad is perfectly nice, but . . ." I sigh. "Never mind, it was a joke."

"Right," he says, and then he laughs.

We get into his car. When he turns on the engine the radio comes on, and the announcer is speaking in urgent tones: ". . . Senator undergoing surgery. The extremist group the Citizen Army has taken credit for the attack, but the shooter is still at large."

"Have you heard about this?" Raul tells me that Senator Joseph Finney was shot as he left a press conference about the economic bill in the capital.

"That's horrible," I say.

"Yeah, but hardly surprising," he says. "Our economy is failing, our government is failing, and no one trusts anyone else. It's like we're on the brink of civil war."

"Come on, it's not that bad," I say. "It's just these extremist groups."

"Well, they're definitely a handy excuse for violating our civil liberties," he snaps, and his snapping takes me by such surprise I don't know how to answer.

A second later he apologizes. "I had a bad experience," he explains, and tells me about walking home from a party late one night and getting stopped and searched by two policemen. "I wasn't doing anything wrong, and they were threatening me, saying I had no business to be loitering around in this neighborhood. Even though I was two blocks away from my own house." His hands are fists around the steering wheel.

"That sucks. I'm sorry. . . . But civil war?" I say.

"Yeah, maybe I was exaggerating." Raul sighs. "Do you want to change the station? Put on some music?"

I spin the knob till I find a tune I recognize. The singer pleads to be forgiven—wailing, crying, begging for forgiveness. It's way too much, so I change the station again, eventually settling on some peppy pop song.

The night is dark, darker than usual. There are not many other cars on the road. I lean back in my seat and gaze out the window. There are storm clouds covering the stars. "I think it might rain," I say, and right on cue, it starts drizzling.

By the time we reach the theater, it's pouring.

"I'll drop you off first so you won't get wet," says Raul.

But I insist I don't mind, so he pulls into the nearest parking space. He unsnaps his seat belt and twists around to shuffle through the objects on the backseat of his car. "I think there's an umbrella somewhere around here," he says.

"It's fine, don't worry about it."

Raul throws a soft bundle into my lap. "You can wear this."

I shake out the fabric. "Isn't this your work uniform? I don't want to ruin it."

"It's waterproof, stainproof, and rip-proof. Practically indestructible," he assures me, so I drape the blue jacket around my shoulders.

We get out of the car and run through the rain. Somewhere along the way, Raul grabs my hand. It's colder outside than it's been in weeks, and I'm grateful for both the protection of his jacket and the warmth of his fingers.

When we get inside, I offer to buy his ticket, since I invited him, but then he offers to buy my ticket, so as a compromise I buy the tickets and he buys a bucket of popcorn, a box of chocolate caramels, and two large cherry sodas. I stare at all the food in the flimsy cardboard tray. "Think you got enough?" I ask.

"Want nachos too? A hot dog? A chili-cheese dog?"

"All of the above, please."

"Really?"

"I'm kidding. Let's get seats," I say.

"You look cute in my clothes." Raul smiles.

I look down at the gleaming blue fabric. The sleeves are so long they cover my hands, the jacket hangs to my thighs. "It's huge on me," I say, and give him a gentle push, careful not to upset his balance since he's carrying all that food.

As we make our way across the diamond-patterned carpet, I am suddenly uneasy, as if I've forgotten to do something crucial. Like turning off the stove before leaving the house. A small detail to remember that becomes a big problem when forgotten. I wring my brain, trying to figure out what it is. Shouldn't my broken memory key help with this? It doesn't.

"Where do you want to sit?" asks Raul.

"In the middle. Is this okay?"

The movie begins. It's a thriller about a beautiful female spy who infiltrates a terrorist group; it's all slinky sneaking and furious fighting and designer disguises and sparkly parties, and it's thrilling enough that I don't notice I've eaten half the bucket of popcorn until my mouth is crackly with salt.

I sip my cherry soda while the beautiful spy is at home, her real home, and her husband, her real husband, is napping in their bedroom while she sweeps the floor in the kitchen. Apparently, even female spies have to clean house.

I put down my drink when the hallway window eases open and the masked assassin somersaults inside. He creeps through the darkness, tucks a tiny ticking box into the corner, and creeps back out. Then he slams the window shut.

The beautiful spy whirls around at the sound.

My mother whirls around at the sound.

I'm standing just outside the kitchen, half asleep and very thirsty, watching as my mother walks across the room. She opens the door. I squint to better see the strangers on the step. There are two of them, a man and a woman, both wearing blue jackets, their faces half in shadow

You have to come with us, says the man.

There is a thunderous explosion and the screen goes up in flames. The assassin has detonated his bomb, and as he runs from the fiery scene he removes his black mask to reveal he is no anonymous assassin: he is the beautiful spy's partner, the handsome spy who has been posing as her husband. This false husband disappears into the night, a triumphant grin on his face.

And my head is throbbing, my heart thrashing—but not over this treacherous plot twist. I've unearthed the secret buried in my memory; I've discovered the fact that may make all the difference: the strangers who came to our kitchen that night, the man and the woman, are both wearing blue jackets. I look down at the jacket I am wearing at this exact moment. Raul's blue jacket.

The beautiful spy drags her true husband out of their burning house, but it's too late. He's dead.

"I knew he was the bad guy, almost from the beginning," Raul says as we walk across the parking lot. "Did you like the movie?"

"Yeah," I say automatically.

It's no longer raining. The ground is slippery wet and the air smells sweet in that after-rain way. There's a cool breeze, but I'm holding Raul's jacket in one hand. I don't want to wear it. I don't even want to be holding it. I can barely stand touching it. When we reach his car, I thrust it at him. "Thanks for letting me borrow this."

"You're welcome." He tosses it into the backseat.

"Is that the uniform for everyone who works at your retirement home?"

"Only the attendants. The nurses wear scrubs and the doctors wear lab coats, usually." Raul backs out of the parking space. "Should we do something else now? Get some food?"

"I have to go home," I say.

"Are you sure? It's not so late."

"I'm sure," I snap. Then I realize that in my agitation I'm being rude. I don't want to be rude, not to Raul who is so nice. Not to Raul who could help me locate those blue-jacketed strangers. "I'm sorry," I say. "I would normally love to get some food after eating all that popcorn and chocolate, but I'm exhausted tonight. Next time?"

"Next time," he says.

Then I say, so unsmooth, "Um, yeah, so I've been thinking I should visit Ms. Pearl at the retirement home. What's a good day? I'm working tomorrow but I can come the day after."

"Is that Wednesday? I'll be there. If you get there around noon, we can have lunch together." Raul smiles his nice smile.

"Great. I'll invite Wendy too. Because she has a car, so she can drive."

"Good idea," he says. Then we talk more about Ms. Pearl, and he tells me what a hustling card player she is, so I'd better watch out when we visit, and it's not until he parks in front of my house that I remember—

What, are you going on a date or something? says Tim as he parks his car in this same parking space.

Shut up, Tim.

Gritting my teeth, I push the past into the past, and when Raul turns to face me, I turn to face him. His expression is so hopeful it makes me ashamed all over again about the other night. Quickly, I move toward him. Just as quickly, he moves toward me. His lips are soft and taste like cherry soda. My fingers curl up his neck and tangle in his hair. His hands slide across my back. And it's nice, like he's nice. It is very nice.

"Guess what. No, you'll never guess what," I say as soon as Wendy answers the phone. I'm in my room, lying across my bed, head flopped over the side.

"Is this about your date?" she says.

"How'd you know about that?"

"Psychic powers."

"Impressive," I say. "So Tim told you?"

"Isn't it sad that I have to rely on my brother to get personal information about my best friend?" says Wendy.

"It was last minute. I would have told you," I say.

"Sure, sure. So were you out with Raul? How'd it go?"

"We saw that new spy thriller. But that's not what I want to talk about."

"Honestly, the *movie* is not exactly what I want to talk about, either!"

"Those strangers in the kitchen that night—they were wearing blue jackets that are exactly the same as Raul's blue jacket," I say quickly, so quickly that my words all bump together. Then I wait for her reaction. And wait.

"Wendy? Are you there?"

"I'm here. But . . . are you telling me Raul abducted your mother?"

"The jacket is his work uniform. So those people in the kitchen must have also worked at the retirement home—"

"—and maybe they still do!" she says.

Then we plan our plots and plot our plans, and after we hang up I'm too excited to sleep. I no longer care about all the excruciating headaches, or the disorienting moments of anger and sadness; I no longer feel guilty for lying to my father and not getting my memory key repaired. What I now know makes it all worth it.

Though, if I'm going to be honest, there is another reason I haven't gotten my key fixed.

I close my eyes and imagine her face.

The memory comes faster than ever before.

My mother's doll speaks in her squeaky high voice; she invites my doll to a tea party. My doll accepts in an even squeakier, higher voice. After the tea party, both dolls go to school. Mama and I play together for hours. We play until I'm a moment before sleep, still atop my bed, mouth still salty from the popcorn.

Yes, this is the other reason why I haven't gotten my key fixed. There is grief in remembering, but there was always grief. At least now there is also her voice, her smile, the cool touch of her quick hands. My mother.

13.

WHEN MY ALARM CLOCK STARTS BEEPING, I GROAN AND COVER my face with my blanket. Beep. My head hurts. Beep. It really hurts. *Beep*. But I have to get to work. *Beep*. So I heave myself out of bed. *Beep*. And smack my alarm clock into silence.

Oh, beautiful silence.

I take five pain pills. Then one more.

Dad is in the kitchen, drinking his coffee and reading the *Tribune*. He says good morning without lifting his eyes from the newspaper. I wonder if he's still mad at me. If so, how unreasonable: he saw the document that said I went to a medical technician.

Except I actually didn't.

Shame momentarily overcomes pain.

Lora, it takes a lot to get your father angry, but once he's angry, he stays angry for a while, says my mother. *He's stubborn.*

I look up, expecting to find her sitting across from me at the table. Of course, there's no one there. My head throbs. One good thing about Dad's annoyed silence is I don't have to make an effort to keep up conversation; I focus on eating my cereal. My skull thunders as I chew.

Then I'm off to the library, pedaling so slowly my bicycle keeps tipping off balance. When I get there, I ask Cynthia if I can work at the circulation desk. I need to sit down. She frowns. "You don't look so good. Maybe you should go home."

"It's only a little headache. I'll be fine."

"All right. But if you start feeling any worse, you better tell me."

I slump at the circulation desk. A kid comes over and tells me this long story about visiting his grandma, and missing the train, and missing the bus, and that's why his books are late. He asks if I'll waive the overdue fees. I say no. He asks again. I snarl in response, and he leaves teary-eyed.

Maybe I shouldn't have snarled quite so ferociously.

Maybe I shouldn't be working the circulation desk.

Maybe I shouldn't be here after all.

Fortunately, the pills kick in by lunchtime. I get a sandwich from the deli and hurry back to the library, to the computer area. I sit at the end of the row, at my usual machine in the corner, and look up the Grand Gardens retirement home.

According to its website, the building was recently constructed and features all the modern conveniences; the grounds are extensive with delightful walking trails and a small fish pond. Residents rave about the food and the staff and the activities. There is a waiting list. All in all, Grand Gardens sounds like a lovely place. Nothing fishy other than that fish pond.

Until I find the article about Grand Gardens' annual benefit dinner.

For the past seven years, the event has been cosponsored by a major corporation, a corporation known for its wholesome values, exemplified by its charitable giving to programs for the community. The article speculates that this corporation will soon be known as much for its philanthropy as for its innovations in medical technology.

This corporation is, of course, Keep Corp.

In the afternoon, when my shift is almost-but-not-quite over, I sneak outside to call Wendy and tell her about the article. "I think Keep Corp was involved in my mom's car accident," I say.

"Wait, Lora, slow down. Maybe those people in the blue jackets took your mother away during the night, but she must have come home in between that time and the time of the accident because she was driving to work when it happened, right? So first of all, the blue jackets are from the nursing home—"

"Retirement home."

"—not Keep Corp. And second, there's no definite connection between the blue jackets and the crash," she says.

"Except the jackets came just six hours before the crash. Six hours before is a definite connection," I say.

Then Wendy says nothing; she lets the line go to silence, lets the fizzy phone silence express her skepticism.

"They could have threatened her or drugged her or did something else that caused the accident. My mom was a very careful driver," I say.

"But what about the in-between time?"

"It doesn't matter," I say, and try to believe it.

"Why not?" she asks.

"Those two strangers are connected to the retirement home, and the retirement home is connected to Keep Corp. That can't be a coincidence," I insist.

Wendy sighs. "Are you at the library? Come over when you get off work."

"I'll come now," I say.

Mrs. Laskey lets me into the house and directs me upstairs, where Wendy is reclined on her bed, sketchbook propped in her lap, nibbling on a pencil. I close her bedroom door behind me. I wonder if Tim is home. Not that I care if he's home.

"What are you drawing?" I ask Wendy.

"I'm not drawing, I'm thinking. I think better with a sketchbook."

"Right. So, what are you thinking?" I sit down next to her.

"We should go to the police," she says.

I shake my head. Five years ago the police had their chance to properly investigate my mother's death, and they failed.

"Then you should tell your dad. I'd feel better if he knew," she says.

"Let's wait until after we go to Grand Gardens. I'm afraid he'll freak out. He's been in such a horrible mood lately," I say, and although this is true, the words feel false—not a lie, but not the whole truth, either.

"Fine. We'll wait a day." Wendy nods. Then she asks about Raul.

"He's good," I say.

"Come on, tell me everything. Sharing is caring."

"When they say sharing is caring, they don't mean that kind of sharing."

"No changing the subject," she says.

I tell her because it's the only way to stop her. I tell her we went to the movies and I bought the tickets and he bought the snacks. I tell her he drove me home and there might have been a few minutes of kissing in his car.

Wendy pinches my cheek. "My little girl is growing up!"

I swat her hand away. "Stop that, my head hurts," I say, and as soon as I say it, I wish I hadn't. I know what comes next.

"Your . . . head hurts?" She peers at me, as if a hurting head is something that can be observed. Then she taps my arm with her chewed-up pencil. "Lora, now that we know those strangers worked at that nursing-retirement home, you should probably get your key fixed. I'll take you."

"I'm fine," I say.

"But what if it's eating your brains?"

"I've figured out how to control it. I can stop the memories when I want, or make them happen when I want. It's pretty convenient."

"Really." She squishes her face, doubting. I've always disliked this about Wendy, and I dislike it now: how she constantly questions what I tell her, poking hole after hole until my words shrivel down like deflated balloons.

It's even worse when she's right.

"Really." I stand up and tell her I have to go.

Then I go.

During dinner, I watch the absentminded professor from across the table. He is taking too-large bites, the food falling from his fork. He gobbles his glass of water. He slops butter on his bread. Then he looks at me. "Aren't you hungry?" he asks.

"Why did Mom go into medical technology?"

If he is surprised by my question, he doesn't show it. "Your mother always had a gift for the sciences. She won first prize in her grade school science fair, did she ever tell you about that?" He smiles a small smile, the smallest smile.

I shake my head.

"She built a three-dimensional model of the human heart using macaroni. Impressive for a nine-year-old, don't you think? She wanted to be a doctor one day, a surgeon."

"What changed her mind?" I ask.

"She always said she got interested in medical technology at the university, but I think it also had to do with her grandfather. You know he had Vergets disease, don't you? She was in high school when his memory began failing. Jeanette deferred going to college for two years so she could help take care of him."

"She did? I didn't know that," I say.

"There was no one else who could stay with him during the day. Her mother worked long hours, and Austin was already away at school. They didn't have the money to hire help, and they didn't want to put him in a nursing home. But her grandfather was in bad shape. He'd wander away if you stopped paying attention for a second. Once the hospital called to say he'd fallen in the street. He was all right, just scratched up and disoriented. But none of them had even realized he left the house. They thought he was napping in his room.

"After that, your mom decided she would stay home with him. Her mother and sister argued, but you know how your mom is once she makes a decision. There's no changing her mind." My father sighs as he adjusts his eyeglasses. He doesn't seem to notice he's spoken about her in the present tense.

"Her grandfather didn't have a memory key? Why didn't they get him a key? There were memory keys by then, right?" I ask.

"She didn't know why her mother didn't consider that option," he says. "She thought it might have been because her grandfather's decline was too fast; he was so far gone by the time they realized the breadth of the problem."

"Still," I say. "They should have tried."

"That's what your mom thought as well. I think that's why she ended up majoring in medical technology, and why she went to work at Keep Corp," he says.

"So she only had to defer two years?"

"That's when her grandfather passed away."

I don't know what else to say. I feel like I've learned more about my family history in the past several days than I have in the previous seventeen years, and this new knowledge sits heavily on my shoulders. "Oh," I say, finally.

"Yes," my father says, returning his attention to his dinner.

"Dad, are you sure there was nothing unusual about the night before the accident?" The words spill from my mouth. I spent the afternoon practicing this question in my head, trying to get the phrasing and intonation just right—nonchalant yet sympathetic. But it comes out clumsily accusing. A statement, not a query.

"Pardon?" His fork hovers halfway between mouth and plate.

"I know something happened that night. What happened?"

He looks not at me, but at my plate of uneaten food. "I don't know what you're talking about. Eat your dinner."

"Don't lie to me, Dad. You got so mad at me for lying to you, how could you lie to me now?" My voice is shaking from the effort to keep from crying, shaking from the effort to keep from screaming.

My father sets his fork down on his plate. The clock on the wall ticks louder and louder to fill the silence. In the distance, a woman laughs.

Finally, he says, "It doesn't concern you."

"But it does. It's about my mother."

"Lora," he says.

"My mother," I say again.

"That doesn't entitle you to know everything."

"Why not?" I demand.

"It's for your own good." He is calm. I hate how calm he is.

"I don't understand why you should be the one to decide that."

"I'm your father. I'm protecting you."

"You're not protecting me. You're protecting yourself!" I shout.

Then I turn away, I run away, I go up to my room and slam the door. My head is beating, blasting; my head burns as if it's made of fire. I gulp down pain pills, one after the other, not bothering to count out the total, and sit down on the hard edge of my bed.

She was my age when she decided to give up college to take care of her grandfather. How selflessly mature she was. How selfishly immature I am. Yet how can I help it when my father insists on treating me like a child?

Why won't he tell me the truth? What is the truth?

Whatever it is, I won't stop until I know.

I promise myself.

I promise her.

14.

THE HORN HONKS AWAY THE MORNING CALM. I GATHER MY notebook and keys and pill bottle and wallet and phone, and stick my head out the window and yell: "Be right there!" Then I race downstairs and outside, to the car parked in the middle of the street, where it would block traffic if there was any traffic to be blocked. The passenger door opens.

"Ready for adventure?" Wendy asks from the driver's seat.

"I guess so." I duck into the car.

"Me too!" someone says behind me.

I twist around to look at the backseat. I untwist to look at Wendy.

"He insisted. What could I do?" she says.

"You could have told him no," I say.

"I'm right here," says Tim. "I can hear you both."

"So?" I glare at him.

"So what?" He glares at me.

"Children, if you can't behave I'm sending both of you home," Wendy says in her most mature tone of voice, the one she uses on strangers and teachers.

"How could I resist a visit with Ms. Pearl?" says Tim.

"Doesn't Keep Corp need you?" I say.

"It's my day off." He shrugs.

I frown at Wendy. We were supposed to plan our strategy on the drive over. She gives me an I-know-and-I'm-sorry shrug followed by a we-could-just-let-him-into-our-plot raise of the eyebrows. I shake my head.

"Did you bring the papers?" I ask, referring to her sketches of the strangers.

"Sure did," she says.

"Great." I begin planning our strategy in my head. We'll start with Ms. Pearl; I think it will be safe to show her the sketches. And I'm sure she'd be happy to fill us in on any oddness about the place. But—

"Lora," says Tim. "I understand we get to meet your *boyfriend* today?"

"He's not my boyfriend," I say, without turning around.

Wendy smiles an I'm-really-really-really-sorry smile.

We arrive just before noon. The building is wide, not high, with two rectangular wings jutting out from the circular center. The exterior is made of a stony white material and looks expensive. The windows are large and clean and look expensive. The lawn is neat and lush and looks expensive. Grand Gardens is, appropriately, grand.

When we come into the lobby, Tim sidles up to the reception

desk and tries flirting with the lady behind it, an older woman with a silver halo of hair and a face drawn on with makeup. Tim compliments her necklace, a roping chain that also looks expensive, and she glares suspiciously at him, as if he's about to yank the necklace right off her neck.

It's nice seeing someone immune to Tim's charm.

Wendy intervenes. "Sorry, ma'am, is this boy bothering you?"

"Yes," the woman says, and it's unclear whether she is answering the question or inquiring about our intentions.

"We're here to visit Ms. Pearl," I say.

"Visiting hours begin at noon. You may return at that time."

I glance at the ornate clock on the wall behind her. It's less than ten minutes till twelve. "Is Raul working today? We know Raul."

"Visiting hours begin at noon," the woman says again. Her gaze shifts to her computer. Clearly, we've been dismissed. We go outside to wait.

"What did you do to offend that woman?" Wendy admonishes her brother.

"Nothing! I was being my normal friendly self."

"That explains it," I say.

"Why don't you call Raul?" says Wendy.

"Yeah, why don't you call *Raul*?" says Tim.

I call, but the line goes to voice mail. I leave a message informing him that we're here. "He didn't answer," I tell them.

"Guess he doesn't like you that much after all," says Tim.

I shove him. Hard. "What's your problem?"

"What's *your* problem?" he mutters, rubbing his shoulder.

Wendy rolls her eyes. "Children, it's noon. Shall we try again?"

This time, the lady condescends to let us enter and directs us to the recreation room. We walk down a very long hallway, turn left, down another very long hallway, and through a set of double doors. Despite the casual name—suggesting Ping-Pong tables in basements, battered couches, and video games—this recreation room is as grand as the rest of the place. Bright light falls through the large windows onto thick rugs. The walls are a warm yellow. Elegant furniture is arranged in perfect conversational clusters.

Ms. Pearl is installed in one such cluster, between two elderly men on a brocade-upholstered sofa. We make our way toward her, heads turning as we pass. We are the youngest people there by several decades.

"Ms. Pearl!" says Tim.

"Timothy Laskey, what are you doing here?"

"We came to visit you," he says.

Ms. Pearl dimples and claps and invites us to sit down. "I'm sorry, young ladies, please remind me of your names again. I'm afraid my memory is not what it used to be." I'm slightly offended that she remembers Tim's name and not mine, when I was the one to rescue her from a speeding car just last week.

Though I shouldn't be surprised. Obviously, unfortunately, Tim is unforgettable.

But Ms. Pearl is so happy to see us, I can't stay resentful. She introduces us to her gentlemen friends, Earl and Henry, and asks us the standard questions about what we're doing with our lives. Wendy tells her about her art, and working at the summer camp. Tim tells her about his med-tech studies and internship. I tell her about my job at the library, and that I'm not sure what I'm going to study when I get to college.

"You know, Lora, I still remember your essay about P. B. Fishman, the memory key inventor. That was an excellently researched paper. Far beyond sixth grade work."

"You remember *that?*" I'm shocked she remembers, and shocked she thought it was excellently researched, and shocked she remembers thinking it was excellently researched. I am also embarrassingly pleased.

She nods, but her gaze drifts past me. "Look who it is," she says.

We all turn around to watch as Raul approaches. He is wearing his blue jacket. The sight of it makes me not like him, and I don't want to not like him, so I concentrate on his cheery face as I grin and wave and call out his name. I am very aware of the fact that Tim is sitting just three feet away.

"I was hoping you'd visit today." Raul smiles his nice smile at us. At me.

"Of course," I say, smiling nicely right back.

"Hey, Raul. This is my brother Tim," says Wendy, and the two of them grip hands—half handshake, half high five, as guys do—and it makes me feel funny. Weird-funny, yes. But a little ha-ha funny, too.

We make plans to meet for lunch in the dining room. Then Raul has to go back to work. But before he leaves he sets his hand on my shoulder. "See you later," he says.

I glance at Tim. He is looking at me. Our eyes meet. Tim glances away.

"Raul is such a nice young man," says Ms. Pearl. "Isn't he a nice young man?"

The gentlemen friends, Earl and Henry, grunt in agreement.

I nod at Wendy. She takes out a folder from her bag. "Ms. Pearl, do you know these people? We think they might work here," she says.

Ms. Pearl lifts her glasses from her chest, where they hang on a thick gold chain, and sets them on her nose. She examines the sketches while Earl and Henry peek over her shoulder. Tim is so unperturbed I wonder what Wendy has told him. I look inquiringly at her, but her gaze is conveniently steady on the old folk.

Earl, who has been dozing on and off during our conversation, becomes animated. He points excitedly at the sketch of the woman. "That young lady is familiar."

"She works here?" I lean forward in my chair.

"No, I don't think so." Earl slumps back into the sofa. "I believe I knew her a long time ago. I'm sorry, my memory isn't so good."

Ms. Pearl pats him consolingly on the knee. "Girls, I'm

afraid I don't recognize either of these people. Are you sure they work here?"

"Five years ago they worked here, maybe," I say.

"I wasn't here then, but Henry was," she says. "What do you think, Henry?"

Henry strokes the few hairs he has left on his head. "No, I've never seen these two before. I'm sure of it. Absolutely sure."

"Absolutely sure?" I remember Raul telling me one of the men has a mild case of Vergets, and neither of them, like Ms. Pearl, have memory keys. I'm trying to figure out which man is which, but perhaps it doesn't matter because they seem similarly incapacitated. It makes me angry. It's irresponsible of them not to have keys. *An essential, preventative measure*, I hear my mother say.

"Absolutely sure?" says Henry, sounding less absolutely sure than before.

"May I ask why you don't have memory keys?" someone says in a loud voice. "After all, your memories are your most precious belongings; they make up your sense of self. Memory keys preserve that, they keep you *you*. And you're not the only one who benefits, it benefits those around you, all your loved ones."

It's my mother. It's my mother's words, it's my mother's voice, but when I look for her I don't see her. I decide it was an aural memory.

Then I notice everyone is staring at me.

Because it was me. I was the one speaking her words, in her voice.

Ms. Pearl smiles gently. I know that look. It's the look she would give a student who tried hard but ultimately gave the wrong answer. "You make some good points, Lora, but I must admit it can be nice to forget a few things every once in a while and just live in the present," she says. Her gentlemen friends grunt in agreement.

"I'm sure that's true." I am mortified by my outburst.

"So you haven't seen these people here before?" Wendy points everyone's attention back to the sketches, and I'm grateful.

"Perhaps they worked in the south wing," says Ms. Pearl.

"There's different staff for each wing?" asks Tim.

"Oh, yes. In the south wing, everything is different."

"How so?" asks Wendy.

Ms. Pearl glances at Henry, who glances at Earl, who glances at Ms. Pearl, who glances back at Henry. Then Ms. Pearl speaks. "People go there when they're gone."

Wendy gasps. "You mean, like, dead?"

"No, no. When they're very sick. Or the Vergets advances to the point that they need more care." Ms. Pearl gently clears her throat. "Children, you must excuse us. We have a lunch engagement. But perhaps we could meet here later for a game of cards? Yes?"

"Yes, Ms. Pearl," we say in unison.

She rises, and is followed by her two gentlemen. When Earl turns, I notice the broad scar on the back of his hairless head. It's curved like a smile, a painful, red smile. So Earl is the one who had to get his key removed because his body rejected it. And Henry is the one who has Vergets.

Wendy sighs. "That was disappointing."

"You'll probably have better luck asking the staff," says Tim.

"Raul might know who to talk to, don't you think?" says Wendy.

"How much did you tell your brother?" I ask her.

"She didn't tell me anything," says Tim. "But it doesn't take a genius to figure out the two of you are up to no good. So fill me in already."

"It's none of your business," I say.

"Come on. Don't you trust me?" he asks.

I blink. There's Tim with his new girlfriend, their arms around each other, their faces so close together they might as well be kissing, and the sight hurts so much that when I turn away and glimpse my reflection in the hallway mirror, I'm shocked that I'm not bloody, I'm not bruised; I'm shocked that I can appear so normal on the outside when I'm breaking on the inside.

I blink. There's Tim on the porch swing, his lips against mine, his mouth slightly beery, but not unpleasantly so, and I cannot believe this is happening, *finally* happening; I am feverish with happiness, I feel it sparkling in my cheeks and chest and fingers and toes, I feel it in my lips against his lips, and I'm so happy.

I blink and there's Tim, opening the door for me, grinning.

I blink and there's Tim, scowling because I laughed at his haircut.

I blink and there's Tim, waving his water gun as I run away shrieking.

I blink. There's Tim gazing at me, his eyes steady, his face hopeful as he apologizes for hurting me, saying that it was just bad timing . . .

And I feel as if I'm about to shatter into pieces, cracked apart by all my contradictory feelings for him. My hand slips into my pocket, fingers curl around cool plastic, and I close my fist, clutching so tightly to the bottle of pain pills that my nails cut into my palms. I compose myself. Then I look at him.

There is Tim, sitting in a brocade-upholstered chair in the recreation room at Grand Gardens, looking at me inquisitively. He asked me a question, I remind myself, and now he's waiting for the answer.

What did he ask? He asked if I trust him.

"No," I say. "I don't."

"But Lora . . ." says Wendy, smiling a concerned smile.

This time, I sense it coming and I grit my teeth. I straighten my shoulders.

But I can't push back the past; the memories are too strong.

Wendy is smiling a concerned smile. But also frowning in frustration. But also pointing a nagging finger at me. Wendy is rolling her eyes while I'm talking. I'm mid-sentence and she walks away.

I blink.

Wendy bangs on the door, then comes into my room scolding: *Why aren't you coming, Lora? You promised you'd come!* She says it with such outrage, as if I've heartlessly betrayed her, instead of merely canceling the double date we had planned with her singer boyfriend and his drummer friend.

I'm sorry. I'm tired, I say.

That's not allowed. Wendy glares, but then she notices my swollen eyes and red nose and blotchy face. Her expression softens. *Lora, what's wrong?* she asks.

And I'm already struggling to hold in my sadness; I cannot hold in one thing more. *It's Tim*, I confess, and I tell her about seeing him with his new girlfriend, I tell her about the night we kissed, and I tell her that I've liked him for a very, very long time.

Wendy rubs my back while I cry and I'm glad I told her.

I'm glad until she sighs and says, *I can't believe you like Tim. You know better, Lora, you really should know better.*

"Lora?" says Wendy, smiling a concerned smile.

I grit my teeth. I straighten my shoulders.

But I can't push back the past; it's too strong.

The memories are perfectly clear, painfully clear. They fall like an endless line of dominoes, each one knocking down the next, and I am flattened by every one.

Greg Lange asks me how serious it is between Wendy and her boyfriend . . .

Nick Jordan tells me Wendy is the most talented person in the whole school . . .

Girls cluster around Wendy, oohing over her dress, ahhing over her shoes . . .

Wendy complains about yet another boy who likes her . . .

Wendy advises that I should try being friendlier . . .

Wendy says she's trying to keep me from moping around . . .

And on, and on, and I hate it, and I hate her.

My best friend. I hate her.

But I also hate my jealousy, my insecurity. I hate how she bosses me, but I also hate myself for letting her boss me. I hate how she wants attention and gets attention, but I also hate myself for pretending that I don't want it when I don't get it. Yes, I hate Wendy, but I hate myself more. Much more.

"Lora, are you all right?" says Wendy, smiling a concerned smile.

My hand hurts. I'm clutching the pill bottle so tightly that my fingers have cramped around the narrow tube. Still, I don't let go. I don't let go even as the pain strikes my skull, pain like a punched face, a snapped limb, a broken heart. Pain like a dead mother . . . almost.

Now Wendy is speaking, and so is Tim, but from inside my headache it sounds like they're yelling at me from some vast distance. I can't understand what they're saying, and I don't want to understand. All I want is to get away from here, from them.

I prop myself up to standing and stagger out of the room. Down the long hallway I go, feet stumbling over air, one hand stretched forward, fingers feeling for direction, while my other hand stays wrapped around my bottle of pain pills.

Footsteps echo behind me. Voices call out my name.

I tell them to leave me alone. I shout it.

Then there are no more footsteps, no more voices, nothing.

I swallow five small tablets, one at a time and haltingly, for I don't have any water and my mouth is dirt dry. I'm not quite sure how I managed it, but I made it outside, and now I'm sitting on a wooden bench, listening to a thundering chorus of bird chatter—there must be dozens of them around, yet I can't see a single one—while the breeze cools my flushed face. The pain seeps away so slowly, I don't notice it going until it's nearly gone.

"Lora?"

I don't answer. I don't look to see who it is. But the person walks over and I'm relieved to find it's only Raul. There are no memories with Raul. He is a blank slate, a new beginning, a clear conscience.

"Can I sit down?" he asks.

"Of course." I wonder how he found me. They must have told him I was out here. I wonder what else they told him. He looks worried. I wish he didn't look worried. "Did you see Wendy and Tim?" I ask.

"Yeah. Wendy said you weren't feeling well."

"That's all she said?" In the midst of all my anger, I'm grateful to her, and the feeling makes me flinch.

"She told me you went out for some air."

I nod. I sigh. "I'm sorry about all this trouble," I say.

"What trouble?" he asks.

"I guess, uh, nothing."

Raul seems disappointed that I don't tell him more—that I don't tell him everything—but he's too nice to insist. Instead he asks what I think of Grand Gardens. I say I certainly wouldn't mind living here one day.

"Me too. It's expensive, though. Better start saving now."

"Except for the south wing. Ms. Pearl made it sound scary."

"That's because she's worried she'll end up there. They're all worried. Really, the south wing isn't scary at all, except the residents are older or sicker, and need more care. They don't have all the socializing and activities and field trips."

"What do you mean *no field trips*?" I ask with mock-outrage. But it's not much of a joke, so he answers me with serious explanations about wheelchairs and medical equipment.

After a while, Raul asks if I'm feeling better. I tell him I am.

"Should we meet Wendy and her brother in the dining room?" he says.

"I'm not hungry," I say.

"Well, I should eat something before I get back to work."

"Of course," I say sheepishly. "Go. I'll stay here."

"You're sure?" He looks puzzled.

"What time do you get off? Can you give me a ride home?"

"Yeah, but I'm here until four. You want to wait till then?"

"I don't mind." I grin broadly, perhaps too broadly.

"But what are you going to do for all that time?"

"I'll walk around Grand Lake. Maybe I'll visit my aunt. She lives nearby."

"You must be really mad at your friends," he says.

I feel a fresh rush of anger. Then one of remorse—all those memories, those screaming, kicking memories, happened so long ago that any hurtful offenses should already be forgiven and forgotten. But if I can't forget, how can I forgive?

"Yes," I say. "I am."

After Raul goes back inside, with instructions to tell Wendy and Tim they can leave without me, I get up from the bench. I walk across lush grass, past stately trees; I circle the fish pond and pause to study the orange fish glimmering at the bottom of the shallow pool, unmoving except for an occasional flick of fin or tail.

But all the while I'm thinking about the man who fell off the ladder and damaged his memory key. The man who damaged his memory key, attacked his wife, and had to be physically restrained for his own protection.

Why do I refuse to get my key fixed?

It's madness.

It *must* be madness to sacrifice my health and my friendships and my father's trust for the sake of a memory. It *must* be madness to exchange all that is real for dreams of the past.

And when I told Wendy I'd figured out how to control my key, that I could stop and start it on command—that's no longer true, if it was ever really true. For while it's become easier to summon memories into being, it's become harder to send them away. I obviously wasn't able to manage it in the recreation room.

I look up. I'm at the other end of Grand Gardens now. Although Raul said there's nothing really scary about the south wing, I imagine people moaning in pain, bodies crashing against the walls in attempts at escape. But of course there's nothing like that. The windows are dark. The place seems uninhabited. Or abandoned.

Until I hear a sound, a squeaking. I tilt my head and see a man on the second floor, straining to open a window. It doesn't open far. The man disappears. My gaze drifts and lands on another window, caught there by a sense of movement. The blinds are up, but I can't see inside; it's too dark. I step slowly forward.

A moment passes before I make out what I'm seeing. The picture assembles slowly, like those optical illusions that require minutes of staring before the image becomes clear. A figure by the window. A woman. One arm across her chest, the other arm folded up so her fingers can gently tap against her cheek, as if she is in deep thought.

I've seen this pose a hundred times before, and all those hundred times beat through me at once.

She is standing at the window, tapping her face in deep thought.

She is sitting at the kitchen table, tapping her face in deep thought.

She is reclining before the television, tapping her face in deep thought.

She is pacing across the room, tapping her face in deep thought.

My mother.

15.

THE WHITE-HAIRED WOMAN BEHIND THE RECEPTION DESK, THAT same impossible woman from an hour ago, an eternity ago, stares up at me. I grip the counter and glance at the doors to the south wing. They're closed. I wonder if they're locked. But I make a second attempt at speech because my first attempt was—I admit it—fairly incoherent.

"I'm here to visit someone." I'm still talking too fast, but now she raises one brown-penciled eyebrow and I take this as a sign that she understands. "On the second floor, in the south wing, please," I say.

"Name of the resident?"

For a second I don't know what to say.

Then I say, "Jeanette Mint." Then I say it again. Then I spell it. Then I begin spelling it again. She tells me she got it. She clicks through her computer. I notice I've left smudges on the countertop and attempt to wipe them away. I smudge it worse. She clears her throat. I stop wiping.

"There's no resident here with that name," she says.

"What?" I say.

She gives me a look that is her response: she knows I heard what she said.

"Are you sure?" I ask. "Jeanette Mint. Will you please, please look again?"

The woman heaves a ten-ton sigh, but returns to her computer. A moment later, she shakes her head. "There's no one here with that name. No Jeanette, no Mint."

My voice is half shout and half whisper. "But I saw her."

No, that's impossible. All of this is impossible.

Without thinking, I step toward the closed doors. Perhaps the woman says something, though if she does, I don't hear her. I reach for the handle and push with all my weight. Perhaps the woman yells for me to come back, though if she does, I don't hear her.

I nearly fall over as the door flies open.

Then I'm running, running as fast as I can. Perhaps I pass people who tell me to stop, ask me what I'm doing, though if I do, I don't see them or hear them. All I see is that figure at the window. One arm across her chest, the other arm folded up so her fingers can gently tap against her cheek. I soar up the stairs and count the doors to my destination: one, two, three, four.

I stop. This is it.

The door is flat-white, unadorned, unremarkable. There's no doorbell, only a brass knob. With great concentration, I bend my fingers to form a fist out of my right hand and tap my knuckles against the flat-white, three gentle taps.

I wait. Then I knock again, less gently this time.

Still there is no answer and no sound from within the room. There is, however, the clatter of quick footsteps down the hall. They are coming for me. They are coming to take me away from her. My palm covers the brass knob. The door eases open. I'm inside.

And there's nothing.

Well, there is a bed and a nightstand, a lamp in the corner next to a chair upholstered in velvet. But there is nothing. No one. Only me and a thin skin of dust covering the entire room.

I touch my face and find my cheeks wet. I hadn't known I was crying. But now that I know, I sob harder, my body shaking so much I have to sit down on the bed. There is no blanket on the mattress, not even a sheet. It has clearly been a long while since this room was last occupied. I am choking, I am drowning in my disappointment.

For the first time I admit the truth: I thought I would find her here even before seeing that figure in the window; I thought I would find her here the moment I matched Raul's jacket with those worn by the strangers who took her from our house that night. Of course, I never spoke my expectation aloud; I did not even think it into actual words. Partly because I was afraid to jinx it, partly to avoid humiliation should I be proven wrong.

But now I'm humiliated anyway. It serves me right for imagining that the last five years of my life had been a lie, for daring to believe she could be alive, for trying to undo the past. My mother is dead. I have to remember. She is dead.

A woman in green scrubs comes into the room and says I have to leave. I tell her I know. I do not look at her. She takes me down the hall, down the stairs. I can't stop crying. I'm so embarrassed. I wish I could stop crying. We walk through the reception area. I ignore the lady behind the desk, though I feel her gaze cutting into me.

"Is your car in the parking lot?" asks the woman in green scrubs.

I shake my head.

"I'm sorry, I have to escort you off the premises," she says, not unkindly.

"I understand." My voice breaks and I would be even more humiliated if I had not already reached my maximum level of humiliation. We go past the parking lot to the front gate.

"This is fine," she says. "Do you know where you're going?"

"I think so." I look directly at the woman for the first time. She is fair-skinned and fair-haired and I guess she is about the age my mother would be if my mother were still alive. But she's dead, I have to remember. No matter that when I shut my eyes she is close enough that I can count the strands of silver in her hair, smell the soft-sweet of her skin. My mother is dead, no matter how much I remember.

"You take care." The woman smiles sympathetically, and her smile wounds me. I have to explain. I have to make her understand.

"I saw someone by the window, but there was no one there when I got to the room. I guess I'm seeing things now. It's been a strange week," I say. Then I look away, embarrassed again, embarrassed still. "I was just so certain I saw someone in there, someone I knew."

"It was probably one of our residents. She likes to wander around to the empty rooms. It's not allowed, but we never manage to catch her in the act. When we go look for her, she's always back where she's supposed to be." The woman shakes her head, chuckling a bit. "Guess you couldn't catch her either," she says.

All at once, I stop crying.

Now I am walking toward Grand Lake Park, walking on the narrow sidewalk next to the wide black road. Now I am trying not to hope, but of course I am hoping. For now that my secret fantasy has been revealed, it won't return to hiding. And how ridiculous the fantasy: that my mother is not dead, that she resides in a luxurious retirement home and spends her days wandering around to the empty rooms.

Why would she go there? Why would she stay there?

I close my eyes and when I open them, I'm hungry, really hungry, stomach howling complaint. I glance at the clock. It's dinnertime. Dad is teaching an evening class and won't be home till late. Mom is in her study, all afternoon she's been in there. I go to her closed door and press my ear against the wood. I hear nothing. I lean on the closed door. It opens slowly, creaking softly.

She is sitting at her desk, pen in hand, writing in her note-book. She does not look up from her work. Maybe she does not notice I'm here. *Mom?* I say quietly, careful not to startle her. She hates being startled.

What do you want? Still, she does not look up from her work.

When's dinner? I'm hungry, I say. She flips a page and continues scribbling. Her usually neat bun is falling off her head, the hair in wisps on her shoulders. *I'm hungry*, I say again, in case she didn't hear me the first time.

Finally, she looks up from her work, looking at me as if I've only just appeared. *I'm busy. Order something, okay? I need some peace and quiet right now.*

What should I order? What do you want?

All I want is some peace and quiet, she says.

Fine, I snap. But there is no satisfaction in snapping at someone who is not paying attention; already she has returned to her notes and does not notice me stomping away.

An hour later, when the deliveryman arrives with our dinner, she will come downstairs, drawn by the smell of hot food, and ruffle my hair, kiss my cheek, pull up a chair and a fork, and act as if nothing bad happened between us. And I will let my hair be ruffled, let my cheek be kissed, let her sit beside me, and act as if I am nothing but pleased to see her.

A week later, while I eat my breakfast, my father will stumble into the kitchen and tell me she's gone.

"Watch it!"

"I'm sorry," I say to the jogger.

"Pay attention!" he shouts as he runs past me.

I stare out at Grand Lake. The beach is crowded with

people enjoying the beautiful day. A woman plays with her two small children at the edge of the lake. They squeal as they splash their bare feet into the water, and she laughs.

Peace and quiet, my mother says.

There's a rattling in my hand. The bottle of pain pills. I unscrew the top before remembering that I've already taken a couple tablets, not long ago. But I gulp down one more, anyway, because my head is aching again.

Except maybe it's not my head that aches, not exactly my head. I don't know. Something hurts.

16.

I WALK OVER TO MY AUNT'S APARTMENT BUILDING EXPECTING she won't be home since it's a weekday afternoon and she's never home on weekday afternoons, but today she is. I give my name to the uniformed man behind the front desk, and when I get upstairs she's waiting at the door. "What a wonderful surprise!" she says.

"I was in the neighborhood. Are you busy?"

"Oh, I'm always busy, but never too busy for you. You just caught me. I'm leaving for the airport in an hour; I'm going to the capital for Joe Finney's funeral. You know about that, don't you?" she says.

I nod. Joseph Finney was the senator who'd been shot after a press conference a couple days ago. He had died from his injuries. "Were you friends with him?" I ask.

"We were allies, an even stronger bond. He was a good man. I can't believe they still haven't found the shooter." Her expression warps and I see anger, I see fear.

"What does the Citizen Army even want?" I ask.

"It's hard to tell. Sometimes they say they want to bring the entire government down, other times they say they just want a political voice. The only thing the Citizen Army is really consistent about is destruction."

I touch her arm. "You're careful, right? You have bodyguards and stuff?"

"Don't worry, my dear. I take all the necessary precautions." She seems both moved and amused by my concern.

Aunt Austin asks if I'm hungry and tells me I'm welcome to whatever I find in the refrigerator. "I'm sorry I can't prepare something for you, but I have so much to do before I leave," she says.

Then she goes to her bedroom to pack, while I ramble around in her kitchen. There is plenty to eat, but I'm surprised to find that her leftovers consist entirely of food in take-out containers. I always imagined my aunt returning from a long day at work and cooking herself an exquisite three courses. Maybe because she always makes us fancy meals when we visit. Or maybe because of the way my mother used to talk about her sister.

Whenever Mom made a particularly bad dinner—burned the chicken or added too much salt to the sauce—she would shake her head in solemn disapproval of her own self and say, "What would Austin think? I'm so ashamed." But then she would laugh, clearly unashamed. In any case, it makes more sense that my aunt would come home exhausted and order in.

I warm up a bowl of soup, eat all of it, and throw out the

container. Still hungry, I cut a slice of bread from the loaf on the countertop. I cut another piece and top it with a dollop of egg salad from the refrigerator. Finally satisfied, I go looking for my aunt. Now that I've eaten, I feel calmer. My mind is working again.

Aunt Austin is still in her bedroom, briskly folding clothes. The room is all white: white walls, white carpet, white furniture, white linens on the white bed. The only blot of color is an orchid in a white pot on her white dressing table.

"Did you eat, my dear?" She smiles at me.

"Yes, thank you," I say. "Can I ask you something? About my mom?"

Her hands freeze mid-fold. "What about her?"

"What was she like when she was little?" I ask, having decided this is a reasonable question for a girl to ask the sister of her allegedly deceased mother.

"She was stubborn and impulsive. Slightly naughty. Not so different from adult Jeanette." Aunt Austin finishes folding what she's folding.

"Naughty?"

"I was always having to cover for her. Sometimes literally: I would cover her mouth with my hand when I knew she was about to say something she shouldn't. She was always saying something she shouldn't. But I tried to be patient. It was my duty to take care of her."

"You were only a few years older."

"After Daddy died, our mother had to work long hours to

support us. She was at the factory twelve hours a day, and when she came home she always had some beading or other handiwork to do to make a little extra money. Jeanette and I had to fend for ourselves."

"It must have been tough," I say softly.

Aunt Austin sighs as she looks around at her immaculate room. "When I remember how poor we were back then, it makes all of this seem unbelievable."

"You've worked hard." I nod as if I understand, though I know I can't possibly understand, not really. All I understand is the comfort of that two-story, one-family house in a nice residential neighborhood in the most southern part of Middleton—the house I've lived in my entire life.

"I worked no harder than my parents." She clears her throat, a quietly bitter sound. "I was lucky. Being born here made all the difference, for me and for Jeanette."

"That's why your parents immigrated. To give you those opportunities," I say.

My aunt shakes her head. "Daddy had his own ambitions. But they came here with nothing, so he had to take the first job he could get while he learned the language, which he did, quickly. He started as a busboy at a restaurant downtown, and worked his way up to manager at a much nicer place. All the while, he saved his money because he planned to start his own business. But then the heart attack . . ." She goes to the window and straightens the white curtain. Once it's straight she keeps straightening.

"He'd have been proud of you," I say.

"I hope so." She is still straightening the curtain. She straightens until it's crooked again.

"Didn't your grandpa also live with you?" I ask, hoping I haven't disrupted the mood. Aunt Austin is not prone to reminiscence. She is not often nostalgic, almost never sentimental.

"Yes," she says. "Grandpa moved in just before my father died."

"So he was home with you while your mother was at work?"

"He read his newspapers and watched us play. Jeanette was his favorite. He spoiled her too much. But I can understand why, she was such a happy kid. Even though she drove me crazy, we were best friends. We had our made-up games and our secret jokes. Sometimes we'd just look at each other and start laughing." Aunt Austin steps over to the potted orchid on her dresser. The flower seems especially vivid in all this whiteness, with its arcing green stem and bright purple blossoms.

"I felt so bad when I went away to college," she says as she studies the plant.

"Because then your grandfather got sick," I say.

"Yes, then our grandfather got sick," she says.

"Why didn't your mother get him a memory key?"

"She wanted to. He refused."

"My mom thought it was because Grandma thought he was too far gone."

"Jeanette thought that because that's what she wanted to think. Even if he were too far gone, even if we had to use our last cent to pay for it, our mother would have gotten him a key if he'd been willing. She knew her duty to her father-in-law. But the truth is, Grandpa had given up. He was ready to go. Jeanette believed what she wanted to believe. She always did."

Aunt Austin frowns as she presses her fingers into the soil at the base of the orchid. "I need to water this before I go," she says.

"Should I get some water?" I ask.

"That's all right. I'll do it." She brushes the dirt from her fingers and comes toward me. "Lora, what a strange and terrible thing it is that you, your mother, and I have all lost the person we loved most at such a young age. For me it was my father. For Jeanette it was our grandpa. And for you—"

"I still have my dad," I say quickly.

"Yes, you're lucky to have Kenneth. Even though Jeanette and I loved our mother, she wasn't there for us the way Ken is for you. She was always working, and when she wasn't working she was always so tired. She didn't understand her daughters, not like Daddy. In the old country, his parents were intellectuals, so he knew what we were striving for. He was striving for the same things. But my mother's family were peasants. For her it was only about survival. Not that I blame her. Your grandmother did not have an easy life." She takes my hand. Her fingers are warm.

"And I have you," I say.

Aunt Austin blinks once, twice, and smiles. "Yes," she says. "Thank goodness we have each other."

Then she glances at the white clock on the white wall. "I'm afraid I've got to go, my dear. The car will be here any minute." She returns to her suitcase, inspects the tidy stacks, nods approvingly, and flips down the cover of the bag. But then her hands pause, palms hovering as if they don't know what to do next.

"Everything okay?" I ask.

"I loved your mom, Lora. I really . . ." Her gaze drifts downward as her fingers jolt back into action. She zips her suitcase closed and turns to me.

"You are an extraordinary young woman and I know you can do anything you set your mind to. What I'm about to say is very important, and it's a lesson I learned the hard way. Are you listening?"

I nod.

"You can't let your life be defined by the loss of your mother." Her face is earnest straight lines, her eyes imploring. "Do you understand?" she asks.

"I understand," I say.

Aunt Austin stares intently at me, so intently I'm afraid she can see everything: all my suspicions and hopes and fears, my misbehavior at Grand Gardens, my falling-out with my friends, my lies to my father. She stares at me so intently I'm afraid she can see I just lied to her too, that I don't really understand, because how could I possibly understand?

She stares. She speaks. "Good," she says.

17.

MY AUNT TELLS ME I CAN STAY IN HER APARTMENT WHILE I wait for Raul, but asks that I'm careful not to spill anything on the carpet or furniture. She shows me how to work her television, though her television works no differently than any other television, and she gives me instructions on how to lock her front door, though her locks work no differently than any other locks.

After she leaves, I lock the door as instructed. Then I go into the kitchen, look through the cabinets, and find a box of chocolate cookies. I eat one. No, two. Next I go into the living room and flip through the television channels for a while. Finally, I decide it's been long enough. Aunt Austin is probably halfway to the airport by now, and not coming back for a forgotten something. Not that she would ever forget anything. And so I do a little snooping.

My intentions are less insidious than they sound. I'm mostly interested in the normal snooping everyone does in other people's homes, browsing the pictures on the walls, the books on the shelf, the bottles in the bathroom. It's only because my aunt's miscellaneous stuff is all tastefully concealed—in built-in closets and cabinets—that my snooping feels slightly sinister.

And so I'm glad to quickly find what I'm looking for. I remove the photo albums from a cabinet and bring the whole stack of them to the cream-colored couch. The top book is recent: Aunt Austin posed with various official-looking people, smiling her congresswoman smile. I set that one aside. The next is better, familiar. Many of these photos I've seen before, at my own house, in my own albums.

There I am, ecstatically hugging a package wrapped in silver paper. The memory beckons, but immediately I grit my teeth, straighten my shoulders, and I manage to send it away. I'm happy to discover I can still control my malfunctioning key. Sometimes. Somewhat.

I turn to the next page. There's my mom and dad in matching red sweaters, arms around each other. There's my mom and aunt standing proudly behind a table that's nearly buckling under all the food atop it. In both pictures my mother looks happy. She must have been happy.

But it's the next album that's the most interesting to me; this one contains the oldest photographs. First, several black-and-white shots of my grandparents looking very young and very serious in their formal clothes. Then two little girls smiling for the camera. I recognize my mom by the twist of her mouth and my aunt by the tilt of her chin. There are many more of the sisters, and in one of them they sit with an elderly man. My great-grandfather, I guess, my mother's beloved grandfather. He stares solemnly at me, as if unaware of the girls grinning on either side of him.

I study my great-grandfather's face, the thinning hair, the sagging skin, the stern line of his mouth. I wonder if he already had Vergets when this photo was taken, whether his memories had already lost their sharp edges. But his gaze seems alert.

Still, I feel sad.

A blaring noise startles me out of my thoughts. I quickly close the album, imagining that Aunt Austin has come back to find me snooping. But it's only my cell phone ringing, echoing loudly in the white stillness of the apartment. I follow the sound to my backpack, and check the caller ID before answering.

It's Wendy.

Leaving my phone on the table, I go into the bathroom and smooth my aunt's scented lotion on my hands. I smell my palms, they smell like roses. As I close the medicine cabinet, I notice the tube of prescription painkillers perched in the corner, and stop closing. The pills are the same kind the doctor gave my dad when he threw out his back shoveling snow two winters ago.

I pluck the bottle from the shelf, thinking of my recent headaches.

I blink. I'm still standing in the bathroom, in front of the medicine cabinet, but now the room is sweetly fragrant: I am nine years old and while reaching for my aunt's scented lotion,

I've knocked over a bottle of perfume, and now the bottle is in pieces and the perfume is a puddle and the air is thickening with smell, smothering smell, too sweet, too fragrant, and I can't breathe, and I turn around, and there is Aunt Austin, standing in the doorway. She looks at me. She looks at the broken glass. She does not say anything; she doesn't have to.

I blink. I put the tube of prescription painkillers back on the shelf, setting it precisely in place.

Then I return to the living room. My cell phone is still ringing and I cannot believe it. Won't Wendy take a hint? No, of course not. Wendy has never taken a hint. She is constitutionally unable to take a hint.

I'm about to shove my phone under a pillow when I see it's not Wendy calling this time. It's Raul. He tells me he's leaving work so I give him directions to my aunt's building.

After I hang up, I pace around the room, thinking about what happened with Wendy and Tim, and I start getting angry again. Then I start getting sad. Wendy is my best friend. And Tim, despite the stupid *whatever* between us, is also my friend.

Yet I don't see how either relationship can be salvaged. There's too much hurt, too much history.

Wendy's voice in my head says: *Just fix your memory key, stupid.*

It's not that easy, is my pretend retort to pretend Wendy.

I stop pacing. I sit on the couch and open up the photo album again. Past the pictures of my great-grandfather, I find the pictures from my aunt's wedding. They're surprising to me,

though I'm not sure why. They could be any old wedding portraits.

Perhaps that's why they're surprising, the ordinariness of
them, just two people in love. My aunt looks much now as she
did then: tall and thin and determined. She wears an ivory
dress with oddly ruffled sleeves. In her hands is a small bouquet. The mysterious Jon Harmon stands next to her. He is also
tall and thin, with black hair and glasses. He doesn't actually
look very mysterious. In fact, he seems kind of nerdy with his
thick glasses and tweed suit and wide-collared shirt.

The intercom buzzes. It's the uniformed man downstairs,
calling to tell me that Raul is here. As I go unlock the properly
locked door, it occurs to me that Aunt Austin would probably
not approve of the fact I'm having a boy over without a chaper-
one. I hope the doorman doesn't tell on me.

Raul comes in with his blue jacket slung over his shoulder,
and it reminds me of the fact I was escorted off the premises
of Grand Gardens today, and I wonder if Raul knows, but he
smiles at me so nicely that I decide he doesn't know. "Fancy
apartment," he says.

"Yeah, my aunt's a fancy person. How was work?"

"Endless." He half sighs, half yawns.

We go into the living room and stretch out on opposite
ends of the couch. The cream-colored sofa is so long that only
our feet overlap. Raul nudges my heel with his socked toe.
"That tickles," I say, gently kicking him away.

"Sorry."

"No, it's okay."

"Okay."

"Want to watch TV?" I turn on the television and skip through the channels until I find a documentary about tree frogs, which seems close enough to marine biology that I suppose Raul will be interested.

But when I glance over at him he's asleep. He looks like a little boy with his eyes shut and brow furrowed, with his mouth curled into a slight frown. A minute later, he begins to snore, and I giggle, hand over mouth to cover the sound.

I'm glad he's here. Raul is nice. He's cute and smart. He seems to really like me. And I like him back, don't I? I do. I must.

A lion roars, startlingly loud, on the television. The tree frogs have gone to commercial, and this commercial is advertising a show about noisy lions. I grab the remote to turn down the volume, but I'm too late.

"What? What is it?" Raul jerks awake. "Did I fall asleep? I'm so sorry."

"It's okay, it's my fault. I bored you to sleep."

"No, it's not, I mean, you didn't. I'm sorry." He is blushing.

"It's okay, really." I feel bad for teasing him.

"Okay," he says uncertainly.

"Hey, do you want to see some pictures?" I smile at him.

"Sure." He smiles back.

I turn off the television and show him the photographs in the family album: little me, my father, my mother, my aunt. I point out my gap-toothed smile. Raul makes the appropriate comments about what a cute kid I was.

Then he abruptly stands.

"Is something wrong?" I ask as he strides across the room to where he left his blue jacket. I look away. I hate the sight of that jacket.

He returns and hands me an envelope. "I forgot. This is for you."

My name is written in shaky script on the front. I flip it over and unseal the flap. Inside are two folded papers. The first is a sheet of stationery with a message written in that same shaky script. It reads:

Dear Lora,

I'm writing to properly thank you for helping me away from that car. The disregard people have for traffic laws is truly appalling. Thankfully there are Good Samaritans like you, keeping the world safe for the rest of us. I was very glad to see you at Grand Gardens today.

Pertaining to our intriguing discussion about medical technology, I've enclosed some information that may be of interest to you.

Yours truly,

Ms. Pearl

The other item in the envelope is a leaflet with black type

on green paper. At the very top, in large letters, are the words KEEP CORP OUT. Raul asks what it is, so I read aloud: "The KCO is an organization dedicated to spreading awareness about the memory key industry. Did you know Keep Corp has successfully blocked other companies from producing memory keys even though their patents should have expired decades ago? Did you know Keep Corp's overseas factories employ children under fourteen? Did you know the government has stopped funding efforts to find a cure for Vergets disease?

"We at the KCO are deeply concerned about the increasing power Keep Corp has over our government, and our lives. You should be too. For more information or to find out how you can help, please contact us at . . ."

I drop the sheet of paper on the floor. "Ridiculous," I say.

Raul gazes at the leaflet and I can tell he wants to pick it up. "There *was* that scandal about twelve-year-old kids working at one of their factories," he says. "But then they shut the place down and said they hadn't known."

"My mom would never have worked for Keep Corp if those things were true." I speak with certainty. But I am not as certain as I sound. How can it be that the more I learn of her, the more I remember of her, the less certain I feel?

All I want is some peace and quiet, says my mother.

"Your mom worked for Keep Corp?" asks Raul.

"She did," I say, gritting my teeth.

"But she doesn't anymore?"

"Do *you* think those things are true?" I ask.

"I don't know enough about it," he says.

"I'm going to the bathroom," I say, getting up to go.

I move slowly around the white-tiled room, phrases from the KCO flyer stuck in my mind, stuck like a song. *Stopped funding . . . Vergets disease . . . Children under fourteen . . . Increasing power . . .* I shake my head, trying to shake out the words, and concentrate on what I'm doing: soaping my hands, rinsing them, opening the medicine cabinet to get out my aunt's rose-scented lotion.

On the shelf is the tube of prescription painkillers, and despite my intention of taking out the lotion, I take out the painkillers. The top comes off with a pop. I slide a single tablet into my hand. The top goes on with a thump.

I stare at the tablet on my palm. I know I shouldn't take it. Not with Raul waiting for me, not after I've already ingested so many drugstore pain pills today. I reach for the bottle again, to put the tablet back. But then I decide that my aunt can't mind if I borrow just one little pill, in case of emergency. So I wrap my one little pill in a tissue to take with me.

In the living room, the KCO leaflet is on the floor where I left it, and Raul is flipping through another one of the photo albums. I pluck the leaflet from the rug, fold it up, slip it back into the envelope with Ms. Pearl's note, and shove it into my bag. The single prescription tablet gets tucked in there, too.

"I recognize some of these people," says Raul.

I zip my backpack closed and go to look at what he's looking at. It's the book I skipped, the one of my aunt with various strangers in various kinds of business and formal attire. I explain to Raul that my aunt is a congresswoman. He seems impressed. He points and asks, "Is that her with the vice president?"

But my gaze has drifted to a different photo. "Dad," I say.

"What?" Raul tries to turn the page, but I'm holding it down, heavy-handed.

"That's my dad," I say, my voice utterly toneless.

In the picture, my father's hair is thicker and less gray than it is now, and he's also thinner. He sits at a table cluttered with wineglasses and small plates, smiling the same slightly stiff smile he wears in all posed photographs. However, even as I notice these details, my attention is not on the familiar figure of my father but on the figures seated next to him.

The two blue-jacketed strangers.

18.

RAUL DRIVES ME HOME AND ALL THE WAY THERE I'M THINKING that I don't know how I'm going to face my father, but when we pull up in front of the house the windows are dark and the driveway is empty, and I cannot believe that after all my dreading he is not even there.

"Don't you think so?" asks Raul.

"I guess so," I say. I have no idea what he's talking about.

"Finally! Someone agrees with me!"

"Um, yeah."

Raul smiles his nice smile. Then I let him kiss me. His lips are gentle. He touches my waist, and his hands are gentle too. I try to forget myself as I kiss him back, but I can't. I can't forget anything.

And I'm tired of this, of him, of everything. I'm so tired. I lean away from his mouth and out of his arms. I thank him for the ride.

"Let's hang out soon?" he says.

I say yes because yes is easier to say. And I am so, so tired.

Inside the house, there's a note on the kitchen counter, the usual note-leaving-place. *Lora, there's a work dinner tonight. Sorry for the late notice. There are leftovers in the fridge, but here's some money if you want to order in.*

Under the page is a twenty-dollar bill. I leave the cash and replace the note on top of it. I check the messages on our answering machine. There's only one, and it's Keep Corp demanding I come in for a checkup. "We're registering increased levels of damage from your memory key," scolds the technician. I tap the delete button.

Then I take the incriminating photo out of my backpack. In the picture, the two strangers are not wearing blue jackets but formal wear: the man in an immaculate suit, the woman in a sequined gown. It doesn't matter. I know their faces. I remember them exactly.

I call Aunt Austin, hoping she might be able to provide explanation or context or something or *anything.* The line goes straight to voice mail. She must still be on the plane. I slam down the phone.

Alone in the gloom of the kitchen, I feel so . . . so . . .

I grit my teeth. But it's too late. I'm in my bed crying. My pillow mushy with tears. Then it's the next night and I'm in my bed crying. Then it's the next night and I'm in my bed crying. Night after night after night, it's the same. My pillow mushy with tears. She's gone. She can't be gone. She's gone. It's the next night and I'm in my bed crying. She can't be gone, but she's gone. Night after night after night, it's all the same. My pillow mushy with tears.

Until my father comes. He sits on the side of my bed, like *she* always did, and the mattress bends under his weight. Though it's dark in my room and my tears blur my eyes, I can tell he's tired. He doesn't sleep much either, I know.

He pats my head. His hand is stiff. But as he continues patting, his touch gets smoother. And somehow, after some time, I stop sobbing and sleep. I don't wake until the morning, and when I do, my father is snoring in the chair by my desk. The sun is dazzling through the window, bright against the white walls, and warm on our faces.

I grit my teeth and I'm alone in the gloom of the kitchen.

We had managed it together, Dad and I, we had rebuilt ourselves a normal, everyday life. We were teammates. We were pals. We were all we had left. But now? Now I don't know what we are.

The doorbell rings and I move automatically toward the sound. I've already unlocked the door before I remember to ask who it is.

"It's Carlos Cruz," answers the sexy voice.

I stumble backward. But it's too late to pretend no one is home, so I fix on a frown and yank open the door. "What are you doing here?"

"Lora Mint, how nice to see you again," he says. "I was in the neighborhood so I thought I'd stop by to see how your article is coming along."

"My article?"

"How different generations have different attitudes about memory keys."

"You know we're not actually writing that article," I say.

"I'm just teasing." Carlos chuckles. He's dressed casually in jeans and a T-shirt, formfitting jeans and formfitting T-shirt, and if Wendy were here she'd surely be swooning. Stupid Wendy.

"Why are you in the neighborhood?" I ask, not swooning.

"I was at that used bookstore, the one on Pine Street? The one Jeanette—your mom—went to all the time. You know which one I'm talking about?"

"Of course," I say because I do know that bookstore, even if I did not know that my mother went there all the time.

"It's where she bought all her lousy romance novels," he says.

I glare. What did he know about my mother's reading habits?

"I'd always tell her a scientist had no business reading such garbage." His smile doesn't seem to be directed toward me, but inward, toward some part of his own self. "But Jeanette was a romantic at heart," he says.

I glare. What did he know about my mother's heart?

I tell him I have to go. By that I mean *he* has to go.

But he acts as if I've invited him in: Carlos Cruz steps forward and I have to force myself not to step back. I hadn't before noticed how tall he is. He looms over me now.

Then he pounces so quickly I don't realize he's snatched

the photo from my hand until I see it in *his* hand. The photograph of my father and the two strangers. I had forgotten I was still holding it.

"What's this?" he asks.

"Nothing." I grab for the picture but he lifts it too high for me to reach. "Give it to me. Give it back!" I shout.

"Sorry, here you go," he says, and taps the photo down onto my open palm. His apology is undermined by the laughter in his voice.

I am mortified by his amusement; he makes me feel as if I were the one behaving inappropriately, not him. I move to shut the door, crash it right on him, but then Carlos speaks again, seriously this time, and his words stop me.

"You're so much like your mother," he says.

My fingers freeze on the brass knob. "I am? How?"

Instead of answering my questions, he asks his own: "That's your dad in the photo, and the others are from your sketches, right? Who are they?" His tone is easy, friendly, but the gleam in his eyes is hard and sharp as a blade.

I shake my head. I tell him again that I have to go.

"All right, Lora Mint. I'll see you next time." He arranges his handsome features into a smile, but that gleam in his eyes does not change.

I close the door.

I lock the door.

Then I look at the photograph crumpled in my fist. As I smooth it flat, I remember Wendy speculating that Carlos Cruz was in love with my mother. She says, *A tragically doomed love. I wonder if they*—I blink.

Standing at the window, I'm confused to see my mom emerge from a car driven by an unfamiliar man, but when she comes into the house she assures me it was only her coworker, a kind friend. She nods at me with her lips twined, her cheeks pink.

Lying in my bed, I'm startled awake by thunder, and startled more when I realize that thunder is actually my dad shouting. I suppose he must be shouting at my mother, but why would he be shouting at her? I try to listen to what he's saying, but all I can hear is *You . . . You . . . You . . .*

Standing at the door, I grip the doorknob as Carlos Cruz speaks of my mother's habits and her heart. He smiles tenderly and it's a true expression on his handsome face, perhaps the only true expression I've seen on his handsome face.

I blink. I grit my teeth.

Then I go get my bag from the hallway and cram the photograph back into the inside pocket. The zipper sticks. As I tug it free, a torn sheet of paper flutters to the floor. It's the list of Jon Harmon phone numbers, the one Wendy printed out.

An idea occurs to me.

I return to the kitchen and open the small drawer that holds our odds and ends. Extra keys. A flashlight. Broken pencils. Batteries used and unused. My skin is poked and jabbed as I sift through the mixture. Finally, my fingers brush smoothness. That's it. I pull out the little leather book.

After my mother died, my father packed up the contents of her closets, along with whatever was left in her study after those solemn men claimed her papers for Keep Corp, and moved all of it up to the attic. But her address book, stored in the communal drawer, stayed.

I flip through the yellowed pages, staring at my mother's print, small and meticulous and so familiar. It hurts to see her handwriting. But I rub my eyes clear and turn to the *H* section. Han, Harvey, Hockey, but no Harmon. I frown. My mother was fastidious about proper classification—she was a scientist, after all—but perhaps a former member of the family merits an exemption.

I turn to the *J* section. And there I find him.

19.

EVERY FEW MINUTES I TURN TO GLANCE AT THE CLOCK ON THE
wall behind me, until Cynthia the librarian comes by and asks
if there's something wrong with my neck, have I strained a
muscle? I tell her I'm sorry, I tell her I'm fine. "How's Gouda?"
I ask, hoping to distract her from my distraction with dog talk.
This strategy always works.

"You can take your lunch break now," she says, and returns
to the reference area. Apparently, the dog talk strategy does *not*
always work. Maybe I'd feel guilty if I weren't so anxious about
meeting Jon Harmon in just four hours and twelve minutes.

I go outside to eat my lunch. When I'm done, I pull the
bottle of pain pills from my pocket and take two tablets—it's a
minor headache, nothing worth thinking about, probably just
jitters. Then I get out my phone and check my voice mail.

There's a message from my father asking where I've been;
he says he feels as if he hasn't seen me in days. This is more or
less accurate. I call him back because I know he's teaching a
class at this exact moment, so the line will go to *his* voice mail.

When it does, I tell him I won't be home till late. I tell him not to wait up.

There's also a message from Wendy, the third message in the past twenty-four hours. I didn't listen to the earlier ones, and I don't listen to this one. Maybe I'm being unreasonable. Wendy would say I'm being unreasonable because she always says I'm being unreasonable. She would say I'm overreacting because she always says I'm overreacting. She would say, Lora, this isn't you, this is your memory key.

What Wendy doesn't understand is that my memory key *is* me.

When my shift finally ends, I go to the back room to gather my things together. Cynthia is in her office. "I know it's tough out there," she says and I think she's talking to me before I realize she's actually on the phone.

After a pause: "Kira, it's not a good idea," she says.

After a longer pause: "That's ridiculous. I'm not censoring you!" she says.

I don't mean to listen, I don't want to listen, but here I am, listening. For I can't help being curious: at the library, censorship is enemy number one. It makes no sense that Kira is accusing her librarian mother of censorship.

"I only want what's best for you." Cynthia says this so quietly I have to strain to hear her. Then I realize that I'm straining to hear her, so I grab my backpack and tiptoe out of the room, catching the door and easing it shut behind me.

It takes twelve minutes to get to the coffee shop, and another minute to lock up my bike, and another minute to unknot my knotty nerves. The place is small. Inside there are fewer than a dozen tables. I search for a tall, thin man with dark hair and glasses. My gaze climbs around the room. Is he late? Has he changed his mind and decided not to come?

A stout man in a blue polo shirt comes toward me. "Lora?" he says.

I stare at him. He couldn't possibly be Jon Harmon.

"I'm Jon Harmon," he says, chuckling. "You know you have your mother's frown?"

I would never have recognized him. Whereas he once was strikingly skinny, he is now strikingly round. Whereas he once had a thick tangle of dark hair, he is now completely bald. He's not even wearing glasses. It's hard to believe he is the man in those wedding photographs. "You look different from the pictures I've seen," I say.

"I bet." He pats his belly.

"I mean, I didn't mean. I'm sorry if . . ."

"Don't worry. If I saw those old photos, I bet I wouldn't recognize myself." He chuckles again, and this time I do too.

We find a tiny table in the corner. The coffee shop—with its exposed brick walls and flickering candlelight—seems slightly romantic, which makes me uncomfortable about being here with a stranger, even if he is my former, future uncle. For a moment, I wish Wendy were here, so we could exchange glances over the absurdity of it all. The moment passes.

"Last time I saw you, you had just started walking," says Jon Harmon.

"I thought you and Austin divorced before I was born," I say, and instantly regret it, for it seems rude to remind him about his divorce first thing.

But he doesn't appear offended. He nods. "Your mom and I were still friendly. We'd run into each other once in a while, reminisce about the old days."

The waitress comes over and greets Jon Harmon with an exclamation and a kiss on each cheek. He introduces us, and I try not to get impatient while they swap neighborhood gossip and banter about the weather. She asks what we'd like. I order an iced tea, he orders a coffee and a plate of cookies. Then she goes, and as soon as she goes I say to Jon Harmon, "You must be wondering why I called."

He needs no further prompting; he bursts effortlessly into story: "Yes, I'm glad you called. Let me start by giving you some background—I don't know how much you know about me and your aunt. Now that was a marriage doomed from the start. Not that Austi isn't great, because she is. She was my first love. We worked together in the governor's office, and the two of us would have the most exciting debates all day long. Can you imagine?" he asks.

I tell him I can, though I can't. Neither can I believe he calls her "Austi." No wonder it didn't work out.

"But after a while, I began losing faith in the political machine. Eventually I decided I wanted to work outside the system. Austi thought I was throwing my career away, all the things we worked so hard for. I thought she was being naïve. Still, I hoped we might get back together, but then she filed the papers. Austi had her path."

"She still does," I say, sad for him. And for my aunt.

"She's done well for herself, and she'll go even further. She has what it takes."

I nod. My father says the same things about Aunt Austin.

"About your mother," he says, and I lean forward in my chair. But then the waitress interrupts us with my iced tea, Jon's coffee, and a tiny plate of tiny cookies.

"Can I get you anything else?" she asks.

Jon asks for a glass of water. Then he nudges the plate of cookies toward me, so I take one. He takes one too, and hums approval as he eats it. "These are my favorite," he says. "Coconut."

"Yum," I say, my cookie still in my hand. "Mr. Harmon, about my mother—"

"Mr. Harmon! Please call me Jon. Unless you want to call me Uncle Jon. You can call me Uncle Jon, if you'd like."

"Jon," I say firmly. "What were you saying about my mom?"

He chews. He swallows. He coughs his throat clear. It occurs to me I might not be the only one who's nervous. Finally, he speaks. "I know you have questions about your mother. I also have questions."

"What questions?" I ask.

"About what happened. About how she died," he says.

I sit still. My heart is jerking around inside my chest, but I sit very still. I'm excited to have found someone else with questions about my mother's death; I'm excited that that someone is willing to talk to me about his questions; yet my excitement feels a little like fear. My voice trembles as I ask him to explain.

Flourishes and digressions aside, Jon Harmon's story is this: a few days before the car accident, my mom came to see him. This was unusual. Although they'd bump into each other here and there, and phone occasionally if there was a specific reason (such as when she put him in touch with Carlos Cruz, handsomely creepy journalist), they never spent much time together. After all, Jon was Austin's ex-husband, and Jeanette's loyalties were clearly and completely with her sister.

So he was surprised to see her, but welcomed her into his house. He made coffee, they exchanged personal updates, and then she told him the reason for her visit. My mother had come across a set of unusual structural definitions in a line of memory keys in development at Keep Corp. She didn't get specific about the science, but told him she was worried there was something inappropriate going on. She asked him for advice.

"Why'd she go to you?" I say.

"My old firm worked to expose corporate corruption and compensate the victims. We won more than a few lawsuits over the years," says Jon. "So I told her I'd help her. I'd even come out of retirement if she needed."

"You're retired?" I ask. He seems young to be retired.

"More or less." His round face is pink, but I don't know if he's blushing or it's the candlelight. "The work was hard: long hours, sad stories. And these companies would go to any length to stop us. The tires of my car were slashed, the windows of my house broken, and . . ."

"And what?"

Jon stares at the lemon in his glass of water. "I was assaulted one night, coming home from the office. They broke both my arms. It could have been a lot worse; they were only delivering a message, they didn't want to kill me. But I started having panic attacks. Insomnia. My partner said I'd better quit before I had a total breakdown. The timing was right: we wanted to start a family. So now I'm a stay-at-home dad. We have two kids, a boy and a girl, seven and four. Best decision I ever made, though I still get the occasional nightmare. Still keep my phone number unlisted."

"I'm so sorry," I say, wishing I had something better to say.

"It was awful. But it's over."

"And you've remarried?"

"Technically, no. Gay marriage isn't legal in our state."

I stare at him, and he stares right back. I forcibly loosen my tongue in my mouth. "Yeah, it's really unfair," I say, and I mean it, though I can't help thinking about Aunt Austin and what this means for *her*. But I remain focused on what's important. "What else did you say to my mother?" I ask.

"I told her to collect all the information she could without drawing attention, so we could evaluate whether to go public, or to the authorities, or directly to the corporation."

"Then what happened?"

"I didn't hear from her again. A few days later I found out about the accident."

I am suddenly furious.

"Why didn't you tell anyone about this?"

"I tried. After the funeral, I called your father. But he was so distraught, I don't think he understood. I considered talking to your aunt, but we hadn't been on speaking terms in years. I thought about going to the police, but I had no evidence, barely any information at all."

"So you did nothing," I say.

"I hate to make excuses, but I was a mess. My panic attacks started up again. I knew how companies like Keep Corp worked, I knew they'd be brutal and relentless. I had no leverage against them."

"Except that they murdered my mother."

"It could have really been just an accident," he says unconvincingly.

We sit there in silence. We sit there in silence for a long time.

"I wanted to forget. I told myself I was better off forgetting. But of course I couldn't," Jon says eventually.

"I know the feeling." I almost laugh.

I take out the photograph and ask if he recognizes the people in it. He moves it closer to the flickering candle. "That's your dad, right? I don't know the others. Who are they?"

"I was hoping you'd tell me."

"I'm sorry, I don't know." He hands the picture back. "Lora, I want to be very clear about something. I told you about my conversation with your mother because you deserve to know. But under no circumstances should you go after Keep Corp yourself, do you understand? There's nothing we can do for Jeanette now."

I look at him. He gazes back sternly. But that doesn't make his expression any less sad. Maybe it's his anguish that makes me tell him, or maybe it's the challenge in his words. Maybe it's because Jon Harmon was the one my mother confided in years ago, or maybe it's simply because I need a ride to Grand Gardens.

"I think she's alive," I say.

Then I tell him about the two strangers and their blue jackets, blue jackets that are the uniform at a certain retirement home. I tell him that at this certain retirement home I saw—from afar—a woman who looked exactly, *exactly*, like my mother. It's possible I exaggerate, but I'll say almost anything to smooth the skeptical arch of his eyebrows.

"Have you talked to your dad about this?" he asks.

"Not yet." I stare at the tiny plate of tiny cookies, now a tiny plate of crumbs. "I don't want to get his hopes up if it turns out to be nothing."

"You have to tell your dad," says Jon.

"But what if I'm wrong? I can't do that to him," I say, and my distress burns my face and shakes my voice, for my distress is true even if my words are not, and Jon seems to recognize that.

He sighs so heavily the table trembles. "I still think you have to tell him. But you're right that we've got to find out if she's there," he says.

"So you'll help me?"

He sighs again. "I'll help you."

We decide we'll go tomorrow. Jon argues we should wait until we're better prepared, but I insist. Because tomorrow I have the day off, and the next day I have to work, and the day after that Jon is busy, and the day after that I have to work. And I cannot, *cannot*, wait another week. He seems to understand. "Well, I'll try my usual contacts, but this may be too short notice," says Jon.

"I have a friend who works at Grand Gardens," I say.

He brightens. "All we need is a list of patients. If Jeanette is there she'll be under a false name, but perhaps we can find it by checking out everyone else."

"Residents," I say. "They call them residents."

"Right. We'll need a list of residents, then. Can your friend get that for us?"

"I don't know. I'll ask him," I say.

We leave the coffee shop and solemnly shake hands—though I think Jon Harmon might have liked a nice uncle-niece sort of hug—and agree to talk in the morning.

I bike home in a daze, past buildings and cars and people and houses, without noticing any of it. And even though

I'm ready-for-bed tired, I don't rush. Because the night air is so fresh on my skin and the road so smooth underneath my wheels. Because I am trying not to hope, but of course I am hoping.

When I come into the house, I am carefully quiet and do not turn on any lights. Yet as I climb up the stairs, my father calls out from his room. "Lora! How was your day? What'd you do? Where'd you go? Who'd you see?"

I pretend I don't hear him and go into my own room. A few minutes later, there is a shuffle of feet in the hallway. I flop down on my bed. There is a soft knock. I shut my eyes. The door inches open. I slow my breathing. Inhale. Exhale. Inhale.

The ringing telephone wakes me.

It's after ten o'clock and my father is gone. While faking sleep, I had fallen asleep. I'm still dressed in my clothes, my face unwashed, my teeth unbrushed. Disoriented, I reach for the ringing phone.

"Why haven't you called me back?" says Wendy.

I sit up, struggling to clear my bleary head. "I've been busy."

"Don't give me that crap," she says.

"What?" I'm taken aback by the wrath in her voice.

"I know things are weird for you right now, but you've been totally unreasonable lately. Abandoning us at the nursing home? Freaking out on our way to Carlos Cruz's? You're being a really bad friend."

"I'm sorry," I mumble, ashamed.

"It's your memory key. You've got to get it fixed."

Instantly, my guilt dissolves. Instantly, I'm wide-awake. "No, you're just upset that for the first time, I'm seeing you for what you really are. Bitch."

Wendy is quiet for a moment. "You don't mean that. Take it back."

But I will take nothing back. I have all the evidence I need to support my statement; the memories are organized neatly, color-coded and cross-referenced, in my filing-cabinet brain.

"Listen, if you don't get your key fixed," she says, her voice hardening.

"What?" I say, my voice just as hard. There's no threat she can make, no warning she could give, that would persuade me to let Keep Corp into my head.

"I'll tell your dad," she says.

I hang up on her.

20.

ONE BY ONE, THE OTHER CHILDREN LEAVE WITH THEIR PARENTS, until it's only me, some slobbering boy, and Mrs. Sunny in the classroom.

Then it's just me and Mrs. Sunny.

When Mama finally comes through the door, I run to her and she lifts me up and squashes my cheek against her cheek. I imagine and reimagine the moment, making the memory last long in my mind. I make it last until the throbbing becomes unbearable. Only then do I grit my teeth and open my eyes to morning.

My father has already left for work so I have the house to myself. I go downstairs for a glass of water and a couple of pain pills. Then I call Jon Harmon to tell him I couldn't get the list of Grand Gardens' residents from Raul.

The truth is I didn't ask. Late last night, I lay in bed and imagined asking him for help. I'd have to tell him about my mother. He would be sympathetic; he's a very sympathetic guy. But what if he said no? What if he said he was sorry but he couldn't risk his job? I imagined my anger. My anger was an inky black, staining our clean new connection.

Jon groans. "That makes everything more complicated. Fortunately I have a friend whose father happens to reside in the south wing of Grand Gardens. What do you think of that?" he says.

"I think we're going to visit him today," I say.

Jon Harmon's car, a boxy sedan, is old but in fine shape, no dents or dings. The back is slathered with crooked bumper stickers, the wordiest and least catchy bumper stickers I've ever seen: SUPPORT OUR TROOPS BY ENDING THE WARS; YOUR SOCIAL INACTION IS SOCIAL ACTION; SAVE THE ENVIRONMENT AND THE ENVIRONMENT WILL SAVE YOU!

"Save the environment and the environment will save you?" I ask.

"Darren and I made those with the kids. Coming up with those slogans is harder than you'd think." Jon is wearing another polo shirt, but today's shirt is mint green. He stares at me curiously. "Now what do we have here?"

"I had to." I'm blushing but he probably can't tell. For in order to avoid being identified as that wacky girl who ran all around the south wing the other day, I've put together a disguise. First, a wide-brimmed straw hat with a clump of fake roses affixed to the front. The hat was from a Halloween costume, the year Wendy and I dressed up as old-fashioned-lady zombies (her idea: old-fashioned ladies, my idea: zombies).

Second, a large pair of black sunglasses. Third, on a whim, I slipped on my mother's peach dress. So now I'm that wacky lady in a wacky outfit.

"You look very nice. Mind telling me why you're so fancy?"

"It's a long story," I say.

"Good thing we've got plenty of time." He gives me a steely-eyed look he must use quite effectively on his kids, and I tell him. Partly because of that steely-eyed look, mostly because he should be prepared in case they recognize me and throw me out again. I leave out the part where I'm hysterically sobbing in the empty room. I do admit I was escorted from the premises.

He shakes his head. "When we get there, you let me do the talking."

"Naturally." I straighten my sunglasses.

Jon whistles at his first glimpse of Grand Gardens, and with good reason: the stone exterior shimmers in the bright sunshine, the windows sparkle, the grass glitters with dew.

We climb out of the car and slowly approach the building. I'm wearing a pair of high heels, which was a dumb decision. My ankles are shaking in my impractical shoes. Though maybe it's because I'm nervous. I'm so nervous.

In the lobby, my stomach flops when I see that familiar white-haired lady behind the reception desk. She tilts her head. "Yes?" she says.

"How are you on this lovely day? We're here to visit Marty Goodman." Jon smiles. His smile goes unanswered.

"Your name?" she demands.

"I'm Jonathan Smith," says Jon Harmon. "Marty's daughter put me on the list of approved guests."

The woman clicks around on her computer, and reluctantly tells us we may wait here for an attendant. Then, for the first time, she looks directly at me. Her eyebrows—brown and penciled—coil in irritation.

My breath stops. It's all over. I'm about to be kicked out.

"I like your hat," she says.

It takes all my self-control not to laugh as I thank her.

The attendant comes, a glum woman in a blue jacket. We follow her down the long hallway. My high heels scratch against the floor. When there is no risk of the reception lady overhearing, Jon chuckles and tells me he likes my hat.

"Thanks, Mr. *Smith*." I grin and remove my sunglasses.

"Right here, room 124," says the attendant. She knocks, but opens the door without waiting for an answer. When I come into the room, I see why she didn't wait.

Marty Goodman is propped up in his bed, but even so he seems more horizontal than vertical. He's the whitest man I've ever seen, and everything about him is white, not just his skin and his hair, but his lips are also white, and even his blue eyes are glazed pale. On either side of him are humming-buzzing-beeping machines, their tubes and wires disappearing under the thin blanket covering his thin body. My throat tightens. I now understand exactly what the residents of the north wing feel about the south wing.

"Hi, Marty," says Jon. "How're you doing?"

The man's eyelids flutter as small sounds sneak from his white lips.

"I'm Nicole's friend Jon. Remember me? We met at her birthday party, years ago." He sits in the chair next to Mr. Goodman's bed.

"You don't have to stay, we're fine now," I tell the blue-jacketed attendant.

"It's standard policy for guests in the south wing to be chaperoned during their visit," she says. Her expression is bored. This is obviously a line she's repeated a hundred times.

Jon and I glance at each other.

Then Mr. Goodman grunts, and we all turn to him. The words come slowly. "How . . . is . . . Nicole?" he asks.

"She's good. She's coming to visit you next week," says Jon.

Mr. Goodman's lips flutter. "Ni . . . cole . . . ," he whispers.

"Where's the bathroom?" My voice is so shrill that everyone looks at me in surprise. Even Marty Goodman. Even myself.

"The public restrooms are down the hall, on the left," says the attendant.

I go into the corridor. Both sides of the hallway are lined with closed doors. So many doors, all of them closed. I take off my hat and cover my face with my hands. How foolish I was to hurry our visit; how stupid I was not to ask Raul for help; how sad I am for Marty Goodman. So foolish, so stupid, so sad.

After a minute, after two minutes, I drop my arms back to my sides. Then, because I don't know what else to do, I walk down the hall to the bathroom. As I reach for the door it sweeps open, and I fall onto a woman in green scrubs.

"I'm sorry. I'm so sorry," I say.

"No harm done." The woman smiles. But her smile fades as she stares at me, as she tries to recall why I am so familiar to her. I know why she is so familiar to me: she is the fair-haired woman who escorted me out of here two days ago. I turn away, but it's too late. I shouldn't have removed my sunglasses. I shouldn't have taken off my hat.

"You're back," she says. "You're not supposed to be back."

"I'm here with a friend to visit Marty Goodman," I say quickly.

The woman nods. "It's nice for Mr. Goodman to have visitors," she says. Then she moves so I can enter the restroom. It's a moment before I realize she is not going to report me.

"Can I ask you something?" I blurt out. "You said the person I saw was probably one of your residents. You said she's always wandering around the empty rooms. You remember, don't you? Will you take me to see her? Please," I say. "Please."

"I can't do that." She frowns.

"Please," I say. "I think I know her."

"It doesn't matter. I can't." She is still frowning, and I know she is about to walk away from me. Perhaps she will report me, after all. I am desperate.

"I think she's my mother," I say.

She stops mid-step. "Jean Lee?"

"My mother's maiden name was Lee. Her name was Jeanette

Lee," I whisper. My hand is still on the bathroom door, pressing it halfway open; I'm stuck in this in-between position while the woman stares at me, studying my face as if it's a problem to be solved. I know she must be trying to decide whether I'm delusional, so I try to look as non-delusional as possible. My efforts are complicated by the fact that I'm clutching an enormous hat with a clump of plastic flowers on the front.

The woman makes a sharp sound through her teeth. "If you bother her in *any way*, you'll have to leave immediately," she says.

"Yes, thank you," I say. "Thank you."

We go up to the second floor. Halfway down the corridor, she stops in front of a door and looks at me. "Ready?" she asks.

I nod because I can't find the voice to answer. I nod, even though I'm not actually ready. The woman knocks. We wait. I think I hear a sound. It's a moment longer, the longest moment, before the voice shouts from inside the room: "Come in!"

The woman in green looks at me, then at the knob, signaling for me to turn the knob to open the door. But I am unable to lift my arm. I don't know what to do or how to do it. Finally, she sighs softly and reaches around me. Just then, the knob glides away, as does the whole door.

"Hello," says my mother.

"I brought you a visitor," says the woman.

Mom smiles at me. For a moment I'm afraid this is not actually happening and I am merely in another memory. But when I grit my teeth and straighten my shoulders, all that happens is gritted teeth and straightened shoulders. Besides, my mother is older than when I last saw her: her hair has more white in it, her skin has new lines. However, her smile is the same.

Exactly the same.

This is real. This is really happening.

"Hello," she says.

"Hello," I manage to say, and there is so much more I want to say, but I don't know where to begin. I don't know how to begin.

My mother takes my hand. She gazes into my eyes.

Then she asks me who I am.

21.

WHAT I FEEL IS ALL THE DISORIENTATION OF AN ABRUPT AWAK-
ening, but not as though I've woken from a dream; it's as if I
have woken *into* a dream. There is a lot of talking, and I am
doing some of that talking, yet I'm not quite sure what's being
said. Then the woman in green—apparently her name is Nina,
and she's a nurse here—goes to find Jon Harmon, while my
mother invites me to sit down.

She asks if I want something to drink and before I can
answer she brings me a glass of water. She asks if I want something to eat and before I can answer she is rummaging inside
her closet. She brings me a box of crackers.

"These might be a bit stale," she says. "I'm sorry I don't
have anything better."

"It's okay," I say.

We sit at the wooden table in the corner of her room.
There's a half-completed puzzle scattered across the top. It's
a nature scene: grass and sky and wildflowers. When I glance
up, my mother is watching me.

"Lora," she says.

"Yes." I reach for the box of crackers. I take one, though I don't really want one.

"I'm sorry," she says again.

"These crackers aren't stale," I say. Though they are. Very.

"No, I'm sorry about before. I was confused. I didn't recognize you at first. You're all grown-up now. I can't believe how grown-up you are."

"Yeah, I guess so." It's true that I've increased inches and hips and chest since we last saw each other. But I'm still her daughter.

"I'm glad you're here," says my mother. She smiles.

"But why are *you* here? You should come home," I say.

Her smile fades. "Yes," she says, fidgeting with a puzzle piece.

"Don't you want to?"

"Of course I do." She tries to fit the piece into a corner. It doesn't fit. She tries again. "But I can't. They won't let me go," she says.

"Mom, I thought you were dead."

She drops the puzzle piece. "What? I didn't know. I'm so sorry."

"It's been terrible. I've missed you so much, and so has Dad."

Her forehead rumples. "Your father. Kenneth. Is he here now?"

"No, it's only me and Jon Harmon."

"Yes, Jon Harmon. Do I know him?"

"Aunt Austin's ex-husband. You don't remember?"

She says his name again and shrugs.

"It was a long time ago," I say.

The door opens and in comes Nurse Nina, and behind her is Jon, red-faced and barreling toward my mother. "Jeanette! I can't believe this," he says, grabbing her into a hug. She pats his shoulder, looking stunned.

I go over to Nina and ask her if my mother can leave.

"Leave? What do you mean?" she says.

"Can she come home with me?"

"If you get the approval of her guardian or whoever brought her here."

"Whoever brought her here." I repeat her words as the meaning sinks through me. Someone brought her here. Obviously someone brought her here. I'm desperate to know. I'm terrified to know. "And who's that?" I ask.

"I've no idea. What I can do is have the front desk call her guardian and tell them you want to take her home. We'll also need her doctor's consent."

"Why do you need that?"

"Because of her memory," says Nina.

"What about her memory?" I ask. And as soon as I ask, I know. I know why my mother didn't recognize me, why she doesn't think she can leave, why she couldn't remember Jon Harmon, why someone brought her here in the first place.

"She has Vergets," I say.

But Nina shakes her head. "It's not Vergets. When your mother came here, her key had just been removed. After years of normal use, the body can reject the memory key. It happens very rarely, but it does happen."

"I don't understand," I say. I don't.

"I'm sorry," says Nina.

I look at my mother. She is looking at me. "It's all right," she says. "My natural memory is underdeveloped, but I've been working to improve it. I've designed a regimen of memory exercises that I do every day. The puzzles help too, and my studies."

"Your studies?" I ask.

"Yes, and you've gotten so much better," Nina interrupts. "I'm surprised they haven't transferred you to the north wing."

I want to laugh. Even with her erased mind, my mother is as methodical as she always was. But I don't laugh. I cry.

"No, Lora. It's all right." My mother touches my elbow, and at her touch I come apart. I fall on her shoulder and weep into the collar of her shirt. Slowly, her arms come around my back, first one, then the other. She used to hold me like this all the time.

But as my tears slow, I begin to notice the ways it's different now. Now I am taller than she is. Now my ear doesn't quite fit into the nook above her collarbone. Now there is tension in her limbs and spine, and a matching tension in my own body. When I let go, she lets go. She takes a step back and touches my peach dress. Her peach dress.

"Do you recognize it? It was yours," I say, wiping my eyes.

"Yes, I think it's familiar." She slides her finger across the silky fabric.

Jon turns to Nina the nurse. "Will you ask the front desk to call her guardian and tell them we want to take her home? And also her doctor?"

"Of course. I'll be right back," she says.

After Nina leaves, closing the door behind her, Jon looks at my mother. "Jeanette, we have to get you out of here before she comes back," he says, very quietly.

"Why, what do you mean?" she asks.

"They faked your death and hid you away!" I say, much too loudly. Then immediately I fix my voice, make it normal. No frustration. No disappointment. "Whatever is happening here, it can't be good. Who knows what they'll do when they find out we've found you."

My mother looks at me but her gaze is far away. She is thinking.

"Yes," she says after a moment. "I'll go with you. But how?"

A short time later, the plump man in his mint-colored polo shirt and the woman in the peach dress, straw hat, and sunglasses walk through the reception area. Perhaps the visitors wave to the lady behind the front desk. Perhaps she does not wave back because she is appalled by this breach in policy—all guests in the south wing are supposed to be chaperoned during their visit. But at least she doesn't stop them. So out they go.

Here's the tricky part: I am still standing in my mother's room, dressed in her sweatpants and T-shirt and sneakers. The shoes are a little tight, a little narrow, but a vast improvement over the high heels now slipping around on my mom's feet.

Of course my idea—that she would dress up in my clothes and leave with Jon—was met with protest. No, no, no. It's ridiculous. Impossible. Out of the question. But I argued that the most important thing was to get her away. It's not as if they could keep *me* at Grand Gardens against my will.

"But we can't just leave you here alone," said my mother.

"Mom, I'm not a little kid anymore," I said. When she flinched, I felt terrible. But it had to be said. This had to be done. "Anyway, you're not leaving me. I'll catch up to you in no time."

Finally, reluctantly, they agreed.

I watch from the window as Jon and my mother walk to the parking lot. When they reach the car, my mom pauses a moment before getting in. She turns to gaze up at the building, as if she wants one last look at the place. But then I realize I'm wrong; she's looking for me in the window. I raise my hand and touch the glass. I doubt she can see me from this distance. But her head seems to tilt in acknowledgment.

The car glides out of the parking lot, down the driveway, and disappears behind a cluster of trees. This is my cue. According to my mother, there is an emergency exit at the far end of the south wing. The alarm will go off when the door opens, but I'll have several minutes before the security guards make it over from the central part of the building. Several minutes to run.

I ease the door open. The hallway is empty. I walk briskly, baggy pants flapping against my legs, rubber soles of my shoes squealing on the linoleum floors. I feel like I'm making a racket, and at any moment someone is going to rush out from behind one of these closed doors.

No one does.

But then I hear them around the corner. A woman is speaking, tone tart with complaint: "So Nina comes and tells me to take my break. I'm just doing my job, babysitting the guests, but she acts like I'm slacking off."

I recognize the voice: it's the glum attendant who escorted us to Marty Goodman. And I don't know what to do. Do I return to my mother's room? Do I continue toward the stairwell? If I continue toward the stairwell, the glum attendant might see me. If she sees me, she might recognize me. If she recognizes me . . .

I don't know what to do. So I do nothing. I stay stopped and still and listening.

Her companion answers in soothing tones. "I'm sure Nina didn't mean it like that. You're just overworked."

"I'm so sick of this place. But I can't quit until I find another job, and there aren't any other jobs. Believe me, I've been looking."

Their voices seem to be drifting away, but I'm not sure. Everything inside me sounds so outrageously loud—my

booming heart, my shrieking thoughts—that I'm having trouble hearing. So I creep closer. I creep to the edge of the wall,
crouch low, and peer around the corner.

Two women in blue jackets are walking down the hall.
Moving away from me, their backs to me. Their backs to me,
thank goodness. I take a deep breath. Then I step, step, step to
the stairwell. And I'm safe. For now.

I jog down one flight of stairs with my head ducked down—
there are security cameras mounted in the corners—and then
I'm at the emergency exit. My palms meet the cold metal bar.
I push down hard. The alarm clangs as the door opens, the
sound slicing the air. I step over the threshold. Then stop.

For standing directly in my way is another person in a blue
jacket. He stares at me with one hand held to his ear, perhaps in
a futile attempt to block out the piercing scream of the alarm.

"Lora? What are you doing here?" asks Raul.

22.

IT'S NOT THE BURN IN MY LEGS OR THE TIGHTNESS OF MY LUNGS
that hurts most. It's my head. My head is pounding. Maybe triggered by the way I'm running hard; maybe triggered by my
fear of getting caught; maybe triggered by exhilaration, I don't
know. All I know is I'd better get to the car soon. It's not the
timing I'm worried about—I can already see the back bumper
of Jon Harmon's station wagon. What I'm worried about is col-
lapsing before I get there.

I should slow down. There's plenty of time, so much time,
in fact, I could have used some spare seconds to explain to
Raul what I was doing at the emergency exit while the alarm
announced my misdeeds.

Instead I ran away.

On the one hand, I feel bad. On the other hand, there's no
possibility of feeling bad, not when my mother is waiting for
me. I fling open the car door, dive into the backseat, and there
she is, turning around to ask me if I'm all right.

"We've really done it now!" Jon cries as he steers us onto

the road, and his excitement must be infectious because my mother laughs and even my headache subsides while I gloat. I stare at her hair, black streaked with white. I stare at her shoulder in her silky peach dress.

Her hair, *her* shoulder, I can't believe it.

Soon we fall quiet. Even though there is so much to talk about: five years to catch up on, plans to make, questions that require answers. Yet everyone seems to have withdrawn into their own selves. Which is fine—my head hurts. It's probably time to get my key repaired. After all, I don't need memories of her now that I have her, herself, in flesh and blood and breath.

I take the bottle of pain pills out of the front pocket of my bag and attempt to remove a couple pills without making any sound. But there is the inevitable rattle, so my mother catches me slipping the tablets into my mouth. "What's that?" she asks.

I show her the bottle of drugstore medicine. "I have a headache."

"Oh, Lora, I'm sorry." She looks regretfully at me, as if it's her fault.

"It's nothing. Just all the excitement." I put away the pills, and that's when I notice my bag is crammed with books and notebooks. My mother said she had a few things to pack, but I thought she meant clothes, not books.

"What's all this?" I ask my mother.

"What's what?" says Jon.

"What are these books?"

"My work."

"You brought your work with you to Grand Gardens?" I don't look at her, I look at the books, the notebooks with their wire spiral spines, the hard cardboard covers of the medical technology textbooks.

"Oh, no, this is all from there," she says. "They have a library, though the collection is sadly limited. But the librarian did order a few special volumes for me."

"Okay." I smile, a small smile. So my mother kept up with her work, despite the challenges of her missing memory, despite the sadly limited library collection. It's good she kept up with her work. I should be glad she kept up with her work.

"Now where am I taking you?" asks Jon. "Home?"

"No, I don't think . . . ," I say. I don't know what to say.

"You're right. That's the first place they'll look for her," he says.

"Exactly." I try to sound like that was exactly my reasoning.

"Jeanette, what happened? How'd you end up at Grand Gardens?" he asks.

"I'm sorry," she says. "I can't remember."

"Nothing?"

She shakes her head.

Jon clears his throat. "Lora, have you called your dad?"

My mother and I say no at the same time. Then she adds, "Not yet," and I add, "But I will." In the rearview mirror, Jon's gaze flicks from her to me, and back again. It's really my mother's expression I want to see, but I can't, not from where I'm sitting.

* * *

Jon Harmon takes us home, to his home, where he makes us hot tea and assembles an impressive selection of snacks—cheese and crackers, cookies, and fruit—before going to make some phone calls. He leaves us sitting in his living room, a room full of furniture and photos, toys strayed here and there: a doll sprawled under the coffee table, a Matchbox car parked next to me on the sofa. It is the opposite of my aunt's immaculate apartment. It seems impossible that she and Jon were once married.

I look at my mother, wanting to comment on the incongruity, wanting to ask her about Jon and Austin. But I don't. I feel suddenly overwhelmed by the imbalance between us: how I remember everything, how she remembers nothing.

"Mom, remember how you used to tell me stories about medical technology at bedtime? My favorite was the one about how P. B. Fishman invented the memory key." I smile at her.

"Yes, it's a good story." She smiles back at me. But because she doesn't say she remembers, I know she doesn't. Of course she doesn't.

Jon comes back into the room. "I've found a place for you to stay," he announces and my mother leans forward as if to get up and immediately go, but he waves her back. "We have time. I didn't use my real name at Grand Gardens, so they can't connect us just yet. Have you had a cookie? Try a cookie. Darren made them."

"Thank you, Jim," she says.

"Jon," I whisper to her. "His name is Jon."

"Jon, I'm sorry. My memory . . ."

"It's all right." He clunks his tea mug down onto the table. Then he tells my mother what he told me, about how she came to him and said she'd discovered something strange about the new line of memory keys at Keep Corp. He asks if she remembers.

"I'm sorry." She shakes her head.

"What have you been working on at Grand Gardens? Anything to do with the keys?" he asks.

"No." She stares down at the bright-striped rug. "The stuff I'm doing now, it isn't at the same level as before. I know that." She seems so discouraged.

"You didn't have the right resources," I say.

"I suppose that's true," she says.

Jon sighs. He sighs and sighs.

"I'm sorry," my mother says again.

"No, it's not you, it's just that none of this makes sense. The faked accident, putting you in that nursing home. Why did they bother? Keep Corp is unscrupulous. Getting rid of you in a car crash is much more their style," he says.

My mother is quiet.

Perhaps she is simply tired. Probably we are all simply tired, done in by the day's adventure. We drink our tea. We eat our snacks. I stare at the family portrait hanging above the fireplace: there's Jon, looking exactly as he does now; his partner, Darren, tall and plump as Jon, but with lots of light brown hair; and their two children, a boy and a girl, with cute freckled faces. They all grin for the camera.

Jon looks at his watch. "Lora, I'll take you home now, all right?"

"Will you come with us? Just for the drive?" I ask my mom.

But Jon answers first. "No," he says, "it's not safe."

"Oh. Well. Okay. Can I come over tomorrow?"

My mother glances at Jon. She nods after he nods.

"Lora," she says. "Will you tell your father I'm here?"

I'm not sure whether her question is inquiry or request. "Yes?"

"All right." She smiles at me, a little uncertainly, but it's okay—even if she can't remember what to do, I remember. I wrap my arms around her and hold her tight. I am glad she has a safe place to stay, though it feels a little like I'm losing her again.

"I'm so happy you're here," I whisper.

"Yes, me too." Her voice is soft, muffled against my hair, but it's still the voice I know by heart, the voice that calls to me from memory and sings to me in dreams. And even though I'm taller now and my ear doesn't quite fit above her collarbone like it used to, it doesn't matter, none of that matters. Not now that we're together again.

Jon Harmon doesn't say much as he drives me home. Though I've known him for only—it's hard to believe—a single day, I already recognize this is out of character. Jon is a talker. But when he parks his car, he seems subdued. "Lora," he says gently. "Will you promise me two things?"

"This isn't my house," I say. "It's a few blocks up from here."

"Yes, but we shouldn't be seen together, just in case."

"Right. Of course."

"Now, Lora, you did an incredible job tracking down your mother. But your involvement ends here. These are bad people, ruthless people who won't let anyone get in their way. You've got your mom back. Let me figure out the rest, okay?"

"What's the other thing?" I ask.

"They won't like it when they find out Jeanette's gone. Promise me you'll be careful—keep an eye out and tell your dad to do the same."

"I promise I'll be careful." I hope he doesn't notice I've made only one-half of the requested promises. "See you tomorrow?"

"Yes. I'll be in touch," he says.

"Thanks." I open the car door. But then I turn back, because there's something more I need to tell him. "I really appreciate everything you've done for me. For us."

"You're welcome." Jon smiles, and for a moment I wonder what it would have been like if he and Aunt Austin had not divorced, if he were my uncle that I'd known my entire life, who fed me cookies and told bad jokes that made me groan till I laughed. For a moment I wish it were so. But the past is irreversible. He has his own family now. And I have mine. Sort of.

I carefully walk the few blocks home, mindful of Jon's warnings, and trying to act normally, but it is so hard to act normally when I keep expecting someone to leap from the bushes and demand to know what I've done with my mother.

So when a neighbor shouts a friendly hello, I gasp in answer. When a gray cat darts around my feet, I jolt as if electrocuted. When a car drives past me, brakes screeching, I have to cover my mouth to keep from shrieking.

When I make it to our front step, unharmed, I wonder if Jon Harmon was overreacting about the danger. Still I lock the door behind me, turn the deadbolt, and seal it with the chain. Then I notice the house is absolutely dark and quiet, and I undo the chain so my father will be able to come in later. Then I frown.

Why isn't my father home? He should be home. He doesn't teach a late class or hold office hours for his students today; today is neither his grocery-shopping day nor his gym day (gym days are usually disregarded, anyway). There is no note in our usual note-leaving place, no messages on our answering machine, no voice mail in my phone's voice mail. When I call his cell he doesn't answer.

Where is he? When will he come home?

And what will I do when he comes home?

I have to tell him, of course. But . . . I unzip my bag, take the photograph out of the front pocket, and look closely at it, as if it might have changed since the last time I looked. But there he is, unchanged, and there they are, unchanged. My father with the two strangers who probably took my mother to Grand Gardens.

I put away the picture and take out Ms. Pearl's KCO pamphlet. I reread: "We at the KCO are deeply concerned about the increasing power Keep Corp has over our government, and our lives. You should be too. For more information or to find out how you can help, please contact us at . . ."

I pick up the phone and dial.

The line goes to a recording and I leave a message. I pace around the kitchen, waiting for them to call back. I pace around the den. I try sitting on the couch, but I'm too anxious to sit on the couch.

Nerves, I tell myself. But it's not just nerves.

I'm sad.

Though I know I should be celebrating. She's alive! Yet my grief remains. My unhappiness is a bulky coat I no longer need now that winter is over, but I don't know how to take the thing off. The zipper is stuck, teeth clenched in cloth.

I still miss her, I realize. I still miss her like she's still gone.

Standing on my tiptoes, I slide a photo album down from the top shelf in the den. I sit on the floor and open the book. As I look at the pictures, I imagine myself into memory. My music recital. Dad's birthday. A family vacation at the seashore. I close my eyes and open my eyes and close them again, imagining, remembering, imagining, remembering, and I don't stop even when my head starts throbbing, I don't stop until I hear the car outside, tires crackling against concrete as it slows to a stop.

Then I run up to my room. I'm not ready to talk to my

father yet. First I have to think out what to tell him. I think, waiting for the thud of the front door. I wait, but the front door doesn't thud. Eventually I go to the window to see what's taking so long. But our driveway is empty. False alarm.

I am about to turn away when I notice something odd. Not that it is particularly odd for an unfamiliar car to be parked in front of our house. Neither is it particularly odd that there is a person sitting inside the unfamiliar car.

But Jon told me to be careful. He said this would be the first place they'd come to look for her. So I turn off my lamp to better see through the glass. Still, it's too shadowy to distinguish more than a man motionless in the front seat.

I blink. My eyes are momentarily dazzled by the sunshine on the silver sedan. I watch from my window, puzzled to see my mother step out of the car. Puzzled as she waves good-bye to the driver, a man with short, dark hair; he's no one I recognize from this distance.

I blink again. It's night again.

I tell myself just because the car I remember is the same make and model and color as the one currently parked in front of our house, that doesn't mean it's the same car. It could be coincidence. It could be that I'm wrong—what do I know about cars, anyway?

I wish my dad were home.

And as soon as I think that thought, his car appears, like magic, gliding down the street and into the driveway. The shadow in the silver sedan sits still. I hold my breath as Dad gets out and walks across the lawn. The shadow in the silver sedan sits still. I hold my breath as Dad vanishes from my sight. Then there's the thud of the front door closing. The rattle of the locks locking.

The shadow still sits still.

I exhale.

My father thumps upstairs and I move toward the sound, wanting to see him, to talk to him, to laugh with him in relief. It feels as if we've just passed through some dreadful ordeal together. I come out of my room to meet him in the hallway. To tell him.

"Lora?" He looks surprised to see me, as if I'm somewhere I don't belong.

"Where were you?" I ask, surprised by his surprise. Surprised by how he is fiddling with the button on his shirt cuff, unbuttoning it then buttoning it again. The absentminded professor is not fidgety. The absentminded professor stares off in the distance; he doesn't dart his eyes around the room, his gaze a scuttling insect.

"Last-minute faculty meeting." His voice sounds strange, out of tune.

"Is something wrong?" I ask.

"No, not at all, nothing at all," he blusters, and this gives him away: Dad gets blustery when he's wrong, and the more wrong he is the more blustery he gets.

All of a sudden my head hurts, it hurts a lot, the pain worse than it's been all week, and the pain has been very, very bad.

How can I tell him about Mom when my head is booming like this? How can I tell him when I know he knows the blue-jacketed strangers? How I can tell him when he is lying about where he was tonight?

I can't.

So I say good night and stumble into my room, shut the door, take out the bottle of pain pills, empty it into my palm, and am dismayed to discover there are only six pills left. I swallow them all, two at a time. Tomorrow I'll buy more.

23.

IN THE MORNING LIGHT, ALL IS CALM AND BEAUTIFUL AS A LAND-
scape painting: the sky clear, the trees still, the grass vividly
green. There is no silver sedan parked in front of our house,
or anywhere else on the block, and I can almost believe I had
imagined that car last night. I can almost believe I imagined
my father's fidgeting hands and blustery explanations. Almost.

When I arrive at the library, I'm a few minutes late for
work, and Cynthia calls me into her office. I worry she thinks I
was eavesdropping on her phone conversation the other afternoon. I suppose I was. But she doesn't say anything about that.
Instead she asks if everything is all right. I tell her everything
is fine.

"Lora, you've always been a responsible employee, but lately
you've seemed distracted. You've been coming in late and leaving early. You've been shelving books in the wrong place and
snapping at our patrons. Are you sure there's nothing wrong?"
Her voice is cool, so is her expression.

"Everything's fine," I say again.

"If this behavior continues, we may have to let you go."

I examine her face for a sign that this is a joke, but find only the straight line of her lips, the blank brown of her eyes.

"We've just been told our budget is going to be cut significantly, and we'll have to downsize. I'm telling you now because I want to give you fair warning."

"I'm sorry. I promise I'll do better," I say.

But inside I'm seething. Maybe I've been distracted lately, but it's only been lately. And Albert, another of the library clerks, is much ruder to the patrons than I could ever be, even at my most distracted. And I thought Cynthia was my friend.

Still, I start my shift determined to be a model library clerk; all thoughts not pertaining to borrowing, returning, or late fees are banished from my brain. I chirp cheerfully to everyone, even the repulsive old man who talks only to my chest. "Have a wonderful day," I tell him. He leers at me as he leaves. Then he leers at me as he leaves. Then he leers at me as he leaves. Then he leers at me as he leaves.

I'm stuck in a memory loop. He leers at me as he leaves. I grit my teeth, trying to force myself to the present. Then he leers at me as he leaves. I straighten my shoulders, trying to force myself to the present. Then he leers at me as he leaves. My head is throbbing. Stupid broken key. Then he leers at me as he leaves.

"Lora," says the next person in line. His voice tows me out from the past. I turn to say a grateful hello, but am unable to speak when I see who it is.

"How are you?" asks Raul.

"Oh." I stare at the book in his hand.

"How are you?" he asks again.

"About yesterday," I say to the book in his hand. "I'm sorry."

"It's okay," he says, and it's the polite thing to say, but he makes it sound like it really is okay. So I look at him then, finally, I look in his face for anger or disgust. But all I find is concern. He is so nice. He is too nice.

"My break is in an hour," I say. "Will you be here for a while? Doing research for your paper on cetaceans? Marine mammals and such?"

"You remembered." He smiles.

"Of course," I say. If I were a more honest person, I would tell him he shouldn't be so impressed. I remember everything.

We meet outside. I have a sandwich, which I offer to share, but Raul says he's not hungry. I ask if he wants some orange juice, but he says he's not thirsty, no thanks. I bite my sandwich. I sip my juice.

"So what happened?" he asks, turning his head all the way around so he can stare all the way at me. His dark eyes are serious. His hair is honey-colored in the sun.

"What do you mean?" I say. As if I didn't know exactly what he meant.

"Yesterday, at Grand Gardens."

"I wish I could explain."

"Then explain."

"I . . . can't. I'm sorry, but I can't."

I truly can't. Because what if he thinks I'm nuts? Or reports me to his bosses? Or just decides he wants nothing more to do with me? I don't know what I'll do if he decides he wants nothing more to do with me. Because with Raul there is no ugly past; there are no nasty words or hurtful actions to remember. I can't give that up.

Raul shakes his head. He is frowning.

"I'm really sorry," I say. I put down my sandwich and my juice. Then I lean over to brush my lips across his lips, and after a second, he kisses me back. His hand finds my shoulder. My hand finds his knee. The dark wraps around us, and I am so happy. I've wanted this for so long. For so long I've wanted to taste the salt-sweet of his mouth, to feel the slide of his fingers across my bare skin, to have his warm body pressed against mine. For so long I've wanted Tim—

Tim? I pull away, I pull myself to the present and smile sheepishly at Raul, as if I'm merely self-conscious about making out in front of my place of work. Which I am. Still, what a cruel joke of memory that was, when a moment before I had been so sure I was immune with Raul. Guess I was wrong.

I pick up my sandwich again. Though I'm no longer hungry, chewing is something to do. Raul smiles his nice smile—his questions about me at Grand Gardens have apparently been resolved through kissing—and asks if I want to hang out tonight. I nod, my mouth full of bread and guilt.

After he leaves, I go back inside the library. There's a

prickling in my head, but I'm not thinking about that. I'm also not thinking about what happened while I was kissing Raul. *Tim.* Raul. The only thing I'm thinking about is how to productively use the remaining minutes of my lunch break. I hurry over to the computers.

It takes some searching, but I find an article that seems to be about the new line of memory keys. I print it out to read later. Then I come across a photo of Keep Corp's CEO with two senators and the secretary of defense at a charity ball. Then a photo of the CEO with a half dozen foreign dignitaries.

As I click through page after page of such pictures, my stomach sinks. Keep Corp is a multinational corporation worth billions of dollars; they're a household name with their clever billboards and heartwarming television commercials. Keep Corp is embedded in our lives, just as their memory keys are embedded into our brains. If I'm right and it's Keep Corp we're up against, what chance do we have?

Abruptly, I stand up. My face is hot and my breath is short, and all I want is to run right out of here. All I want is to race over to Jon Harmon's house. Because all I want is my mother, to sit with her, look at her, talk to her. She is all I want.

But I don't leave. I can't. I am a model library clerk.

I am a model library clerk until an hour later, when the throbbing in my head becomes unbearable. Then I ask Albert, the other clerk, to cover for me at the circulation desk. I go to the back room and blunder around in my backpack, searching for my pain pills, but when I find the bottle it's empty. Because I took the last of the tablets last night.

My headache intensifies. Maybe because I'm panicking, of course I'm panicking—how will I make it through the rest of my shift? It feels like someone has chopped open my skull and is kneading my brains into dough. It hurts so much I can barely breathe.

Panicking, I unscrew the bottle again to check again that it's empty, and of course it is. Panicking, I ransack the inside of my bag, searching for something that can't possibly be there: a dozen tablets miraculously mislaid or the new bottle I haven't yet bought.

Then I find it. A lump wrapped in tatty tissue. The single prescription painkiller pill that I took from Aunt Austin's medicine cabinet.

I stare at the small white tablet. I probably shouldn't take it. I don't know how it'll affect me and I'm supposed to be a model library clerk. I probably shouldn't take it since I remember how my father got when he took these painkillers for his back injury: slow and confused, clumsy. Forgetful.

But agony overcomes reason. Easily.

The pill is chalky on my tongue, bumpy down my throat.

I return to the circulation desk, and in what seems like no time at all, the pain lifts away, flies away, and I fly with it in relief. Yes, I might be slow and confused. Yes, there are a few occasions when I'm forced to ask people to repeat their questions—not so fast please. But the pathetic truth is that I can still do my job just fine. I can check in books and check out books and smile at the patrons, and no one seems to mind if my smile is a little loopy, a lot loopy, all loopy.

There's only one awkward moment when my hand accidentally flops against Albert's and he looks at me with brow raised, quite un-Albert like, and asks if I just touched him. I say no.

So it's only after my shift ends that everything goes bad. As soon as I stand up I get dizzy. Then my headache comes back. Even worse.

"Are you all right?" asks Albert.

"I'm fine," I say, and leave as quickly as I can in my incapacitated state.

Outside is too bright, and I can't look, and I nearly fall. It's not just my pounding head, I'm also nauseated. It's not just the nausea, my whole body is trembling. I totter to the railing, hanging tight to the bar as I stumble down the stairs.

"Lora!"

I wobble around. When I see him, he appears to be shimmering and I wonder if this is just another memory. But then he comes over, puts his arm around me, props me up against his shoulder, and helps me down the steps, and he's so solid he must be real. This must be real.

"What are you doing here?" I ask, feeling too bad to be mad.

"Coming to your rescue," says Tim.

"I don't need to be rescued," I say sharply, try to say sharply, but fail miserably as the world swirls. I touch his cheek, trying to make it stop. My hand rubs his chin, which is pleasantly scratchy with stubble. Tim laughs and pulls my fingers away.

We are at his car. He helps me into the front seat, and asks for my keys so he can put my bike in the back. As I wait, I try to straighten up, to settle my mind, to shake off the hurt. It feels better to be sitting again, but only a little better. My head throbs. Where *are* my pain pills? I reach for my bag. Then I remember there aren't any left.

Tim gets into the car. "It's your memory key, isn't it," he says.

"No, I'm fine," I say. "And I have somewhere to go."

"I know. I'm taking you there."

"Thanks." I close my eyes.

"You're welcome," he says.

My face flops against the cushioned headrest. I want to ask Tim for my pain pills, but I don't know how, and when I do know how, I remember the empty bottle. I remember that prescription painkiller lump wrapped in tatty tissue. I shouldn't have . . .

I blink. My father knows what to do. I know he knows because he's always the one who stays home to take care of me. Now I'm in bed with a stomach-heaving flu and Dad is wiping my face with a cool cloth.

Drink some water. Can you drink some water? he asks.

No. I shake my head.

How about some ginger ale? It'll settle your stomach. Daddy cracks open the can and sticks in a straw. He knows I can't resist a straw. *One sip*, he says and I take one sip. *One more sip*, he says and I take one more sip.

When's Mama coming home? I ask.

Soon as she can leave work.

Will you stay with me till she comes? I ask. He's right about the ginger ale, I feel better already, though I don't tell him that. I want him to stay.

Of course, he says.

My head hurts, I say.

"My head hurts," I say.

"Lora, we're here," says Tim.

I look around. But this isn't Jon Harmon's house. This isn't anyone's house. This isn't any place I recognize. We're surrounded by cars and concrete gray. Another moment passes before I understand that we're inside a parking garage.

"Do you need me to carry you?" asks Tim.

"That's not necessary. I've recovered," I say.

"Great," he says.

With effort, I manage to crawl out of the car and stretch myself upright. But when I stagger forward, Tim takes my arm. I let him. My headache is so bad that I have to.

We walk through a corridor and come into a room where a security guard sits behind a desk. Tim shows his ID badge and the guard scans it. Sliding doors open to a glass-walled atrium. Here there's too much light, my eyes start watering from so much light, but still I look around, for there is so much to look at, and it all seems eerily familiar.

For example, there's the attractive man sitting on a bench, I know I know that attractive man. I squint at him, but he doesn't notice; he's reading a magazine with complete attention. And just behind him, I recognize another face: a little girl with braided hair dances on the beach. But there's something very wrong—though she's just a little girl she's twice my size, and even though she's smiling at me, I'm frightened of her, and why are we at the beach when we're not?

Tim tugs me forward and I realize there isn't any little girl; she's just an image on a huge screen, she's just the girl from the commercial, it's the Keep Corp commercial on a huge screen. Which means the attractive man is the attractive man from the Keep Corp billboard. I laugh at my foolishness.

Around the corner is another desk, or is it still the first desk? There's a pen in my hand and I'm trying to write my name, but the letters are slippery. "That's good enough," a voice says, and I'm relieved, so relieved.

I don't remember closing my eyes, but when I open them again, Tim is gone and I'm strapped into a chair, cold metal pressing each side of my face. "Relax, you're going to be fine," says someone from somewhere behind me. I don't recognize the voice. I twist around in panic, trying to get a look at the person speaking, but my body is anchored and I can't move at all.

"Just relax," that someone says.

But how can I relax with all these voices shouting from memory?

He was struck by this incredible pain, the worst pain in his life.

They had to cut the key out of his brain . . . The body can reject the memory key. It happens very rarely, but it does happen . . . Now he can't remember much of anything because he'd been so reliant on his key.

"Please, you need to relax," that someone says.

But how can I relax when I'm terrified of what will happen if I do?

"Don't worry, you won't feel a thing," that someone says. A mask clamps over my nose and mouth. I try not to breathe. I try not to breathe. I have to breathe.

I breathe and realize I'm about to lose everything.

24.

THE WORLD IS WHITE. I RUB MY EYES, CERTAIN I'M MISTAKEN. I'm not mistaken. Everything is white. There's a white curtain on both my left side and my right, a white wall in front of me, and a thin white sheet covering my body. I look up and the ceiling is white. I turn over to look at the floor. The floor is blue. For some reason, this is comforting.

I realize I'm no longer strapped into place, so I sit up carefully. My head is tender, but not painfully so. I crawl my hand through my hair, searching for the sore spot. My fingers snag on the bandage at the base of my skull.

"Don't touch!" A man emerges from the whiteness, tall in his lab coat, clipboard in hand. "I'm Dr. Trent. It's a good thing you came to us when you did. Your memory key was severely damaged. Have you been getting headaches?"

"Where am I?" I ask.

"Keep Corp's Memory Key Center. Don't you remember?" Dr. Trent is a thin man with salt-and-pepper curls and a narrow face.

"What did you do to my key?" I ask.

"We transferred your data onto a new one. It's the same model as the one you had, so all should be back to normal. If you notice anything out of the ordinary, you'd better let us know right away. The procedure might not be as simple next time."

"You can't just change my key on me!"

"Shush, you'll disturb the other patients," he says.

I look around for the other patients, but all I see is white.

"You signed the consent form." He shows me a sheet of paper.

"I didn't," I say, but then vaguely recall holding a pen.

"You'll feel better after you eat something," says the doctor. He drops a package of crackers and a carton of juice on the table beside me. "Now tell me, have you been getting headaches?"

I think. Yes, I do remember getting headaches. I nod.

"Do you remember how often?"

I think. Yes, I do remember how often. "A couple times a day," I say. And I'm so relieved to remember that I smile at him while he makes a note on his clipboard.

"How long did each headache last, on average?"

"An hour maybe? They'd go away after I took pain pills," I say. And I'm so relieved to remember I tell him I was scared. I tell him I thought my body had rejected my key, and I was going to lose all of my memories.

"You didn't have to worry. Key rejection is extremely rare," he says.

"How rare?" I ask, thinking of my mother. Remembering my mother. All I can remember, however, is the sketchiest sketch of a woman in a peach dress. I feel a pang of loss, a sharpness in my stomach.

But she's back. I remind myself that I've got her back. Remember?

I remember. I try to focus on what Dr. Trent is telling me.

"Rejection occurs in fewer than one in a hundred million patients," he says.

"That *is* extremely rare." I frown.

"Is something wrong?"

I shake my head. "No. I'm just wondering . . . Why didn't I get the newest kind of memory key?"

"Your insurance wouldn't cover the upgrade. Anyway, it's better to reinstall the key you're accustomed to. You don't want things to get too mixed up in your head." He eyes me accusingly, as if he knows exactly how mixed up my head has been.

I take a sip of juice. "What features does the new one have?"

"The MK-545, which came out six years ago, has a data backup system and upgraded filters. Other than that, it's more or less the same as yours, the 485."

"But isn't there a new one coming out soon? What does that one do?"

"Not public yet." Dr. Trent flips through the pages clipped to his clipboard. "If you'll just answer a few questions we'll make sure everything is in order," he says.

"But how did you get the data from my old key onto my new one? Since mine didn't have a backup system?"

"It's a simple procedure. Fortunately, despite the damage, we were able to download the data from your key into our systems, so we could upload it onto a new key," he says. "Now please, let me ask my questions."

"Sorry, go ahead."

"Your name?" Dr. Trent glances at the clipboard. Then he looks abruptly at me.

"Lora Mint," I say, and at the same time, he says, "*Lora Mint?*"

"If you knew, why'd you have to ask?" I smile.

He does not smile back. Slowly and carefully, as if he's weighing each syllable on his tongue, he says, "You wouldn't happen to be related to Jeanette Mint, would you?"

I consider lying, but I don't think I could get away with it. I nod.

"You're Jeanette's daughter, aren't you?"

I nod again.

"I'm so sorry for your loss. Your mother was a wonderful person and a great scientist. We worked together." He looks sad, terribly sad.

"Yes." My eyes are glistening. I am the very image of a girl who has lost her mother. And I'm not even trying.

Dr. Trent shakes his head slightly. Then he clears his throat and asks me a series of questions to make sure my memory is intact. He inquires about things like my first pet, my third grade teacher's name, a positive experience I had in middle school, my emotions upon graduating high school, and what I ate for lunch today. Finally, he makes a note on his clipboard and says, "Good as new. Do you have any questions for me?"

"If someone has their memory key removed, but later changes their mind, can they get a new key put in?" I ask.

His narrow face puckers. "You want to have your key removed?"

"No, no. Hypothetically."

"Do you have any questions about *your* memory key?"

"I know this guy who had his key removed years ago because he didn't like having one. But now he's been diagnosed with Vergets. So can he get a new key?"

Dr. Trent scowls. "I have to say, that is extremely irresponsible behavior. And without examining the patient, I can give you no definitive answer. However, if the area is not too damaged, if there is no inflammation or excess scar tissue, it would be possible."

"That's comforting to know." I grin, ignoring his scowl.

But the doctor has moved his disapproving expression past me. "Can I help you?" he says, and I turn to see who he's talking to. It's Tim. I stop grinning.

"I'm here for the patient. Not that *Lora's* patient. I mean, she *is* the patient." Tim laughs at his own stupid pun. I do not.

Neither does Dr. Trent. "You're not allowed back here," he says.

"It's okay. I work here." Tim brandishes his badge.

"All right," the doctor says begrudgingly. Then he looks back to me. "Well, Miss Mint, it was nice to meet you. Let us know if you have any problems with your new key."

And before I can ask another question, or even just thank him, he's gone.

"How are you doing?" Tim comes to stand beside me.

I glare at him.

"Come on, Lora!" he says. "You were practically passed out at the library. What was I supposed to do? And don't you feel better now? You look better."

"But it wasn't my memory key. It was just these painkillers I needed to—"

"Will you listen to what you're saying? *Just these painkill-ers?* Once you're drugging yourself, it's probably time to admit something's wrong."

"It's not like that," I say. Then I realize it's exactly like that.

Tim sighs. "Let's go. I'll drive you home."

We walk through a maze of hallways: white walls, blue floors, and Keep Corp's octagonal logo everywhere. I keep my eyes on the blue floors and say nothing. I am a bit unsteady, but when Tim offers his arm I refuse. He asks if I can manage stairs and I shake my head. As we approach the elevators, the doors open.

"Timmy! I thought you'd left already!" The girl pounces on him. She is cute, wearing a cute striped dress, tossing her cute long hair. They hug.

"I brought my friend to get her key fixed," he says. "Becky, this is Lora. Lora, Becky. Becky is another one of the interns here."

I say hello and fake-smile. I do a bad job, but Becky doesn't seem to notice, so involved is she with Tim. It's high school all over again, when I would watch him flirt with girl after girl after girl. My breath catches; I'm afraid I might have summoned the memory.

Then I remember my key has been replaced so I no longer have to worry about the past. The realization feels peculiar, not disappointment, but something akin to disappointment. I relax my shoulders and invite the memory to come. I dare it to come. I insist that it come. But I'm stuck in the present, in this slowly descending elevator with chattering Tim and Becky.

"My friend is having a party tonight," she says to him.

"Sounds fun," he says to her.

"I'll call you later," she says to him.

The elevator chimes, the doors slide open.

"This is us," Tim tells me.

"Bye!" Becky waves cutely. "Nice meeting you, Lauren!"

I give her a fake smile, faker than the first, and follow Tim down the corridor, into the parking garage, and back to his car.

"Want to go to that party tonight?" He opens the passenger door for me. But then he stands in the way so I can't get in.

I just glare.

"Lora, give me a break. Stop being such a jerk."

I try to push him aside so I can get into the car. He won't move. So I try to wrestle him out of the way, and somehow my arms get twisted up with his arms, and our bodies smash together, and then we're kissing, kissing so fiercely it's like a battle with desperate stakes, and after a minute, our limbs unknot and rearrange so we're holding each other tight, as tightly as we can, but still struggling to get closer. Mouths open. Tongues tangle. Hot hands on hot skin. We're greedy, we're both so greedy; the more we touch, the more we want to touch.

Then a car drives by and honks. "Get a room!" shouts the driver, and I'm positive Tim is going to pull away, this is where he always pulls away, except he doesn't, not this time. This time he kisses me harder. But . . .

Now I've started thinking. And I have to stop.

Even though to move away from him—to step out of his arms, to separate our lips—takes almost more strength than I have. "I—I can't do this," I say.

"Why not?" Tim leans over and kisses my neck.

"I can't." I push him away. I force myself.

"Because of that guy, what's-his-name? Ralph?"

"Raul. And, yeah, because there's Raul."

I say this even though I had not thought of Raul until this moment. But Raul is a reason that can be easily explained and easily understood. The passenger door is still open so I climb into the car. Tim walks around and slides into the driver's seat.

"You don't *really* like that guy, do you?" he asks.

"I do," I say, which is true. Raul is so nice.

"Good for you, then." Tim grins. It is the poorest imitation of his usual grin. Yet this false smile convinces me in a way that his kiss did not.

"But I like you too," I say, which is also true. I'm tired of pretending otherwise.

"Well, the feeling's mutual." He reaches then—not for me, but for my seat belt. He pulls it across my chest and buckles me in safe, and it's the sweetness of this gesture, even more than his declaration, that crushes my heart.

"If things were different—" I say.

"Why can't they be different?" he interrupts.

"Like I said, there's Raul, and—"

"Look, I'm sure Ronald is an okay dude, but . . . you need to get rid of him," he says with his typical self-assurance.

I'm annoyed. Tim is so certain of himself, and of me. So certain I will do anything to be with him. But that's not true, not now. Even with my key fixed, I haven't quite forgotten.

"Maybe I don't want to get rid of him," I say, sharpening the edge of every word. I wait for his snappy retort, but he doesn't retort; he just turns on the engine and starts driving. Then I wish I could take it back. One small sentence should be easy enough to take back. But I don't. I can't. Even with my key fixed, I haven't quite forgiven.

So I change the subject. "What were you doing at the library?"

"I thought you should know," he says, staring straight out at the road.

"Know what?"

"Wendy told your dad you still haven't gotten your memory key fixed."

25.

I HAVE FIVE NEW VOICE MAILS. TWO ARE FROM MY FATHER, AND both of these are shouted. One is from Jon, asking when I'll arrive. One is from Aunt Austin, saying she'll be returning the day after tomorrow and would like to see me soon. The last is from Raul. He wants to know what I'm doing tonight, if I still want to hang out.

I gaze out the windshield, trying to figure out who I should call, where I should go, but then I flinch when I notice where I already am. And I forget my dad's rage. I forget Jon and my aunt, I forget Raul's niceness and Tim's annoyance. I forget everything other than my fear. The car is speeding toward the entrance of the bridge that spans the river that runs along the northern edge of Middleton. The bridge where my mother died.

"No," I say.

"What?" says Tim, and the needle in his voice stings me, stings me enough to remember that she didn't die. Stings me enough to realize we must have crossed this bridge on our way here, so I shouldn't be as frantic as I am. Still, I am very frantic.

"I can't go this way. I can't. Can we go the other way?"

He doesn't answer but he does change lanes, and takes the last exit before the bridge. Which means he has to drive an extra twenty minutes to get back to the city.

"Are you okay?" he says, voice rough, eyes forward.

"I'm okay," I say, voice soft, eyes down.

When we get to Middleton, I ask Tim if he'll drop me off at Jon's house, and when he grumbles agreement, I give him directions. That is the extent of our conversation for the rest of the drive. There is not much traffic, so even with the detour it doesn't take long to get there.

"Thanks for the ride," I tell him. "And for taking me to get my key fixed."

"Yeah," says Tim, and as soon as my bicycle and I have been removed from his car, he zooms away. For a moment I just stand there, alone in the middle of the street, and try to remember the exact feeling of his mouth on my mouth. But I can't remember. Not anymore.

It's for the best. Because the two of us together is obviously impossible: first he hurts me, now I hurt him; first I'm angry with him, now he's angry with me—the cycle seems doomed to repeat itself over and over and over forever. It makes me sad, though I have no reason to be sad. My mother is waiting for me.

Except she's not. Jon Harmon lets me into his home, guides me to the living room, tells me to take a seat, and takes a seat himself. Immediately a little girl leaps from the floor to his lap.

"This is my daughter, Ginny," he says.

I say hello, but I'm anxious. "Where is she?" I ask.

"I'm here." Ginny stares at me. She has curly hair and a cute freckled face and a very intense stare.

"I know. I meant . . ."

"Don't worry, everything's fine," says Jon. "I'll explain after I put Ginny to bed. It's bedtime now, isn't that right, Gin?"

"I'm four," she tells me. "Almost five."

"Great! When's your birthday?" I ask.

"Today," she says.

"No, honey, your birthday isn't today," says Jon.

Ginny laughs uproariously.

"Yup, it's definitely bedtime." Her father stands, lifting her up with him, swinging her to his chest as she flings her arms around his neck, lays her head upon his shoulder, and he carries her away, their routine movements graceful as choreography.

Jon is gone a long time. And the longer he is gone, the more anxious I get. When he returns downstairs, before he can even sit back down, I start with the questions: Where is she? How is she? When can I see her?

"We'll go right now." He explains that Darren's sister is away on business so they've settled my mother in her apartment, just a few blocks away. He takes me into his kitchen and out the back door. "Just to be safe," he says.

We walk silently through the dark night, across the yard and down the alleyway behind his house. And even though he told me where she is, and he assured me she's fine, and now he's taking me to see her, I'm still anxious. I keep imagining that when I get to where she's supposed to be, she'll be gone.

But then Jon knocks a particular rhythm on a particular door—one long tap, two short—and the door opens, and there she is.

As soon as I see her, I feel better. I smile and reach out for a hug, and in my arms she feels so delicate I'm afraid I might break her if I hold on too tightly, so I'm gentle as I let go. "I'm sorry I'm late," I say.

"It's all right. I've kept busy." She steps aside to let us in, but Jon excuses himself and says he has some things to do at home, and he'll come back to join us later.

So it's just me and my mother. She gives me a tour of the apartment. It's one bedroom, one bathroom, a narrow kitchen, and a square-shaped living room that she has already transformed into her office: the coffee table made of books, the sofa upholstered in notepaper.

Mom clears a small space for us to sit and asks me how I am. I tell her I'm fine. I ask how she is. She tells me she's good. I ask about her day and she says it was productive, a lot of reading, a lot of writing. She asks about my day and I tell her it was okay, just a normal day working at the library.

Then I can't stand the small talk any longer. "Have you remembered more about Keep Corp?" I ask her. "About why they would put you in that home?"

"I'm afraid not." She stoops to pick a stray paper from the floor.

I frown. Then un-frown before she sees. "What about a silver sedan?"

She shifts upright again. "A silver sedan?"

"You told me it was your coworker's car."

"I'm sorry. I don't remember."

"Do you remember Carlos Cruz? He's a journalist and your . . . friend?"

"Carlos Cruz? I don't think so." She tilts her head thoughtfully.

And there's something in the thoughtful tilt of her head that I don't like, so my next question comes out harsher than it should. "Don't you remember *anything*?" I say.

She looks at her coffee table of books. "I'm very sorry, Lora."

"No, I didn't mean . . . It's not your fault."

My mother stands up. "I should have asked before, are you hungry? Can I fix you something to eat? Or drink?"

"Sure," I say, though I'm not particularly hungry. "Thanks."

Five years away and her cooking has not improved at all. She makes a grilled cheese sandwich and somehow the bread burns without the cheese melting. "Is it okay? You can tell me if it isn't," she says. "I'll make you another one."

"It's perfect," I say. And it is. Because how miraculous it is to be sitting here with my mother, eating a sandwich she burned for me. Perhaps she thinks so too: she watches me chewing with a bemused expression.

But no, it turns out she's thinking about something else. Someone else. "I thought Kenneth might have come with you tonight," she says.

"Um. I haven't told Dad yet. There hasn't been a good time." My excuse is so bad, I wait for her to tell me how bad.

She nods.

There's a knock on the door—one long tap, two short—and Jon Harmon is back. He comes into the kitchen holding an enormous shopping bag, carrying it against his chest with his arms wrapped round, the same way he carried his daughter earlier. He eyes my charred sandwich.

"You know what would go perfectly with that? I brought over some vegetable soup. Would you like some soup?" He takes a plastic container out of his shopping bag and ladles its green contents into a bowl. This is one thing he and my aunt still have in common: they both love to feed people.

Jon puts the soup bowl in front of me, and a spoon, and a paper napkin folded neatly into a rectangle, and urges me to eat.

I don't eat. I just look at him.

"What are we going to do?" I ask.

Jon doesn't answer immediately. He puts away the groceries in his shopping bag. He sits down. He sighs. Then he says: "Well, your mom can stay here till the end of the week, when Darren's sister gets back. After that, we'll have to find somewhere for her to go. The farther from Middleton, the better. Perhaps abroad."

"You want to send her away?" There is an ugly taste in my mouth, a bitter taste. The burnt bread of the sandwich, I think.

"There aren't a lot of options. We don't know what Jeanette found out about the new keys. We don't have any leverage against Keep Corp. But someone went to a lot of trouble to make her disappear, so our priority has to be her safety."

"But if we don't do anything she'll never be safe. She'll spend her whole life away in hiding," I say. *Away from me*, I don't say.

I glance at my mother to see her reaction, her indignation, her steadfast refusal. But she doesn't even seem to be following our conversation. She is staring at the wall, and her eyes are far away. How well I know those faraway eyes.

"Lora," says Jon. "You promised you'd let me handle things."

"Except you're not handling things, you're avoiding them!" I say. Then instantly wish I hadn't. Jon has been so helpful, so supportive, and even now he is looking at me with sympathy, not annoyance. With understanding.

"I'm sorry," I tell him. "I didn't mean that."

"I know. It's a frustrating situation."

"What if we went to the police?" I say.

He shakes his head. "When I . . . When they . . ." He clears his throat and tries again. "After I was attacked, the police arrested the two suspects I identified in a lineup. But then the charges were dropped out of nowhere. The company we'd been investigating made it happen through their contacts and influence. Everyone knew it, but there was nothing we could do."

"That's awful," I say. "But this is a different situation."

"The main problem is the same. We don't have solid evidence, something they can't ignore or hush up. Don't underestimate Keep Corp's power."

"Well, what if my mom got a new memory key?" I say.

"She can't. Her body rejected her key," he says.

"I did some research and rejection is extremely rare. Maybe they lied about it or misdiagnosed her case. A new key might help her remember what happened."

"But how would we get it implanted? Not at Keep Corp."

"Why not? She probably still has friends there," I say.

"Friends who think she's dead," he says.

"Excuse me," says my mother.

We look at her, startled.

"Would you mind not talking about me as if I weren't here?" she says, and now there is nothing faraway in her eyes. Her gaze is sharp and so is her voice, and it's a familiar sharpness. I realize it's *her* I'm recognizing; she seems suddenly like her old self.

"Sorry," Jon and I say, sheepishly, together.

"It's all right. My memory has its weaknesses, but my brain still functions. I'm still capable of making my own decisions," she says.

"So would you consider getting a new key?" I ask.

"I'd need more information before deciding, of course, but at this point, my natural memory has developed to the extent where I'm not certain the benefits of a new key would offset the risks involved."

"Oh. Okay. Then would you leave Middleton? Go abroad?"

"Yes. If necessary."

"Oh. Okay." I stare down at my forgotten food.

"It's not that I want to leave—you understand, don't you, Lora?"

"Sure." I pick up my spoon and start eating again. I don't stop until I've eaten it all, the cold soup and the burnt sandwich, the crumbling black crusts.

Jon Harmon yawns. He yawns with his whole body: shoulders curling as his head falls backward. The sound is loud and long. He apologizes, smiling sleepily. "I should go," he says. "But, Lora, you should stay longer if you'd like. Darren or I can drive you home later. Just give us a call."

I glance cautiously at my mom. "Do you mind? I have something to show you."

"Of course I don't mind," she says.

"Thank you," I say gratefully. Then I'm embarrassed for sounding so grateful, as if I had expected her to say no.

My mother carefully uncovers the couch, collecting her papers in some particular but inexplicable order, then we sit next to each other in the square-shaped living room to look at the photo album I brought from home. I place the book in her lap. Slowly, she lifts back the cover.

And there she is with my father, arms linked in front of the bedecked tree. There's little me dressed as an elf. There's the three of us standing in the snow. I wait for my mother to comment on the garish sweaters or my crooked pigtails, but she says nothing. She scrutinizes every picture, and turns the page.

There's Aunt Austin cutting into a chocolate cake. There's me with my mouth smeared with chocolate frosting. There's the two sisters looking at each other and laughing. And there are my parents, leaning sleepily against each other on the sofa.

Still she says nothing. She scrutinizes every picture, and turns the page.

It takes a long time for my mother to get through the album. When she comes to the end, I shift around in my seat so that I can see her face. I am not sure what to expect: maybe sadness or contentment or nostalgia. Maybe tears. But when I see her face there is nothing at all. Her face is blank. I panic.

"Mom? Don't you remember *any* of it?"

She looks at me, notices me looking at her, and her expression immediately transforms into an expression. But still it's not sadness or contentment or nostalgia or frustration.

It's apology.

"I think I do," she says. "A little."

"What little?"

"My sister, have you talked to her? Have you told her?"

"Not yet. She's out of town, but I can call her for you," I say.

"No, why don't you give me her number and I'll call."

"Okay." I smile. I try.

My mother closes the photo album. "Thank you, Lora. This was a good idea. I'm sure I'll remember more as I look through it again."

"We have lots of albums. I'll bring them tomorrow," I say.

"No need to bring them all at once. One at a time is enough."

"Right. Of course."

"And will your father also come tomorrow?" Her voice is soft.

"I'll ask him. I'm sure he'll want to." My voice is softer.

She nods. "It's late, Lora. I'll call Jon to drive you home now."

"It's okay. I have my bike, I'll bike home."

"But it isn't safe. Not at this hour." She lays her hand on my arm.

And suddenly I'm annoyed. I have to restrain myself from yanking free from her touch. I have to restrain myself in order to say, in a reasonably calm tone: "I bike at night all the time. I've been doing it for years."

My mother lets go of my arm. She stands and starts straightening the couch cushions, plucking linty flecks from the fabric upholstery. I watch her, surprised. She never used to fuss like this.

"Then you'd better leave now," she says, "before it gets any later. Just call me when you get there, so I know you made it safely." She does not look up from her tidying.

The sky is empty of stars and moon, so the night is dark. Extremely dark.

I regret not asking for a ride home. And I regret arguing with her. I wanted my mother back so she could be my mother— listening to my worries, counseling me on my complaints, wrapping me with scarves in cold weather, insisting I don't bike home too late at night—so why did I resist when she tried?

How I regret arguing with her. And how I regret not asking for a ride home. Because it's dark, it's late, and there is the issue of the silver sedan.

The silver sedan. As I turn onto our block, I look for it and it's not there. But what *is* there is equally alarming: there's a gleaming black SUV parked across from our house. It's alarming because the car is too startlingly large and too shiningly new in this family neighborhood of dented minivans. It's alarming because the windows are tinted dark, silhouetting the two figures in the front.

I know it could mean nothing. I'm sure it must mean something.

I speed up the driveway and hurry to the door. My hand shakes as I work the key into the lock; my fingers tremble as I turn the key till the lock clunks open. I glance backward. There is movement within the black car. Quickly, I go inside, close the door, bolt the door, chain the door, exhale, and exhale.

Then I call my mother to tell her I made it home safely.

"Good. Thank you for calling," she says.

"Mom, I'm sorry about before," I say.

"What are you talking about?" She sounds genuinely puzzled. I imagine her at the other end of the line with her brow crinkled. Her eyes far away.

"Never mind," I say. Overhead the ceiling creaks and groans, then there is the thud of feet stomping down stairs. I tell my mom I have to go.

My father comes barreling down the hallway as I hang up the phone. He is yelling. Yelling about my memory key and my lies and how Wendy told him everything. It's no surprise.

What *is* a surprise is how my own anger rises to meet his.

"You're such a hypocrite!" I shout. "Are you really going to scream at me for keeping secrets? How can you when you won't tell me what happened to Mom! I know you know the truth. I know it. So tell me, what did you do to her?"

Somewhere amidst all my fury, I am stunned. I have never spoken to my father in this way.

Perhaps he is also stunned. His mouth is still open, but no more comes out.

"I went to Keep Corp today. A med-tech replaced my key. See?" I flip my hair to show him the bandage at the base of my head. Then I lower my voice. "I shouldn't have lied to you, but I had my reasons. Now tell me what happened the night before the accident. You owe me that." I pause to find my breath. "You owe me."

He closes his mouth and, suddenly, he looks old. His hair is thinning. His skin is deeply creased around his eyes. He's thinner and shorter than I remember. When I saw my mother for the first time at Grand Gardens, it was a shock how much she had aged. But because I see my father every day, I hadn't noticed the wear on his face, the narrowing of his body. I notice it now.

"Please, Dad," I say. "Please talk to me."

Finally, he answers: "We'd better sit down."

We go into the den. I tuck myself into the corner of the couch. My father remains standing. It is a moment before he begins his story. But once he begins, he speaks effortlessly, as if giving a speech diligently prepared for a long-awaited occasion. Perhaps because that's exactly what this is.

"It began a few weeks before the accident," he says. He tells me he noticed that my mother was acting oddly. She was working even longer hours than usual and seemed constantly distracted. He'd hear her on the phone, and when he asked who it was, she'd change the subject.

"Jeanette had always been a private person, like you, Lora. But in this case I was certain there was something more going on."

I nod, guessing that this was when my mother had discovered the problem with the new memory keys. I wonder why she didn't tell my father what she found; he was her husband, after all. She should have gone to *him* for advice.

Yet I'm not wholly surprised she didn't. Dad is right about

Mom liking her privacy. And I suppose he's right I can be that same way. It must have been hard for him to be stuck between the closemouthed two of us.

"To this day, I'm utterly ashamed of what I did next." Dad says that in his frustration, he eavesdropped on one of her telephone calls. He heard her talking to a man, begging him to meet her. The man said it was too risky. She said she needed to see him. Eventually, he agreed.

For a few days, my father did nothing. He did not know what to do. He wished he could forget. But he could not forget. So he confronted her, asked about all those late nights. She said she had been working. He asked about all those furtive phone conversations. She said they were about work. He told her if she couldn't tell him the truth, he wanted a divorce.

"That night, she never came up to bed. The next morning, the police called about the accident," he says, gazing at the floor. It feels as if he's forgotten I'm here.

"If only I hadn't lost my temper. Why wasn't I able to control my temper? We could have worked it out. I would have forgiven her. I should have told her these things. If only she had gotten a good night's sleep, if only she hadn't been so upset . . .

"The accident. It's . . . it was entirely my fault."

"No, Dad, it wasn't. It really wasn't."

"I'm sorry, Lora. I'm so, so sorry."

My body moves without my consent, jerking across the room. Before I understand what I'm doing, I've taken the photograph out of my bag and brought it over to my father. "And what about this?" I say, shoving it toward him.

Startled, he takes the picture from me, the picture of him smiling with the two strangers. He stares at it for a minute. "Well, there I am. But I don't know these other people."

"If you don't know them, why are you sitting together?"

"I think this was at a Keep Corp fund-raiser. I must have met them there, but I don't remember who they are. You know how it is at these functions. Meaningless small talk. I always hated going to those things. But Jeanette insisted. Why?"

"Where were you last night? I know you weren't at a faculty meeting."

"I *was* at a faculty meeting," he says slowly. "But afterward I went for a drink with a colleague. A woman. A date. I don't know why I didn't tell you."

"You should have told me."

"Yes, I should have."

"Mom wasn't having an affair," I say, and as soon as I say it I'm sure it's true. But I don't blame my father for his suspicions because they're not so different from my own fears about sexy journalists in unfamiliar cars.

"How do you know?" Dad looks at me in wonder.

"There's something else," I say.

"What? Lora, what is it?"

I tell him.

26.

MY FATHER DRIVES INTO THE PARKING LOT, INTO THE FIRST available space, and shuts off the car engine. Then he just sits there, hands resting on the steering wheel. I want to say something. I want to apologize again. For lying about my memory key. For making assumptions about his guilt. I want to tell him it'll all be all right.

Instead I ask: "Shall we?"

We shall. We get out of the car and walk up to the department store, through sliding doors, down air-conditioned aisles. When I called Jon to tell him about the black SUV loitering outside our house last night—though it was gone by morning—he said we should take precautions today and gave me very specific instructions. When I repeated these very specific instructions to my father, he seemed bewildered.

But he's seemed bewildered ever since I told him about her.

"Dad, hold on!" I call him back to the Personal Care aisle.

"What's that?" he asks.

I show him the bar of lavender soap wrapped up pretty in

its floral paper. "I want to get this for Mom. It's the soap she used to use."

My father says nothing, but when we go through the checkout counter he hands the cashier a twenty-dollar bill before I can take out my wallet. I protest. He says nothing. I let him pay.

Per Jon's instructions, we leave the store at the opposite end from where we entered, through an exit that opens to street level. I glance back to see if anyone comes out after us. No one does. We briskly walk the couple of blocks to Darren's sister's apartment.

But when we arrive at the building, I stop on the front step.

"Is this it? Should we go inside?" asks Dad.

"Yeah. But. Can I ask you something?"

"Yes, Lora?"

"What about that woman? The one you're dating?"

For a moment he looks indignant, as if he's been wrongly accused of some crime. Then he shakes his head. "We're not dating, it was only a couple dates. It's nothing," he says, and he sounds so dismissive that I would feel bad for the woman if I weren't so entirely relieved.

We go inside. I knock the correct rhythm on the door—one long tap, two short—and Jon Harmon lets us in. He takes my father's hand and shakes it with enthusiasm. "Ken, it's been a long time, too long a time."

"Too long, yes." Dad smiles nervously.

"Hello?" says a voice from across the room.

And there she is. My mother. Coming slowly toward us. In my silky peach dress. *Her* silky peach dress. I glance at my father. Her husband. He is staring at his wife with light in his eyes. She stares back at him. Her expression is more solemn.

I realize I'm holding my breath, waiting for something to happen, for someone to come forward, for someone to speak. No one comes forward, no one speaks. Nothing happens. I am not sure what I expected from this moment, but I did not expect this. I exhale. "Hi, Mom," I say.

She looks at me. "Lora," she says.

Then she looks again at my father. "Ken," she says.

"Jeanette," he says. "How are you?"

"I'm fine. And how are you?"

"Good. I'm good."

"I'm glad," she says.

"Yes," he says. "You're looking well."

"Thank you. As are you," she says.

They are both lying. Neither one of them looks well. She is pinched and pale. He is flushed and sweating. Their smiles are painfully polite. I step forward, but a hand hooks my elbow and draws me back.

"Come, Lora, let's give them a chance to get reacquainted," whispers Jon.

I shake my head, but when he pulls me away I don't resist.

In the narrow kitchen, I watch as Jon Harmon moves nimbly from cabinet to refrigerator to sink to stove. His polo shirt today is a soft pink. I wonder how many polo shirts he owns, and in what colors.

"Lora, how are you doing?" Jon brings over a teapot and two mugs, and two wedges of lemon cake on two plates with two forks, and sits next to me at the counter.

"I'm okay."

"Sure? This is a lot to handle. It's okay if you're not okay."

"I'm okay. It's just . . . Do you really think that black SUV was at our house to look for my mom?" I ask.

"I think it's very likely."

"But she can't remember anything! Why should they care if she left the retirement home? She's no threat to them anymore."

"I don't know. But someone wanted her gone, and I doubt that's changed. The sooner we get her out of Middleton, the better."

"It's not fair," I say, and this is the most trite observation, the most tired truth; it's the obnoxious refrain of some little kid's temper tantrum; yet I say it and I mean it.

"I know. The thing to remember is that your mother is alive and well. She can make a new life for herself, and you'll be able to visit her."

"I guess so," I say.

Then we eat our cake and drink our tea, and as we eat and drink, the sound of my parents' conversation seeps into our silence, but through the muffling walls their voices are melodies without lyrics, and I can't even tell whether the song is a happy or sad one.

"Jon?" I set my fork down gently on my plate, so gently there is no clink.

"Yes?"

"Why didn't she tell my dad about what she found at Keep Corp?"

Jon sighs. "It's impossible to know what any relationship is like from the outside. But I'd guess that Jeanette wanted to protect him, to protect both of you. If she told Ken, she would have put him in danger. And if something happened to him, what would have happened to you?"

"Yes, but," I say, then stop because I don't know what else to say. His reasoning makes absolute sense.

But.

I stuff another chunk of cake into my mouth. "This is delicious."

"Darren made it. He's a wonderful baker."

I nod. I swallow. My phone starts to ring.

"Go ahead and answer that if you want," says Jon.

I check the caller ID. It's Raul. And then I feel guilty. I remember kissing Tim in the parking garage. The press of Tim's lips. The heat of Tim's body. I stare at my ringing phone. I feel so guilty.

Kissing Raul is nice too, I tell myself.

Kissing Raul is nicer than kissing Tim, I tell myself.

I apologize to Jon and step through the tiny hallway and into the bedroom and shut the door and answer the phone and tell Raul I'm sorry for not calling him back yesterday. I tell him I've been busy with family stuff.

"Is everything all right?" he asks.

"Everything's fine." I flop down on the bed. Raul is so nice. I could be nicer. I should be. So I hesitate for only a second when he tells me he needs to talk to me and asks if I can meet him. Soon.

"Sure," I say. I'm reluctant to leave my parents, but I know I have to give them a chance to get, as Jon said, reacquainted.

After hanging up, I stay flopped on the bed for a moment longer. On this bed that my mother has slept in these past two nights. The mattress is soft. She always preferred a firm mattress, I remember. For better posture, she said.

I go back to the kitchen, but Jon is no longer there, so I peek into the square-shaped living room. My mother sits at one end of the sofa, my father sits at the other end, and there is a space between them. Her face is no longer quite as pale. She seems calmer. He still looks bewildered.

But perhaps that's because Jon is leaning against the wall and talking about, of all things, his daughter's difficulties at preschool. "She's not very good at sharing," he says.

"She'll learn," my father says sympathetically.

I come to sit in the space between my parents. "Mom?" I say.

"Yes, Lora?"

"How have you been sleeping?"

"Very well. Why do you ask?"

"Oh. Just wondering. Um, I got you a present. Well, Dad paid for it so technically he got it for you, but I picked it out. It's not a big deal or anything, it's just . . . Hold on." I run across the room to get the lavender bar out of my bag.

"It's the soap you used to use. Remember?" I say. "Smell it."

My mother cradles the bar in her hands, admires its floral wrapping paper, but does not bring it close to her face, does not inhale its perfume, does not tell me that she remembers. "Lovely," she says.

"You have to smell it," I say. "When you smell it you'll remember."

She brings the soap swiftly to her nose, and swiftly down again. "What a thoughtful gift. Thank you," she says.

I smile to cover up my confusion. It's not that I expected her to instantly remember everything, but I had hoped for something more than this polite gratitude. I stand up. "I'm going to meet a friend now. I'll be back soon," I say.

"Who are you meeting? Where?" asks Dad.

"I'm meeting Raul at the park. It's just a couple blocks away."

My father looks at Jon. "Is it safe for her to go by herself?"

My father looks at me. "Maybe I should come with you."

"Dad, no!"

"Only kidding," he says. "Mostly."

"It should be all right," says Jon. "Just be careful."

I look back once before leaving. My mother is still holding

the lavender bar of soap in her lap, in the hollow of her hands, and she is gazing longingly at it, as if it's something she wants but cannot have.

Outside it's hot and humid and I have plenty of time before I'm supposed to meet Raul, so I walk slowly. When I get to the park, I choose a spot in the misshapen shade provided by a misshapen tree, and sit cross-legged in the grass. I touch the bandage under my hair. For a moment I wish I still had my broken memory key. I know it's stupid; I certainly don't miss those debilitating headaches. And yet . . .

"Hey, you're early," says Raul.

"You're early too," I say.

"Not as early as you." He sits very close to me.

"True. So what do I win?"

"What do you mean?"

"For being early. I deserve at least a dollar, I think," I say and Raul digs a rumpled bill from his pocket. I wave it away. "I'm kidding," I tell him.

"Right. Of course." He smiles his nice smile, but for some reason his nice smile now makes me want to roll my eyes. So I'm glad when his expression turns serious.

"We have to talk," he says.

My first thought is that Raul knows about what happened with Tim. My second thought is that Raul is going to break up with me. My third thought is that I don't mind.

Therefore, I'm completely unprepared when he says:

"People have been asking questions at work. About Friday, when the alarm went off."

"What did you tell them?" I am trying not to panic—of course people are asking questions; one of their residents has gone missing.

"Nothing. I figured I should talk to you first."

"Who was asking? What did they ask?"

"It was weird. These people showed up, two people we'd never seen before, and management told us we had to answer their questions. They asked if we were working Friday, and did we notice anything out of the ordinary, and where were we when the alarm went off."

"Two people? What did they look like?"

"A man and a woman, both with brownish hair, both wearing suits."

"A man and a woman?" I zip open my bag and take out the photo of my father with the strangers from our kitchen. "Were they, possibly, this man and woman?"

Raul studies the picture. His finger hovers over the man's face, then the woman's face. "Yeah! It was definitely them. Who are they?"

"I don't know. That's the problem." I am still trying not to panic, though this is definitely cause for panic.

"Lora, what's going on?"

"Remember when I said I was dealing with family stuff? Well, this is that family stuff. I'm sorry I can't tell you more," I say.

Then I expect Raul to be annoyed because I'd be annoyed if I were him. But he looks at me with understanding, more understanding than I deserve, and takes my hand into his hand. His fingers are warm. His grip is gentle. How easy it would be to stay here with him in the overgrown green grass, watching the drifting clouds.

But I don't want to. And when I think of the light in my father's eyes when he saw my mother, I realize what I must do. I realize I've put it off too long already. Because as much as I like Raul, I don't *like* him like him. I slip my hand from his hand.

"Raul, you're great, you're a really nice guy, but . . ."

"What?" His eyebrows draw together.

I say a lot of things about how my life is crazy right now, and I don't want to inflict that on him, and how I wish things were different, but they aren't different, and I'm sorry, so sorry. I am terrible at this, having had little practice at breaking up with boys. But Raul listens quietly, doesn't interrupt, and when I'm done he nods.

"I hope we can be friends," I say.

"Right. Friends," he says.

"I'm sorry," I say for the tenth time.

"Okay. Guess I'll see you around." He gets up and walks away. He doesn't look back, not once, and I watch until he's gone. I feel bad, though he didn't take it badly. Then I feel bad that he didn't take it badly. Then I feel awful for being awful. Then I feel a wave of pure relief.

I reach for my cell phone to call Wendy and tell her what

happened. But I stop mid-dial when I remember. We're not talking. And I'm still mad at her. Because she told my dad about my broken key. Because she always thinks she's right. Which means I'm always wrong.

My memory key is fixed, and I am still mad.

I put away my phone. There's no time to waste, anyway. I have to get back to Jon's house. I have to tell them what I've learned. Keep Corp is looking for my mother.

The news does not have the impact I expected. My father looks bewildered. My mother seems distracted. Jon nods and announces he's not surprised. "I checked and there's been no media coverage about a resident's disappearance, no report filed with the police, nothing that would happen in a normal situation," he says grimly.

"Will they be able to connect her disappearance to you two?" asks Dad.

"The nurse can," I say. "She's the only one who knows we were there, in Mom's room. And she knows I'm her daughter. But maybe she hasn't told anyone. It might endanger her job—she wasn't supposed to bring us to her room. Or leave us unattended."

"I don't think Nina would give us away," says my mother.

Jon shakes his head. "We have to assume she's told them everything. But at least they don't know who I am. What we have to do now is arrange for Jeanette to get away, within the next few days. In the meantime, Ken and Lora, you'll act like you know nothing. Maybe you visited your mother at the retirement home, but you left her there, and that was the last time you saw her. Okay?"

"Maybe we should talk to Nina. Ask her for help," I say.

"No!" yells Jon.

We all turn to him in surprise. And I suddenly notice how bad he looks. His complexion is clammy. There are purple shadows under his eyes. I remember him telling me about his breakdown, the panic attacks and insomnia. I remember and I'm ashamed that it's only now I'm realizing that beneath his cheery mask Jon is a stressed mess. Because of us.

"I'm sorry," I say. "That was a stupid idea."

He swipes his arm across his damp forehead. "No, I'm sorry for shouting like that. I'm just a little tense."

"It's fine," I tell him.

Then I don't say another word while Jon summarizes the plan: Dad and I will return to the department store, retrieve our car, go to the bank to withdraw money from the ATM, and drive home. Tomorrow my father will dress in his workout clothes and meet Jon at the gym with as much cash as he has, in order to purchase the necessary identification papers, airplane tickets, etc. They will go together to procure these items from Jon's contacts, and afterward they will return to Darren's sister's apartment to finalize the plans for my mother's departure.

I don't say a word. I wait for someone else to protest. No one does.

"Okay?" asks Jon.

"Okay," says my father.

"Okay," says my mother.

And I want to scream that there must be some alternative, that she doesn't have to go, that we can find another way. Instead I say something ridiculous.

"Can I come along tomorrow?" I ask.

Jon is the first to say no, then Dad. They both say it kindly, firmly.

I look at my mother.

"Lora," she says. "It's for the best."

27.

I CALL IN SICK TO WORK THE NEXT DAY. I TRY NOT TO NOTICE
Cynthia's disapproving tone on the phone. I try not to notice
I'm neglecting my duties after being lectured about neglecting
my duties. I try not to feel bad but I'm feeling very bad when my
father comes downstairs in his T-shirt and athletic shorts and
white sneakers and socks stretched halfway to his knees; I feel
so very bad and so very anxious that I don't even comment on
his dorky gym clothes. All I say is: "Please be careful."

"Of course, Lora." He kisses my cheek.

I watch from the window as he walks down the driveway,
bulky duffel bag bumping against his hip. He gets into his car
and goes. I wait to see if another car comes racing down the
street after him. No other car comes racing. Everything outside
is perfectly, picturesquely ordinary. Neighborhood kids play
kick ball in the grass. The trees bob and sway with the breeze.

For a long time I just stand there, looking out at the fluttering leaves and the snickering kids and the red ball swooping
through the air. Then I get out my phone. I dial. The line rings

and rings and rings, until the answering machine comes on.

"Hi, it's me," I say. "Just wondering what you're—"

"Lora?" My mother picks up. "Is that you?"

"Yeah, Mom, how are you?"

"I'm good. And you?"

"Good. I was thinking, if you're not busy or anything, maybe I could come over? Just for a little while? If you don't mind?"

She pauses before she says: "All right."

"I don't have to, if it's inconvenient."

"It's not inconvenient. Please come."

"Are you sure?" I ask.

"I'm sure," she says.

Though I notice no strangers lurking, no vehicles following, I ride a long and circuitous route around the city, and lock my bicycle a few blocks away from Darren's sister's apartment. Jon and Dad will not be pleased that I am making this trip alone, so the least I can do is to be careful.

"I thought you had work today," my mother says when she opens the door.

"No, no work. I couldn't . . . I hope I'm not interrupting anything."

"Not at all. I was just doing some reading." She leads me into the square-shaped living room. As before, the couch is covered in notepaper, and, as before, she carefully collects them to make space for us to sit down.

I look at her stack of paper and at the books piled up on the coffee table. "How did you keep up with all this med-tech stuff while you were at Grand Gardens?"

"Well, at first I didn't. I couldn't. My memory was so bad. So my doctor recommended that I find an interest or hobby, some topic to focus my mind on, and of course I thought immediately of medical technology."

"*Of course*." I don't mean to sound sarcastic. I sound so sarcastic.

She doesn't seem to notice. "Yes, of course," she says. "The more I studied, the more information came back to me. Not right away, and not everything, not by a long shot. But enough to make me feel more like myself again."

Then I feel bad. What right do I have to resent her enduring dedication to her work if it makes her feel more like herself again? I have no right.

"That's great," I say.

"Yes." She leans back on the couch.

"Yes." I lean back on the couch.

We sit in silence for a minute. Two minutes.

"What is—" I say and "What are—" she says.

"Go ahead."

"No, you go ahead."

"What's that?" I point to the open magazine on the table.

"It's the latest issue of *Med-Tech Quarterly*. Jon got it for me."

"That's nice of him."

"Yes, very nice." She describes the article she just read,

something about the problems with a new kind of neural sensor, and I nod as she talks, but I am looking at her more than I'm listening. I am looking at her shirt and sweatpants, her same shirt and sweatpants from Grand Gardens, and wishing I'd thought to bring some of her old clothes from the attic. She never used to wear sweatpants.

"But I just don't think it's a realistic goal, do you?" she asks, smiling.

"Um. I don't really know," I say.

Her smile fades. "You should read the article. It's fascinating."

"Okay," I say. "Were you going to ask me something before?"

"I wanted to know about your studies. What do you plan to major in?"

"I'm not sure yet," I say. "I'm only starting college this fall."

"Yes, your father told me. But it's good to be prepared, so you can go in and take immediate advantage of the resources available to you. What subjects are you considering?" she asks.

"I really don't know yet."

"What were your favorite subjects in high school?"

"History and math, but I'm not sure I want to major in either of them."

Her lips compress, her eyes narrow. I remember that expression. It's disappointment. "Well," she says. "I'm sure you'll figure it out eventually."

I nod. I don't speak. I don't want to disappoint her again.

My mother picks up her magazine—the latest issue of *Med-Tech Quarterly*—and flips it shut. "Can I offer you a drink?" she asks. "Water? Juice?"

"What kind of juice do you have?"

"There's some cranberry juice, do you like that?"

I don't like that. "I'll have some water. Thanks."

We go into the kitchen. My mother takes a glass from the cupboard. She gets the ice tray from the freezer and cracks the cubes out of the tray. She stands at the sink and fills the glass under the faucet.

"Anyway, lots of kids start college without a major. It's normal," I say.

My mother looks at me. While she is looking at me, the glass overflows. She turns back and for a moment just stares at the water spilling down her hand. Then she grabs the tap and twists it closed.

"I'm sure you're right," she says.

I don't stay much longer after that.

When I tell her I should probably be getting home, my mother nods and walks me to the door. I kiss her cheek and say it was nice to see her and I'll see her again soon. She kisses my cheek and says the same. We are speaking all the correct words and making all the correct gestures, but it all feels off, as if we're actors performing a scene and performing it badly.

And I cannot figure out what we're doing wrong.

So I don't know how to fix it.

* * *

I ride an even more circuitous route going than I did coming, and it's not until I am rolling my bicycle into the house that I realize the circuitous route was unnecessary—anyone following me would already know where I live. I slam the front door shut. Then I notice my cell phone is ringing.

It's her. It has to be her.

It's not her.

I don't recognize the number, but I answer anyway.

"Hello! This is Tonya from the KCO, returning your call. How can I help you?" chirps the voice at the other end. It takes me a second to remember that the KCO is the anti–Keep Corp organization from Ms. Pearl's leaflet, and then my mood immediately improves. Maybe the KCO can help us.

I start small: "Do you have any advice for people who've gotten their memory keys removed?" I ask.

"No, we actually don't recommend key extraction."

"But what about the things you say? About Keep Corp's power? About the child labor in their factories?" My improved mood is already deteriorating.

"Unfortunately, there's no alternative as long as Vergets disease is a threat," she says. "Not yet, anyway."

"Then what do you even *do*?" I don't bother hiding my disappointment.

"At this point, our main goal is to end Keep Corp's monopoly on key manufacture. Their patents should have expired decades ago, but they've managed to get extension after extension. The other med-tech companies are afraid to challenge them because every time someone has tried, Keep Corp has successfully sued." Tonya from the KCO talks quickly, as if she's afraid I might give up, hang up, before she's done.

"In three months, there'll be a rally to increase public awareness," she says.

"A rally," I say.

"If we can end their monopoly, there'll be more regulation of the industry, more transparency. And that's only the beginning! Won't you help make it happen? Anything you're able to do—distributing flyers, making calls, raising money—would help."

"Distributing flyers," I say.

"Sure! We're having a meeting next week. Let me give you the details."

I listen to the details. I hang up the phone. I slip my hand into the front pocket of my bag and fumble around for something. It's only when the top is unscrewed and I'm staring at the blank white bottom that I realize it's the empty bottle of pain pills I've got clenched in my fist.

But my head isn't aching. But my memory key isn't broken. I have no excuse. No excuse other than I'm so frustrated it hurts. Keep Corp wrecked my family once, but it's us doing the wrecking this second time. If only Jon weren't so afraid. If only Dad weren't so bewildered. If only my mother weren't . . . I go into the kitchen and drop the empty pill bottle into the recycling bin.

I come to a decision.

My first move is a text message: *Can we talk?*

After waiting a few minutes, I leave my phone on the table and go upstairs. I wash my hands and face. I brush my hair and tie it up into a ponytail. I make my bed. I put away my laundry. Then I run downstairs to check if I've gotten a text back; I must have gotten a text back by now.

I haven't. I scowl at my phone. It chimes.

I'm at the place.

"The place" is the pizza place in our neighborhood, and it serves what may be the worst pizza in the whole city: never enough sauce, never enough cheese, so much crust. The décor is equally unimpressive; the principal design feature is grime. But the waiters are friendly and they let you stay hours, even if you've only ordered a soda. Probably because the place is almost always almost empty.

This afternoon is no different. Only one table is occupied, the table in the back corner. Tim's regular table. And Tim is sitting there. And he's not alone.

"Hi, Lauren!" says Becky, cute Keep Corp intern.

"Hi, Becky." I wait for Tim to correct her about my name, but he doesn't. He is apparently too busy chewing up the plastic straw in his empty cup.

"That's bad for your teeth," I tell him.

He shrugs.

Becky stands up. She is wearing a fluttery polka-dotted dress and a crisscrossing pair of sandals. Her lipstick is bright red. All of it is cute, just like she is cute. "I better get going before I'm late. Bye, Lauren. Bye, Timmy."

She leaves and I sit down.

"How's it going, *Timmy*?" I say.

"What do you want?"

"What makes you think I want something?"

"Why else would you be here?" He does not look at me. His gaze drifts from the dingy walls, to the plastic menu on the table, to the tiled floors, to the yellowed ceiling, but not to me, never to me.

"I just have a question for you."

"What?" he says.

"What do you know about the new memory keys?"

Finally, he looks at me. "Why do you want to know?"

"It's a long story," I say.

"I don't mind." Tim stares resentfully at me. And I stare resentfully back at him. For he has no right to stare at me so when he was just hanging out with *Becky*, cutest intern ever.

After a moment, his mouth curls. "Don't you trust me?" he asks wryly.

"I do," I say, and realize it's true. Tim may not be the nicest person: he can be selfish and unthinking; he goads and teases and never lets anyone get away with anything. But he is also the one who, when we were kids, soaked me with his neon green water gun then handed me the gun so I could soak him back. Tim is my friend. And I'm tired of pretending otherwise.

"I trust you," I say.

"Yeah?"

"Promise you won't tell anyone."

"I swear it," he says, and if it's possible for a grin to be solemn, his is.

Then my story comes speeding out of my mouth, phrases tripping in eagerness, sentences jumbled, words crowded too close for breath. I tell him about finding my mother at Grand Gardens. I tell him about mysterious cars and Carlos Cruz. I tell him about Jon's plan for my mom to leave the country.

"This is . . . It's totally unbelievable," he says.

"But you believe me, right?"

"Nope. Never."

I glare at him.

"Okay, okay. I believe you! Of course I believe you."

"That's better." I smile. "So what do you know about the new keys?"

"I know they're scheduled to be released at the end of the year. It's weird because there's lots of buzz, but no one seems to know what makes them special. I'll ask around. I'm friends with some recent grads in that department."

"That'd be really helpful. Thanks," I say.

"Do you have that flyer with you? From the Keep Out Keep Corp-whatever?"

"I think so." I unzip my bag. Out comes a sweater, a stack of rumpled documents, a bottle of water, and a book I thought I'd lost.

"Is this it?" Tim yanks a sheet of paper from my pile of mess.

"No, what's that?" I lean over to see. He leans over so I can see. Our elbows bump once, twice. I have to remind myself to read.

It's the article I got at the library about the new memory keys. Now that I'm looking at it closely, I think it's funny I printed it out. The article is not from a newspaper, but a tabloid magazine, the kind that loves a good alien abduction story.

The writer claims that Keep Corp will soon present a new line of keys that will be marketed as innovative memory technology, but will actually be used to transmit data to the extremist group the Citizen Army, enabling them to circumvent security measures and carry out a series of political assassinations. With the government destabilized by these murders, Keep Corp will take power.

"I know that can't be true," I say. "But could it?"

"Are you serious? This is a magazine that claims werewolves are living secretly among us. Why would the Citizen Army help Keep Corp take power?"

"Maybe they don't know about Keep Corp's plans."

"They'll know once they read this article." Tim smirks.

"My mom discovered something bad about the new keys. This is bad, isn't it?"

"Sure it's bad, but seriously, Lora, it makes no sense."

I scowl at him. "Well, let's hear some of your ideas then."

"Glad you asked. I think we should talk to that journalist."

"Who? Carlos Cruz? But we can't trust him!"

"Why not?" he asks.

I point out the inconsistencies in his story: how Carlos said he knew nothing about Keep Corp anymore, but then talked about their new line of keys. I describe his unexpected visit to our house and his interest in the blue-jacketed strangers.

"Honestly, it sounds like he's just doing his job," says Tim.

"No. It's more than just his job," I say.

"You really don't like this guy, huh."

"He's too handsome for his own good."

"So am I, and you like me, don't you?"

I roll my eyes. "You're cute and all, Tim, but Carlos Cruz is really, really handsome. Like movie-star handsome."

"I knew it! You think I'm cute!" He grins triumphantly.

"I don't! I was just being nice. Anyway, this is about Carlos."

"Right, Carlos. I've got an idea, an amazing idea."

We bike over to Tim's house so he can get his car. I tell him I'll wait for him outside. He looks at me with confusion. "It might take a couple minutes," he says. "Wouldn't you rather come in?"

"It's better if I wait here," I say.

His expression clears. "Wendy's not home, if that's what you're worried about. She's with her new boyfriend."

"That's not what I'm worried about."

"Right. Whatever you say."

"And who's this new boyfriend, anyway? The football player?"

He shrugs. "How should I know?"

"She's your sister."

"Exactly. She's my sister. I want to know *nothing* about her love life. Gross," he says. "Anyway, if you're so curious, why don't you ask her?"

I make a face. But when he motions for me to follow him inside, I follow. We go into the living room, where his parents are watching television.

"Lora!" they say. "Wendy's not home, but she should be back soon."

"Oh, good." I wonder how soon.

The evening news is on and they're showing scenes from Senator Finney's memorial service. The president gives a speech about how this is a personal tragedy for every citizen, as well as a tragedy for the country as a whole. He says we must unite across party lines to fight the radical extremist groups that are threatening our nation and our freedom.

"Nice talk, now let's see some action," says Mr. Laskey. His wife shushes him as the camera shifts to people nodding in sorrowful agreement. Suddenly, it's Austin nodding in sorrowful agreement.

"My aunt!" I say. She looks tired, her mouth tight with grief, her face pale above her black suit. Then the camera pans, and she's gone.

"It's so very sad," says the news anchor.

"Yes, a life and a career cut tragically short. Who knows what impact the senator would have had," says the other news anchor.

They segue into a segment about new opposition to the proposed economic bill, specifically the defense budget. A conservative commentator talks about how the liberals are destroying everything the nation has worked so hard to accomplish.

"I can't believe this guy. What an idiot," says Mrs. Laskey.

"You're not even listening to him," says Mr. Laskey.

"I *am* listening, and it's outrageous," says Mrs. Laskey.

I stare at the television. The program goes to commercial. On the screen, it's a dreary day and people are gloomy until a dozen women come running down the street, tossing yellow umbrellas to everyone. The umbrellas glow as they open, and soon everything is glowing: the street, the sky, the formerly gloomy people. Then it all fades into the Keep Corp logo and the caption BRINGING YOU A BRIGHTER YESTERDAY.

I glance pointedly at Tim. He glances pointedly back. But I'm not sure we're glancing about the same thing. His parents' conversation is getting louder.

"You think protecting our country is wrong? You think supporting our troops is wrong? Really?" Mr. Laskey scowls at his wife.

"I think it's wrong that we're spending billions on these useless wars when there are so many people unemployed and hungry here." Mrs. Laskey scowls at her husband.

Tim glances pointedly at me. I glance pointedly back. This time we are definitely glancing about the same thing. We escape outside and get into his car. "They're just enjoying some spirited debate," I say.

"If you say so." He sighs as he turns on the engine.

There's a tap-tap-tap on his side of the car, and we both turn toward the sound.

It's Wendy.

Tim rolls down his window. "Hey. What's up?"

"What are you doing?" she asks her brother.

I don't know whether to look at her or not. So I don't. Then I do. She is with a handsome hulk of a guy, the football player, presumably. His arms really *are* impressive. But after my cursory inspection (of his biceps), I look only at Wendy. I look at the familiar tilt of her chin, the familiar slant of her mouth. She does not look back at me.

"We're going on an adventure. Want to come?" asks Tim, and as I wait for her answer I realize I want her to say yes. I realize I miss my friend, I miss her fiercely.

"Well . . ." Wendy glances at me as if she has just noticed I'm in the car. Her eyes are dead cold. And even though she is standing right there, she seems hopelessly far away. "No, thanks," she says.

"Okay, see you later!" Tim backs out of his parking space and drives down a couple blocks. Then he pulls over to the side of the road.

"Are you all right?" he asks me.

"I'm fine," I say.

"If you're fine then why are you crying?"

"I'm not crying. Not really. Not a lot."

"Just talk to her," he says.

"I called her a bitch," I say.

"Well, she *can* be kind of bitchy sometimes." Tim hands me a tissue.

I wipe my eyes and tell him I'm impressed he has tissues in his car.

He mutters something about allergies. "Anyway, I know she misses you," he says, patting my shoulder.

"Yeah? How do you know?"

"I know her. I know."

"Thanks, Tim. You're a good friend." I smile at him. He smiles at me. Then his hand stops patting, but stays carefully balanced on my shoulder. We look at each other, no longer smiling. We look at each other until Tim looks away.

"Thanks for not making fun of my allergies," he says.

"To be honest, I would if I could think of a witty way to do it."

"Well, thanks for not being able to think of a witty way to do it."

"You're welcome," I say because that is what good friends say.

Tim slows the car as we approach Carlos Cruz's apartment building, then we circle around, looking up and down the street. There are no silver sedans. "So much for your amazing idea," I tell him.

"Could it be in the back?" he says.

We get out of the car and sneak down the alleyway that cuts through the center of the block. There's a small parking lot behind the building, with room for just four cars. There are three cars, none of them silver sedans.

"Maybe he's not home?" I say.

"Let's look. Which is his apartment?"

"That one, I think."

We creep closer, breathing softly, moving slowly, stepping carefully, though the gravel still spatters and sputters under our shoes. The window is open and a breeze flutters the curtains apart, just far enough apart so we can peer inside.

"See anything?" I whisper.

"A light? Is that a light there?" Tim whispers.

"I think it's a mirror," I whisper.

"No, it's a light," Tim whispers.

"No, it's a mirror," says Carlos Cruz as he yanks back the curtains and stares at us through the screen, his handsome face darkened by shadow, and as I stare back at him I remember another handsome face, another attractive man, sitting on a bench, reading a magazine, except that other man was not another man, that man was actually this man.

It was Carlos Cruz I saw that day at Keep Corp.

28.

"MISS MINT, HOW NICE OF YOU TO VISIT! PLEASE, WON'T YOU come in? It's a little awkward talking like this, don't you think?" Carlos smiles hospitably, as if we had come knocking on his door, not peeking through his curtains.

"I'm sorry, it's not what you think," says Tim, and I elbow him. Carlos Cruz deserves no apologies, no excuses or explanations.

"I saw you at Keep Corp," I say, pointing rudely so there can be no mistake. "What were you doing there if you don't have any contacts anymore?"

"Let's have this conversation inside. I just made a fresh pot of coffee. You kids drink coffee?" Carlos is not fazed, not even a little.

"No way," I say.

He sighs. "If you don't like coffee we can go to the bakery down the street."

Tim tugs my arm, pulling me back from the window. "Let's talk to him, Lora. We have nothing to lose," he says into my ear.

"What if he's involved?" I hiss.

"You know he's not involved. You know that you know."

"The bakery makes really good sandwiches," Carlos croons through the screen.

"I *am* kind of hungry," says Tim.

"Fine," I snap. "Let's go."

We sit on the bench outside of the bakery, and before anyone can unwind their really good sandwich from the waxed paper, before anyone can take that anticipated first bite, I turn to Carlos and say: "What were you doing at Keep Corp the other day? I know it was you."

"Well, perhaps I wasn't being completely honest when I said I had no contacts there. The truth is, I've been cultivating a new source in the company," he says, then pauses to smile charmingly. "And why were *you* at Keep Corp?"

"None of your business," I say.

He raises an eyebrow. The message is clear: if I won't, he won't.

"I had a problem with my memory key. I had to get it replaced," I say. "So what kind of information have you gotten from your new source?"

"Your mother's death was no accident."

"What do you mean?"

"According to my source, Keep Corp hired a 'specialty firm' to take care of the problem she posed. I'm sorry to have to tell you this."

"But—" says Tim.

I interrupt. "Why? Why did they do it?"

"I was hoping you'd have some ideas," says Carlos.

"All I know is that she discovered something strange about the new line of memory keys, but I have no idea what it was."

"What about those people? The ones in the sketches you showed me, and in that photograph with your father. Who are they?" Carlos asks.

"They're the ones who took her away. They must have worked for that specialty firm." I describe my memory of that night, of watching the two strangers lead my mother out the kitchen door.

Carlos frowns. "And your father knows them?"

"No. That photograph was from a Keep Corp fund-raiser. He doesn't remember who they are. We still haven't figured it out."

Carlos Cruz strokes his chin as he thinks. He narrows his eyes. "Will you lend me that photo? I'll try to identify those people for you."

I pull the picture from my bag and rip it in two—feeling a little guilty since it doesn't exactly belong to me—and hand over the piece with the strangers. I keep the piece with my dad. "Will you tell me? As soon as you find out?"

"If I can find out, yes," says Carlos.

"Can we eat our sandwiches now?" asks Tim.

We eat our sandwiches now. Tim bolts his down, as if he hadn't been eating pizza at the pizza place just an hour ago.

After gulping his last bite, he gazes pleadingly at me. Or, to be precise, he gazes pleadingly at my sandwich. I continue eating. With pleasure.

"Hey." Tim looks reluctantly away from my food, to Carlos Cruz. "If you have a source at Keep Corp, why would you go there looking for him? Wouldn't that put him in danger?"

Carlos nods. "The problem is, I haven't been able to get ahold of my guy recently. I set up a meeting and he didn't show. I've called him and he hasn't returned my calls. I was worried, so I went by to check out the situation."

"And what did you find?"

"I didn't see him but it seems like he's all right. Still coming to work. I suspect it's a case of cold feet—he said he'd get me some documents that would prove Keep Corp's involvement in your mother's death, but now I think he's scared to deliver."

"What documents?" I ask.

Carlos Cruz shrugs and keeps chewing.

And even though he didn't answer my question, I smile. Because I'm thinking this could be the solid evidence that Jon said we needed. Solid evidence that would give us leverage over Keep Corp. Solid evidence that would make it possible for my mother to stay here. With me.

By the time the baker rattles down the metal grate, closing shop, our sandwiches are finished and our talk is finished too, for the time being. We gather ourselves up from the bench, brush our clothes clean of crumbs, discard the greasy scraps of waxed paper, and exchange some surprisingly cordial good-byes. Carlos promises he'll tell me if he learns anything about the two strangers in the photograph. I promise I'll tell him if I learn anything about what my mother discovered.

"By the way," I say. "What kind of car do you drive?"

He answers in exquisite detail but all I register is that he does not drive a silver sedan, that he would never drive such an uninspired car. "Why do you ask?" he asks.

"Just curious."

"All right, I admit he's good-looking. Like, unnaturally good-looking," Tim says as he drives us home. "Why didn't you tell him your mother's alive?"

"You think I should have?"

"He could probably help her."

"He doesn't have to know in order to help her. Once he gets those documents from his source, I can do the rest," I say.

"*You* can do the rest?"

"I mean, *we*. Jon Harmon has connections, and I'm sure my parents . . ." I stare out the car window, at the sky bruised purple by the setting sun.

"Yeah?" prompts Tim.

"You know what doesn't make sense? If Keep Corp hired people to kill her, how'd she end up in that fancy retirement home?" I say.

"Maybe they had second thoughts? Developed a conscience?"

"For some reason I doubt it."

"Same here," he says.

"I hope this stuff isn't messing up your internship for you."

"I'm actually not surprised there's something shady going on. I majored in medical technology because I'm into tech, and I want to help people. But at Keep Corp, it's so easy to forget the helping people part. Everything is about business and the bottom line."

"Have you thought about working at a med-tech hospital instead?"

"I interned at a hospital last summer and honestly, it wasn't that different." Tim sighs. "Not that I'm complaining when we should be figuring out what happens next. So what happens next?"

"I'll talk to my parents and Jon tonight."

"Then I'll talk to my friends in the key department tomorrow."

"And maybe . . ." I don't finish my sentence. Because what I was going to say was that Wendy might have some helpful ideas, too.

Tim parks in front of my house—windows dark, no one home—and we swivel subtly in our seats, searching for black SUVs and silver sedans. There's nothing noticeably suspicious, but I wonder if this fact is suspicious in itself.

"Maybe I better stay till your dad gets back," says Tim.

"You think? You don't have to."

"Do you not want me to?"

"I want you to. If you want to."

We go inside and turn on every lamp downstairs, blaze the rooms up in light, banishing darkness and shadow, banishing a few of my worries, a little of my fear, though I still wonder where my father is and what he's doing, whether he's all right, whether they are *all* all right.

"Do you have anything to eat?" asks Tim.

"Really? You're hungry?" I say, but I lead him into the kitchen and we make ice cream sundaes with chocolate sauce and whipped cream fizzed from the can. I dig out the ancient jar of maraschino cherries from the bottom shelf of the refrigerator. I know they're Tim's favorite.

"Lora," he says. "About what happened the other day. In the parking garage."

"What?" I almost drop the jar of cherries. "I mean, I'm sorry."

"No, *I'm* sorry. You're with Raul. I shouldn't have presumed."

"You don't have to apologize. You have nothing to apologize for."

"Good." He takes the jar from me. "These are my favorite."

I blurt it out before I think it out: "Anyway, I broke up with Raul."

"You did?" He sets the cherries on the countertop.

"Yeah, so what's the deal with you and Becky?" I ask.

"Becky? We—we're just friends." Tim seems suddenly confused, as if he can't recall how he got here: into this house, into this kitchen, into this conversation; and I'm embarrassed, so embarrassed, about my blurting and my asking. I turn away from him, but before I am completely away he catches my wrist and spins me back around.

Then he kisses me.

It's not the fever of mashing mouths that was two days ago, but something less desperate, more tender. Neither is it the tentative touch of lips that was two years ago, but something more honest. Though we briefly part to smile, and briefly part so he can whisper that my hair smells good, and I can whisper that he has the nicest mouth, our bodies are always resting together, our fingers always entwined.

For a long time we stay like this, and only separate when we remember our melting ice cream. But once separated, I'm immediately uncomfortable. I'm thinking about just-friends Becky.

"Is something wrong?" asks Tim.

And I can no longer ignore what I've been conveniently ignoring: even if Tim was the reason I ended things with Raul, Raul was not the only reason keeping me from Tim. "We shouldn't . . . That was a mistake," I say.

"Because of what happened before?"

I wish I could say no. I say yes.

"You don't trust me," he says.

"No, I trust you," I say, and I do. I do believe him when he tells me there's nothing between him and Becky. But it's not enough.

"Then what's the problem?" He's upset. Of course he's

upset. Because this is how it works, this cycle of hurt and anger, our cycle of hurt and anger. And the only way I can think of stopping it is by telling him the humiliating truth. So I do.

"The problem is I don't trust myself," I say.

For I now understand that what happened before wasn't only his fault: I had been the one to carefully keep his careless rejection, I had been the one to let it sink me down for far too long. And I'm afraid it will happen again. And I'm tired of pretending otherwise. I tell him this, all of this.

Then I wait for Tim to smirk or thunder or inform me I'm overreacting. But he says, "I think I get it," and his face is serious but not angry. His voice is regretful but not hurt.

"Yeah?" I say.

"As long as we can still be friends—we can, right?"

"If your allergies don't interfere."

"Very funny."

Then we eat our melted ice cream and joke about what good friends—no, *great* friends—we'll be. "We should probably have a secret handshake," he says.

"And a password."

"And a special code."

"And a coordinated dance routine."

He groans. "You mean an uncoordinated dance routine."

We smile at each other and I know this is the sensible thing. Still, if I'm going to be totally, absolutely, and completely honest, I have to admit the sensible thing pretty much sucks.

* * *

Tim and I are watching TV when my father gets home. He comes into the den to sit with us, still wearing his T-shirt and gym shorts, but now his white socks are sagging around his ankles. He looks exhausted.

"Is everything okay?" I leap up from the couch.

"Yes, everything's fine." Dad flops into his armchair.

"Good," I say, and sit slowly back down.

"How are you, Timothy? Haven't seen you in a while."

"Except for at the graduation party, Mr. Mint."

"Ah, that's right. That was a nice party, wasn't it?" My father removes his glasses, rubs his eyes, then puts his glasses back on, crookedly.

"It was, but, um, I should probably go now. I have work early tomorrow." Tim stands up and says good-bye, good night, and thanks for the ice cream.

I walk him to the door to see him safely to his car.

"Sorry that was uncomfortable," he says. "I had to get out before I congratulated your dad on the fact his wife is alive. Would that have been inappropriate? You think they make greeting cards for this kind of occasion?"

"If they don't, they should," I say.

We linger awkwardly on the front step, as if we don't know how to say good-bye to each other, though we've said good-bye to each other a thousand times before, but now it seems that we've both forgotten how to do this simplest thing.

Then, simultaneously, we remember: secret handshake.

* * *

When I come back into the den, the television is still on but my father is asleep in his chair. I turn off the TV and he jerks awake. I apologize.

"What? I wasn't sleeping," he sputters.

"Sure, Dad."

"Really!"

"Okay. But we need to talk." I tell him about our meeting with Carlos Cruz, and the possibility of getting some definite proof of Keep Corp's crimes.

My father looks bewildered. I had hoped he would have overcome his bewilderment by now, but apparently he has not. "Who is this guy? How do we know we can trust him?" he says.

"Carlos is friends with Jon Harmon. And Mom, too, I guess."

"Well, I suppose you better talk to Jon about this." My father speaks with no particular urgency and I'm puzzled by his lack of response. This is beyond absentmindedness.

"Don't you understand, Dad? Maybe she won't have to go!"

"But we've already spent the day getting everything together—the papers, the tickets. It's all arranged."

"Arrangements can change," I say.

"Lora," he says. "She's leaving tomorrow."

"No," I say. I gaze down at my hands. My nails are painted darkest red from when Wendy and I got graduation manicures two weeks ago, forever ago, and the darkest red polish is now chipped at the edges, revealing the paleness underneath. "No," I say again. "She can't."

I get up. I walk down the hall to the phone in the kitchen

and call Jon Harmon. I tell him about Carlos Cruz. I tell him my mother doesn't have to go.

"Lora, what did I say about staying out of this?" he bellows. "This is dangerous business! And telling Carlos, of all people! That man would sell out his mother for a story."

"But he can help us," I say, and it feels strange to be defending Carlos after I've thought so many similarly bad things about him. "Anyway, I didn't tell him she's still alive."

"At least there's that." Jon sighs. "Perhaps this will go somewhere, but in the meantime we still need to keep Jeanette safe, and the only way to do that is to get her far away from here."

"Why does it have to be tomorrow?"

"I know it's fast, but you'll have time to say good-bye. I'll call you in the morning and we'll plan something."

"I have to be at the library at noon," I say. I can't call in sick again.

"Then we'll plan for something before noon," he says.

I hang up the phone. I go back to the den. My father has not budged from his chair. "She's leaving tomorrow," I say.

"I know. I told you," he says.

"Don't you even care?" I say.

"What does it matter?" he says.

I look at him with utter disbelief.

But then I notice that he is crying, his face like crumpled paper, his hands clenched in his lap, doing nothing to hide the drip of his eyes. "Dad?" I say, and it's all I say because it's all I *can* say.

"This is a stressful time, that's all." His voice is hoarse.

"Don't worry, Dad. We'll get the proof we need, then she can come home, and everything will be normal again."

"Yes, normal," he mumbles as he lunges out of the armchair. He goes into the bathroom. The door shuts.

I don't know what to do. I sit. I wait. I try to think of what I'll say when my father comes back. I'll tell him we'll figure this out, because we always figure it out, because we're a team—not like a superhero and sidekick, but two sidekicks, fair and square. I'll tell him we'll figure this out and everything will be normal again.

But when my father comes back his eyes are clear, his mouth is smiling, and he doesn't give me a chance to tell him anything.

"Sorry about that," he says briskly. "I haven't been getting much sleep recently; I must be overtired. Aren't you tired? It's late. We should both go to bed. I teach early tomorrow, and you have work at the library, don't you? How's that going, by the way? How's Cynthia? Wow, it's really late. Definitely bedtime."

The only way to respond to his cheery chatter is with cheery chatter. Together we go upstairs and make the smallest small talk until he turns to go into his room and I turn to go into mine.

"Good night, Lora," he says, still smiling.

"Good night, Dad," I say, trying hard to smile back.

29.

I'M SURE THERE MUST BE SOME MISTAKE—MY PHONE CAN'T BE ringing, not at this hour, in this darkness—but yes, it's ringing and so I answer. "Hello?" I gurgle.

"Lora Mint, did I wake you?"

"It's the middle of the night."

"It's nine in the morning," says Carlos Cruz.

"It is?" I glance at the clock. He's right. I untwist my body from the blanket and get up; I go over to the window and pull back the curtain. The glass is streaked with water. The sky is a heavy gray.

"I've got strange news and bad news," says Carlos. "What first?"

"Strange news," I say, scratching the sleep from my eyes.

"I haven't been able to identify your two strangers. Apparently, they don't work for Keep Corp. Nor do they work for that specialty firm."

"Then who are they?"

"Nobody knows, that's what's strange."

"Okay. And the bad news?"

"My source has disappeared. No one's seen him since yesterday."

I sit back on my bed. "It's only been a day. He could reappear."

"Sure, anything's possible," he says. "Which reminds me, I need your friend Tim Laskey's telephone number."

"What? Why?"

"I want him to check on something at Keep Corp."

"How did you know he works there?" I say accusingly.

Carlos sighs. "Are we playing this game again? He mentioned it yesterday."

I frown. I don't remember him mentioning it yesterday.

"Listen, Lora, your friend could help get the evidence we need to prove Keep Corp's involvement in your mother's death. Don't you want that?"

I give him Tim's number.

When Jon Harmon calls a little while later, I don't bother telling him what Carlos said. I know what Jon's response would be: there's nothing we can do, she has to go and the sooner the better, let's make it an hour earlier, maybe three hours earlier, maybe she's already gone.

"Thanks," I say. "See you there."

I retrieve my umbrella from the closet, along with my raincoat and boots, and since the weather's too bad for biking, I take the bus downtown. It drives a different route from the one

I normally take, a route that goes past Keep Corp's trip-down-memory-lane billboards. Even soaking wet, the attractive couple is extremely attractive. They look so happy together. I have to remind myself it's fake.

My phone starts ringing again, and this time it's Tim. I answer, trying to ignore the glares from other passengers. "Did Carlos Cruz call you?" I ask.

"Why are you whispering?"

"I'm on the bus," I say.

"Right, so I talked to Carlos. He wants me to sneak into his source's office and find those documents he told us about."

"That's crazy! I didn't think he'd ask you to do something crazy!" I forget to be quiet, and the other passengers glare harder. I lower my voice again. "What did you tell him?"

"I said I'd do it."

"What? Why? Wait, hold on, it's my stop. I'm getting off." I hop down to the wet sidewalk and wrestle open my umbrella. "Okay, are you still there?" I ask.

And as soon as Tim acknowledges he's still there, I start shouting. "Are you insane? What if someone catches you? These people are dangerous!"

"Don't worry, it'll be fine."

"But, Tim!"

"I have to go. I'll call you later."

"But, Tim!"

He's gone. He doesn't answer when I call him back once, twice, thrice. I'm worried, and I'm scared, and I feel guilty for getting him into this situation. But I also feel guilty because some tiny part of me is pleased—if he finds what he's looking for, then my mother can stay.

After Tim doesn't answer for the fourth time, I give up.

I cross the street and go into the big department store on the corner, the same store I went to with my father on our way to Darren's sister's apartment the other day. I walk straight to the Intimates section, where there is only one customer browsing, a woman wearing a wide-brimmed hat that is somewhat familiar. She is studying the sizing chart on a package of underwear.

"Find what you're looking for?" I ask her.

My mother steps back in surprise, clutching the pack to her chest, and I realize her hat is *my* hat, with the plastic flowers removed. I kind of wish she had asked before cutting off the flowers. I tell myself it's a hat, just a hat.

"You made it, I'm so glad," she says.

"Yeah, Mom. Where's Jon Harmon?"

"He went to pick up my passport." She rests her hand on my shoulder. "Thanks for coming. I was afraid I'd have to go without seeing you again."

And even though I knew she would be going, it feels as if I hadn't known this at all. "What time are you leaving?" I ask.

"My flight is at seven tonight." She drops the package of underwear into her shopping cart. It flops against a tube of lotion. I pick the tube up and read the label.

"Unscented?" I say.

"I have to be careful with fragrances. My skin has become very sensitive."

I remember the lavender soap I bought for her, from this very store. I remember and wait for her to remember. She pulls an undershirt from the rack, examines it, then puts it back. I tell myself it's a bar of soap, just a bar of soap.

"So where are you going?" I ask.

"I can't tell you, Lora, you know that. It's for your own safety."

"But . . . I'm your daughter."

"Yes, and as my daughter will you help me select a coat? It'll be cold where I'm going, the nights are apparently very cold." She pushes her shopping cart toward Women's Apparel, and I trail after her, trying to think of cold places, but I can't think of a single one right now. All I can think of is my father sitting in his armchair, weeping.

"Dad was really upset last night," I tell her.

"Oh, no," she says. I wait for her to say more. But she never says more.

So I say more: "You don't have to go. We'll find a safe place for you here, and once we get the evidence against Keep Corp you can come home. I think we're really close."

"That's good." She holds up a navy blazer. "What do you think of this?"

"Did Jon tell you about my conversation with Carlos Cruz yesterday?"

"He told me. And you know, I think I remember him."

"Who? Carlos?"

"Is he a dark man? Tall?" she asks.

"Kind of dark. Kind of tall." I should be glad she remembers him; I should be glad if she remembers anything. I'm not. "Have you remembered anything else?"

"A little, but it's all in pieces. My sister coming to visit. My grandfather reading his newspaper. A room with a thick green carpet and a large desk."

"That's your office! What else?" I wait for her to say she remembers me. Anything about me. Everything about me.

"That's about it. My memory . . ."

"Your memory?" I say. Then I say it again.

The words seem to act as an incantation, unfurling something within me. Rage. I am suddenly and completely enraged. How could she have been so careless? Why was she always rushing to work? How could she have let herself get killed? How could she abandon me like that?

I don't understand what's happening. This shouldn't be happening, not now, not when my key has been repaired. And she's alive. She is alive, I remind myself. But my anger easily adjusts to the changing circumstances: she was only a half hour away at Grand Gardens—why did she never come for me? How could she have forgotten me? Did I mean so little to her?

"Lora, what is it?" asks my mother.

"You *want* to leave," I say, finally understanding.

"No, I *have* to leave."

"I don't think that's true." My voice is hard and my face is hard. But inside I am soft. Inside I am waiting for her to furiously deny it, to say that she's my mother so of course she would never leave me willingly, that she would never leave me at all, no matter what.

"I can't live like this, Lora, stuck in some small apartment, constantly afraid I'm going to be found. I didn't leave Grand Gardens to be trapped in some new place. I need to have some sort of life."

"But what about me? And Dad? Aren't we your life? Don't you care about us?"

"Of course I care," she says.

"Then why can't it be like it used to be?"

My mother sighs. "But I can't remember how it used to be. I wish I could, I wish it so much. But I can't. I can't be the person you knew. She doesn't exist anymore."

I feel sick. Nauseated. I need to sit down. But there is no place to sit down, so I stand up straighter. "You could try harder," I say. "Why won't you try harder?"

"I have been trying. I really have." Her voice is quiet.

Then there is nothing left to say. So I stand up straighter, even straighter, and stare at a display of bathing suits. I stare at so many stripes, ruffles, and polka dots on sale, and tell her: "If you're going, you better go."

But when I look again she's still there. She stretches one arm out, reaches her open hand toward me. Then we both startle back as sound blares through the store. It's a PA announcement: *Will Millie please report to Men's Shoes. Will Millie please report to Men's Shoes.* The announcement is followed by a silence as loud as the loudspeaker blare, louder even. The silence howls with no shame.

I blink and see my mother standing in our kitchen, arm crossed over her chest, gaze faraway. I see her wandering through the den, not noticing me on the sofa. I see her sitting across from me at dinner, so distracted that when I ask her a question, she gives the answer to a question I didn't ask. She calls my father the absentminded professor, but she has no right. She is the absentminded one.

She is the absent one.

All at once my rage feels hot enough to burn the whole department store down. "Just go!" I shout, and I shout it again. I shout it again, again, again.

And my mother does the worst thing she could possibly do. She does as I ask.

30.

TRAGEDY STRIKES, YET IT DOESN'T SEEM TO MATTER. YOU brush your teeth. You go to school. You come home and eat your dinner. You watch the evening news. Sometimes you wake in the morning not remembering she's gone, and you have to remember it all over. Even so, you still have to get out of bed. You still have to comb your hair. You are not excused.

I walk to the library. I arrive a little before my shift begins, so for a few minutes I stand outside, protected from the rain by a narrow ledge. With one hand, I touch the back of my head. The bandaged place is barely sore. I close my eyes and test my memory key. But no matter which way I bend my thoughts, I stay standing outside the library with my eyes closed. My key is working as it should.

So I go in and get to work. I shelve the books that need shelving, organize the periodicals, mop the puddles on the floor, put up a CAUTION—WET sign. I try to help the one person at the computers, but he doesn't seem to want my help. I mop the floor again. I shelve the three newly returned books.

"Lora, you're so full of energy today," says Cynthia. "I guess you're fully recovered from your illness?"

I stare at her. Then I remember I called in sick yesterday. "Yes, I'm better," I say, two moments too late.

Cynthia frowns and asks me to take over at the circulation desk. She walks away before I can answer.

On this rainy day, there is not much circulating so I pass the time staring. I stare at the floor and ceiling, at the shelves of books. It's an exciting occasion whenever the doors open and someone comes inside. Then I can watch them shaking out their drippy clothes and soaked umbrellas. I can watch them stomp the water from their shoes onto the rubber mat. I can watch and not think.

The doors open. Someone comes inside. And this time I feel no excitement, only panic. Why is *he* here? Why would he go out on this stormy afternoon? Why would he come to the library after what happened the other day?

Raul shakes out his drippy clothes and soaked umbrella. He stomps his shoes on the rubber mat. His gaze wanders across the room. It passes me without pausing. He walks away from the circulation desk, to the computers in the back.

A minute later, I follow him there. Right now I could really use a friendly face, a kind word. A nice smile. "Raul?" I say, stepping cautiously toward him.

He is already at work on a computer. He does not look up right away. And when he does, he looks faintly puzzled, as though he doesn't know who I am.

"Hey, Raul," I say. "I'm glad—"

"Are you kidding?" His lips coil, as if he tastes something sour. Perhaps he does, for he spits out his next words: "Why are you talking to me?"

"I thought we—"

"I'll tell you why. You used me to get into Grand Gardens. And when you didn't need me anymore, you got rid of me. But now you need me again. You need my help. Is that what it is? Well, too bad."

"I don't, I didn't—"

"I shouldn't be surprised. Really, it's my fault for not knowing better. I saw how you treated your friends," he says.

"I'm sorry, but—"

"Forget it." He swivels his chair and attaches himself to his computer: eyes stuck on the screen, fingers fixed to the keyboard. He starts typing. He types very fast.

"Lora," says someone behind me. "We need you at circulation."

It's Cynthia the librarian.

I say that I'm going. I say that I'm sorry. And I go. And I'm sorry.

I sit behind the big desk and check out books for the two people waiting. "Have a nice day," I say to the first. "Have a nice day," I say to the second.

After they leave, I stop smiling.

I hate that Raul thinks I used him. Because the terrible truth is that I did. Though not in the way he said: I didn't need him to get into Grand Gardens. But I used him just the same, I realize. I used him like a bandage to cover up the scabby scars of the past. As much as I tried convincing myself otherwise, it was never him I wanted; I wanted only a distraction from the memories.

I'm so ashamed.

For all this time I resented Tim for treating me thoughtlessly, but I treated Raul the same way. I wonder if he came here today with the purpose of telling me off. If so, I don't blame him.

When Albert comes to the circulation desk so I can take my break, I first go to the computers to apologize to Raul. But he's gone. On the one hand, I'm disappointed. On the other hand, I'm exceptionally relieved.

Next I go to Cynthia's office to tell her I'm sorry for abandoning my post earlier. In response she gazes at me with lifted eyebrows and I worry she is about to lecture me again about irresponsible behavior. But all she says is: "Boy trouble?"

"Um. Sort of."

She nods. I cannot tell whether she is waiting for me to say more or waiting for me to go, and I hate how uncomfortable it is between us when she used to be my favorite librarian. When I still want her to be my favorite librarian.

So I don't go. I say, "Yeah, I was kind of dating that guy, but I didn't really like him, so I broke it off, and I guess he's angry now, and I feel really bad."

"Don't feel bad. They're always angry, but they always get over it."

"I hope so." Smiling tentatively, I ask her how she's doing.

"Good. I'm good. Everything's good." She smiles back but there's something broken in her smile: a crack, some rust, a missing part.

"Everything?" I ask.

Cynthia sighs forcefully, as if trying to exhale more than just air. Then she tells me how worried she is about her daughter. She tells me it's been over a year that Kira has been unemployed.

"I think one reason she's had such a hard time has to do with this political website she writes for. Kira has strong opinions, and these days it seems like employers—even when they agree with her views—are reluctant to hire someone who could be divisive," she says. Then she frowns. "So I did something I regret. I told Kira to stop writing for that website."

"But that makes sense. Why do you regret it?"

"Because it's important to stand up for what you believe in."

"That's true. I see what you mean."

"But I'm also her mother and I want her to be safe. And happy."

"Yes, of course you do," I say, and suddenly there are tears in my eyes, tears on my cheeks, everything wet everywhere.

"Oh, honey, don't trouble yourself over that boy." Cynthia comes out from behind her desk and puts her arms around me.

She pats my back. She hums comfort into my ear. I tell her that
it's okay, that I'm okay. But she doesn't let go. She doesn't let go
until I've finished crying.

After I've washed my face, dried my face, and composed my red
face in the bathroom mirror, I get out my phone and discover
that I missed two calls while I was working. The first was from
Tim.

He left a message: "Lora, I found something. I'm not sure
what it means, but I scanned it and sent it to you, so check your
email. I'm going to put it back, then I'll call you again."

But he didn't call again. So I call. His line goes to voice
mail.

The second missed call was from Wendy. She did not leave
a message.

I walk over to the computers. The promised email from
Tim is in my in-box. There's no message, only an attached file.
I download the file, print it out, and read it. Except I can't read
it. It's a complicated diagram, all geometric lines and techni-
cal terms. Like something you might find in the latest issue of
Med-Tech Quarterly.

I call Tim once more. His line goes to voice mail once more.

And suddenly, I'm afraid.

But if I think too much about my fears I might start sobbing again, so instead I think about that missed call from
Wendy. Why would she call me? She seemed so angry yesterday. I remember the mean things I said to her, and the

condescending way she acted toward me.

I saw how you treated your friends, said Raul.

I pick up my phone again. I dial. She answers on the first ring.

"Lora, thank goodness," Wendy says, her voice too high, too sharp.

"What's wrong?" I ask.

"It's Tim. He's been arrested. For trespassing. At Keep Corp."

"What?" I wait for her to tell me she's joking.

Instead she tells me that the security guards found Tim somewhere he wasn't supposed to be and were unconvinced by his explanation that he got lost. "My mom's at the police station now, but they won't release him. She's freaking out. What are we going to do?" she says.

It's a good thing she can't see my face. I am able to compose my voice enough to tell her, in a fairly convincing tone, that I'll talk to Jon Harmon, that he has experience in these situations and will be able to fix this, no problem. But my face, if she were able to see my face, she would not believe a word I said.

"Okay, then call me back," says Wendy.

I dial Jon's home number. The line is busy. I hang up and try again. Still busy. I try his cell. No answer. I realize I've stopped breathing. I tell myself to breathe. I tell myself to calm down. I have to focus. I take a breath. Then I call my aunt.

It should have occurred to me sooner that if there's anyone who can help Tim, it's Aunt Austin. She's a congresswoman.

Also, an all-around intimidating person. I am so relieved when she answers. "Lora, hello," she says. "I'm glad you called. I just returned last night. My trip went smoothly. The service was sad, but tastefully done."

"Good," I say. "I was wondering—"

"My dear, it's very hectic here, but I'd like to see you. I know it's horribly inconvenient to ask on such a rainy day, but would you be able to come by my office? I'll have my secretary order us a nice snack, some pastries? I know how you like pastries."

"Yes, but my friend Tim—"

"When can you get here? In twenty minutes? A half hour?"

"Twenty minutes, but I wanted—"

"Perfect. I'll see you very soon, then."

"Aunt Austin, hold on," I say too late. The line clicks. I sigh. At least she won't be able to hang up on me once I'm sitting in front of her.

I walk over to Cynthia's desk. She looks up from her work. "Yes, Lora?"

"I have an emergency. And I have to go. I'm so sorry. Albert is at the circulation desk, and it's not busy today, so I hope it's okay." I am nervous. I'm afraid I'm making it uncomfortable between us again. I'm afraid of losing my job. Not that my job matters much at this moment.

But Cynthia nods and tells me I can go. "I hope everything is okay," she says.

"Thanks. I hope so, too," I say.

Then I put on my coat and my boots, and run out into the rain.

There's a long line of people waiting at the security checkpoint in my aunt's office building. In addition to the standard metal detector and x-ray machine, the guards are pulling visitors aside to have their palms swabbed for chemical residue. When it's my turn, I set my bag on the conveyer belt, and my raincoat, and my rain boots, and I step through feeling vulnerable in my state of semi-undress. At least I'm not pulled aside for additional checks.

I reassemble my outfit and take the elevator upstairs. Another guard is stationed in the hallway. I show him my visitor's pass and he points me through the door. At the reception desk, I give my name to a man with spiky hair and a dazzling smile. He cheerfully tells me to take a seat.

Several minutes go by. I take Tim's diagram out of my bag and stare at it, hoping that if I study it for long enough, I'll understand it. I don't. Eventually I put it away, too agitated to look anymore. If only I hadn't asked Tim for help. If only I hadn't given Tim's number to Carlos Cruz. If only I had told Tim he didn't need to do it because my mother is leaving and nothing can stop her.

The cheerful receptionist clears his throat. I glance at him hopefully, but he only looks at my foot tapping the floor, his smile less dazzling than before. I hadn't realized my foot was tapping. That's how agitated I am. "Sorry," I say, clamping sole against carpet.

"No worries." His smile dazzles again.

The longer I wait, the more confused I am to be waiting. Aunt Austin is partial to punctuality, and I am right on time. But I know she is busy, undoubtedly busier than usual since she was away these past few days. Still, she invited me and she wouldn't have invited me if she were otherwise occupied.

But now fifteen minutes have passed since I arrived. My foot is tapping vigorously and I can't make it stop. The cheerful man calls me back to his desk and I'm worried he is going to scold me for fidgeting. "I'm sorry," I say preemptively.

"No, Miss Mint, *I* am sorry." He gently places down his phone. "The congresswoman's assistant has just informed me she was unexpectedly called out of the office. My apologies. She's usually extremely organized, but her schedule has been chaotic lately, with all the economic bill stuff."

"What happened? Is everything all right?"

"I'm sure everything is fine. I cannot tell you more than that."

"But Austin is my aunt," I say.

"Really? I didn't know that. Let me tell you, your aunt is fabulous. She gets things done, unlike so many of those career politicians." The cheerful man rolls his cheerful eyeballs.

"Where'd she go? Are you sure everything is all right?" I say.

"Well, since you're family, I suppose I can tell you." He glances around, then lowers his voice. "She was called home for an emergency," he says dramatically.

"What emergency?" I'm ready to smack his smiling face.

But now he is looking past me. "Hello!" he says over my shoulder. "It's horrid weather out, isn't it? I hope you didn't get too wet."

I turn around, hoping it's my aunt. It's not. It's a man in a gray suit accompanied by a woman, also in a gray suit. They nod in response to the receptionist's greeting, their expressions solemn. They do not seem to recognize me.

But I recognize them immediately.

They are the ones who took my mother away.

31.

"THOSE PEOPLE WHO JUST CAME IN, WHO ARE THEY? THEY LOOK familiar," I say. My voice sounds normal. Impossibly normal.

The receptionist grins. "I'm sure you've met them before. They're your aunt's aides. They've worked with her forever."

"Forever," I say.

"Not literally forever. But years and years."

I try to process this information, that the blue-jacketed strangers work for my aunt, that they've worked with her for years and years. I cannot process this information.

"I have to go," I say slowly. Slowly because my tongue seems to have swollen inside my mouth. In fact, all of me seems to have swollen. My lungs strain thickly inside my chest. My skin feels about to burst. I stagger out of the office, past the security guard, into the elevator, and back down to the lobby.

I remember Aunt Austin in her bedroom, standing over her suitcase. *I loved your mom, Lora. I really,* she said, then zipped her bag closed without completing the sentence.

I remember my mother sitting on Jon's couch. *Why don't*

you give me her number and I'll call, she said, and I gave her her sister's number.

Fumbling my phone from my pocket, I try Jon's house again. Again I get a busy signal, tinny and echoing in my ear. I try his cell again. Again it goes to voice mail. So I try Darren's sister's apartment. I leave a message on the answering machine—"It's Lora, pick up, pick up, pick up!"—but no one picks up.

Then my phone rings.

"They're not going to release him until the judge sets bail. His lawyer says this is unusual for a trespassing charge, and she's going to fight it, but it sounds bad, Lora, it sounds really bad. Did you talk to Jon Harmon?" Wendy says all of this in one breathless rush.

"I'm going to his house. Do you want to meet me there?"

"Yes! I'm going crazy waiting," she says.

"We've got to hurry. Before it's too late," I say.

"Too late for what?"

"I'll tell you when we get there. Hurry, okay?" I give her Jon's address. Then I look around for my bicycle, and realize it's at home. Then I look around for my umbrella, and realize I left it in my aunt's office. So I pull my hood over my head and race outside. The rain has eased; now it falls in thin, sharp needles.

A bus is pulling away from the stop on the corner. I chase after it, waving. I run two blocks to catch up. "What's the big rush?" the driver asks when I get on.

I shake my head.

Traffic is bad because although it's no longer pouring, the roads are soaked and slippery. I groan at every stop, every red light. When I get off the bus, the other passengers are probably glad to be rid of me, but I don't care. I dash up the street to Jon's house and ring the bell. Then I wait.

And wait.

And wait.

The door opens.

"Hello," says the man. He is short and slim, with a lot of red-blond hair.

"Hi. You must be . . . Darren." It takes my damp brain an extra second to recall the name of Jon Harmon's partner.

"And you're Lora," he says. "It's so nice to finally meet you. Please, come in. I'm sorry to have kept you waiting, I was upstairs."

Darren hangs my coat in the closet while I step out of my dripping boots. He invites me to borrow some slippers and I choose the plaid pair closest to my size. They are still much too large. "Would you like something to drink?" he asks.

I shake my head impatiently. "Where's Jon? And my mom?"

"I was hoping you'd know. No one was here when I got here," he says, waving me into the living room. He sits in the armchair, normally Jon's armchair, and I sit on the sofa.

"I called the apartment. There was no answer there either," I say.

His pale eyebrows come together. "Where could they be?"

"Could they still be at the department store?"

"The department store?"

"The one on Greenfield Avenue," I say.

"Ah, yes, that one." He gazes at me, eyes gleaming. "Lora, I can't imagine what it must be like for you. To have thought your mother was dead, and then find out otherwise. You must be so happy," he says.

"Of course, I'm very happy." I nod. Darren is not what I expected. He is intense, almost uncomfortably so, in stark opposition to Jon's laid-back cheerfulness.

"I truly admire the way you got your mother out of Grand Gardens. What an elegant plan you came up with, and so quickly," he says.

"Thank you," I say, idly scratching at an itchy place above my ear, but there's no relief, only increasing discomfort. I force my hand down, clamp it underneath my leg. The irritation is not on my head, it's inside my head. I've forgotten something.

"And you didn't even panic when you got outside and bumped into your friend who works there, what's his name, Ralph, Ron . . . I'm so bad with names."

"Raul," I say, distracted, as I try to remember what I've forgotten.

"Yes, Raul. How's it going with Raul? He seems so nice."

Then my full attention is abruptly on Darren. How does he know about Raul? I haven't told Jon about Raul. How does he know I saw Raul outside the retirement home? I haven't told anyone about seeing Raul outside the retirement home.

"How do you know about that?" I ask.

But now Darren is the one distracted. He is gazing out the front window. I turn to see what he sees, and I nearly choke when I see it. A silver sedan is pulling into the driveway. The car door opens and a tall man unfolds out. He holds his hands over his face to protect against the rain as he strides quickly to the house. The doorbell rings.

"Finally," says Darren. "Now don't move. I'll be right back."

I don't move. I can't move. So complete is my confusion. So complete is my fear. There is the creak of the door opening, and a bang as it closes. There is the low murmur of deep voices. I cannot make out what they are saying. Perhaps because they are speaking so carefully quietly. Perhaps because I am remembering what I had forgotten.

The only part of me that will budge is my gaze, so I push my eyes away from the window, away from the silver sedan in the driveway, and over to the family portrait on the wall above the fireplace. There's Jon Harmon, bald and beaming, and the two kids, cutely freckled. But I'm focused on the other man in the photograph. The other man is tall, unlike Darren, who is of average height. The other man is plump, unlike Darren, who is slender. The other man has brown hair, unlike Darren, whose hair is a reddish blond. The conclusion is obvious. Darren is not Darren. But if he's not Darren . . .

I've got to get out of here.

I stand. But then there's a clatter of footsteps and Not-Darren reappears. "Sorry for the interruption," he says. "You stay put while I talk a minute with my friend. We'll be right here in the hallway, so don't worry about a thing. You might as well sit back down and relax." Not-Darren smiles at me, and I know that he knows that I know. I sit back down. He nods approvingly as he goes.

I've got to get out of here.

But how? I ease myself up and tiptoe to the window. With great tenderness, I tug on the frame. The wood jiggles, but won't lift. I search for a latch or a lock or a lever, fingers crawling into dusty cracks and corners, but then I'm distracted by a flash of color. I look through the glass and am appalled by what I find.

Wendy is walking toward the house.

Her umbrella is open high above her head, and that's what caught my attention because her umbrella is hot pink. I tap on the window. Then I tap more frantically. I can't let her fall into this trap I've fallen into. For that's what this undoubtedly is: a trap. Set for my mother, but now that Not-Darren has caught me, he's keeping me instead. Or in addition.

I tap as loudly as I dare, then consider more drastic action, looking around the room for something heavy, something I can use to smash the glass.

Wendy stops mid-stride. She sees me.

I shake my head and wave my arms and mouth a million desperate words. When she nods I exhale with relief. Now she will walk away, she will go for help, she will save herself, and maybe, hopefully, me.

But instead, Wendy dashes out of my sight.

But instead, the doorbell rings.

No, no, no.

The two men fall silent. A moment passes before they begin whispering again. Then one of them treads toward the door. I run to the fireplace, to the iron poker resting against the bricks, thinking I can use it to smash the window, the room, anything, everything, and create a diversion so that Wendy can get away.

But as I reach for the poker a hand grips my arm and pulls me backward. "Lora Mint," says a voice in my ear. I turn around.

It's not Not-Darren.

This man is tall. This man is thin. This man has salt-and-pepper curls and dark eyes. I know this man. He's the doctor from Keep Corp, the one who replaced my memory key. The one who said my mother was a wonderful person and a great scientist. The one who looked at me with such grief when I told him I was her daughter. Dr. Trent. Driver of the silver sedan.

"It's you," I say. I glare.

"Quiet," he says. "You don't want anyone to get hurt, do you?"

This quiets me instantly.

Wendy's voice soars nimbly through the stillness. "Are you Jon Harmon?" she asks. "I'm the journalism student who called to interview you about your experiences in activism. I know I'm early for our appointment, I hope you don't mind."

"No, I'm not Jon. He's not home right now. You'd better come back later, when he's expecting you," says Not-Darren.

"Do you know when he'll be back?" asks Wendy.

"I'm afraid I don't," says Not-Darren.

"*Get out of here*," Dr. Trent hisses.

"What?" I'm sure I heard him wrong because I was focused on the conversation between Wendy and Not-Darren. I stare at the doctor. His face is narrow eyes and narrow lips and nothing revealed.

"Is there another exit? A back door?" he whispers, releasing his hold on my arm.

"Through the kitchen?" I say.

"Then go that way. Now." Dr. Trent is obviously exasperated by my confusion.

But I still don't understand. "Go?" I say. "Go where?"

"Anywhere! Just get out of here!"

I take a step toward the door, then turn back.

"Why?" I ask. "Why are you letting me go?"

For a moment, I think he's not going to answer. I take another step toward the door, and another, before he speaks. "I owe your mother this much," he says softly. "Now, go!"

I go. I sneak across the hallway. Wendy is still chattering to Not-Darren, even as his responses get impatiently short. Still she prattles on, telling him how important this article is to her, and how hard it is to get a regular column at the school newspaper, and how she's always wanted to be a journalist, even when she was a little girl. Terrified as I am, I'm still able to admire Wendy's act.

In the kitchen, I undo the deadbolt. But when I ease open

the back door, the hinges screech, they scream, they wail. I freeze.

I freeze and wait for the thunder of footsteps. What I actually hear is much worse. "Wait, I recognize you," Not-Darren says to Wendy. "You're Lora's friend. Cindy? Mindy? Winnie? I'm so bad with names . . ."

He continues guessing, but I've stopped listening. I leap outside, across the wooden deck, down the stairs, and into the yard. My feet slip in the muddy grass, and I realize I'm still wearing those too-large plaid slippers. I kick them off as I race around to the front of the house.

"Wendy!" I shout. "Wendy, run!"

She hears me. She sees me. She runs.

Not-Darren reaches for her, but trips over the hot-pink umbrella she has dropped in her haste. He swiftly recovers, sprinting down the front path. But Wendy has a head start, and with those long legs she's very fast.

"Car! Over there!" she yells, pointing at the end of the block.

I follow her. The concrete is painfully hard against my socked feet. The rain is coming down in dense drops. Wendy unlocks her car and we both dive inside, shut our doors, lock our doors. Only then do we look behind us.

Not-Darren is nowhere to be seen.

"Let's go," I say to Wendy. My voice is wobbly.

"Yes, let's," she says to me. Her voice is wobbly, too. She starts the engine and pulls out of the parking space. We have to pass Jon Harmon's house, and as we approach, Wendy accelerates.

"No," I say. "Not so fast."

She raises her eyebrows, but slows down. I stare out the window. Not-Darren stands on the sidewalk, holding Wendy's open umbrella over his head. The umbrella glows pink on his face. Dr. Trent is on the porch, calling out. But it appears as though Not-Darren does not hear him. Perhaps because he is too busy watching us as we drive past. I'm unnerved by his expression. He doesn't look angry or disappointed or frustrated.

Instead, Not-Darren is smiling as if he doesn't mind that we've escaped. He is smiling as if it was his plan all along to let us go. He is smiling as if we're playing a game and he's just realized he is going to win.

32.

"HE KNEW WHO I WAS." WENDY IS CLENCHING THE STEERING wheel so tightly that her hands are bumpy knuckle and nothing else. "How did he know? I've never seen him before in my life."

"He knew all these things he shouldn't have known. I don't know how."

"Should we call the police? I think we'd better call them," she says.

"Turn right and go down two blocks," I say.

"Where are we going? We should call the police."

"We have to find my mom. I told him the department store. If she's there—"

"Wait, what? What do you mean *your mom*!" she cries.

"She's alive. Here, just park now, here." I get out of the car and hurry to the building. Wendy is right behind me, screaming questions at me. I batter the correct rhythm onto the door—one long tap, two short—and immediately it swings opens.

"What are you doing? Where's Jeanette?" asks Jon Harmon.

"You don't where she is?" I say.

"She's late. She was supposed to be back ten minutes ago."

"She's not still at the department store, is she?"

"No." He looks confused. (I realize it was hours ago I'd met her there.) Then my panic becomes anger. "Why didn't you return my calls?" I ask him.

"I tried. What's going on?"

"Keep Corp's at your house. Tim is in jail. And . . . If my mom isn't at the store, where is she?"

"They're at my house?" Jon frowns.

"Where's my mother?" I ask.

"She went to see her sister. But what about my house?"

"She went to Aunt Austin's?"

"Yes, but what about Keep Corp *at my house*?" yells Jon.

"I have to go, right now, I have to go. Can I borrow your car?" I ask Wendy, and grab the keys from her hand before she can respond. I race out of the apartment and I'm almost down the hall when she comes after me.

"Lora! You can't leave like that!" Wendy grabs my arm.

"It's okay. Tell Jon what happened, and he'll help Tim."

"I will. But you're not wearing any shoes."

I look down at my feet. I'm not wearing any shoes.

"Hold on." Wendy kneels to unlace her sneakers.

"You'll need them," I say.

"You'll need them more. I'm not letting you go unless you take them."

"Fine." I slip on her shoes and tie them tight. Her feet are larger than mine.

Then I remember something else. I take Tim's diagram out of my backpack. "Here, I don't know what this means, but maybe Jon can do something with it. In case . . ." I don't finish the sentence out loud; I don't finish the sentence in my head. I turn to go.

"Lora!"

I glance back. "Yeah?"

"I missed you," she says.

"I missed you, too," I say.

"Be careful, okay?"

"I will."

Then I'm running outside and instantly soaked, the wind washing through my hair, my eyes weeping rain. The wet sky is the same dark gray as the wet road, and I'm so grateful for Wendy's car and Wendy's sneakers. And Wendy herself.

In this rainy bad weather, I drive as fast as I dare drive. And, fortunately, there is not much traffic. Until I come to the exit for Grand Village. The off-ramp spirals me down to street level, and into a crowd of unmoving cars.

"An accident," I whisper to myself as we roll forward half an inch.

"Ridiculous," I whisper to myself as we roll forward another half an inch.

I turn on the radio and flip through the stations, listening

for information on traffic delays. I speed past reports of flood-
ing, electrical outages, a person critically injured by a falling
tree, but it's too much to listen to so I turn it off, and, anyway,
we're suddenly moving. Forward the car goes, slowly still but
surely down one block, and another, and another, until I come
to the place where the problem began.

I look. I look away. I look, even though I don't want to look.
An ambulance and two police cars are there: lights flashing
yellow through the murk, sirens off so the only sound is the
falling water and the rough shouts of the emergency workers as
they carry their burden across the road. A white sheet settled
like snow over hills and valleys on the stretcher. The still ter-
rain of a motionless body.

And I remember that it was a stormy day like today that my
mother died. My tense body tenses more. I inform myself I'm
wrong. She never died. She's alive and I am going to find her
and I can't get distracted by some other tragedy.

I look away. I keep driving.

One more mile and there it is: the ultramodern condominium apartment building, gleaming and imposing as
always, immune to the indignity of bad weather. I pull up in
front, into a parking space I'm not sure is an actual space, and
run inside.

I am met with silence. And shadow.

No neatly uniformed man stands behind the front desk,
waiting to greet me. No light glitters down from the massive
chandelier to illuminate the marble floors. "Hello?" I say, my

voice skittering across the abandoned space. No one answers. The lobby has the look and feel of a forsaken place.

"So much for security around here," I say, trying to talk normally, trying to destroy the perfect quiet of this deserted room, but one wavering voice does nothing against this vast emptiness. As soon as a syllable trips out over my lips, it disappears.

I continue walking, though the farther I go, the darker it gets. The seeping daylight wavers and weakens in the windowless elevator vestibule. Squinting, I fumble for the button. Find it. Press it. Press it again. Nothing happens.

"The power's out," I say aloud.

Of course the power's out. That's why the lights aren't lit. That's why the security guard is missing; he must be fiddling with a fuse box somewhere. I'm reassured by the simple explanation. I'm reassured until I realize this means I have to find another way to the fifteenth floor. And the only other way is painful and obvious.

I feel my way around the corner, past the mailboxes, sliding hands across the walls, wet shoes slipping on the floor. At least it's not completely dark inside the stairwell. A pale backup light flickers overhead. I put my hand on the railing and begin the climb.

At first I go quickly, for ten floors I go quickly, until my legs start complaining and my lungs start protesting, so I slow legs and lungs until my feet are a steady thump, thump, thump on each ascending step. I force myself up the final flights and push my way out of the stairwell. And step into black nothing.

I stumble. I reach out my arms. I stumble again. I stumble down the hallway, across the thick carpet. I stumble again as my palms slam a vertical surface. Which means I'm at the end of the corridor. Which means I'm in front of my aunt's apartment. I find the knob and twist. Then the door—inexplicably unlocked—glides open.

And I'm shocked by what I find inside.

All the usual order has been violently destroyed. There are books splayed on the floor and chairs turned over and the coffee table is leaning at a dangerous angle. Paintings and photographs have been ripped down, leaving ugly scars in the wall. The cream-colored couch has slashes up and down its body, and from each cut bleeds fiber filling.

Away from the chaos, a woman stands at the window, staring out at the rain, one arm across her chest, the other arm folded up so her fingers can gently tap against her cheek, as if she is in deep thought. Suddenly, she whirls around.

"Lora, what are you doing here?" asks Aunt Austin.

"I know what you did," I say accusingly.

Then I notice her eyes are wet.

"My dear, you shouldn't have come," she says. She weeps.

"You took my mother away from me."

A sob breaks open her face.

"Why did you do it?" I am trying to be firm, but it's impossible when she is crying like this; I've never seen my aunt cry like this. Not even at my mom's funeral—but then, she knew it was no true funeral. This last thought kicks.

"Why did you do it?" I ask again, and this time I'm screaming.

"They were going to have her killed! It really would have been Jeanette in that car if I hadn't sent her away."

"You should have gone to the police!"

"There wasn't time. I had to do something before . . ."

"Tell me," I say. "Tell me exactly what you did."

She nods. She pulls a handkerchief from her pocket and wipes her swollen eyes. "An associate of mine told me that Jeanette was in trouble. I tried talking sense into my sister, but she was stubborn as she always was—always *is*. She refused to accept the fact she was in danger. So I had to take action."

My aunt explains she had the car accident staged, and that the recovered body came from a medical lab. Meanwhile, she arranged for my mother to be taken to safety at Grand Gardens.

"Then you let us think she was dead," I say.

"I was trying to protect her. I was trying to protect *you*."

"For five years I thought my mother was dead," I say.

"It was necessary. Jeanette discovered confidential information about a certain project at Keep Corp. She went to the man in charge, her colleague and supposed friend, and told him she didn't approve of his project, that she was going to the authorities about it, and he should cooperate. Instead he reported her to his superiors. They hired people to get rid of her, and they would have, if I hadn't intervened."

"And Keep Corp let you do it?"

"I called in favors. I used every connection I had."

I shake my head. It makes sense, yet nothing make sense. I point at the wounded walls, the mutilated sofa. "What happened here?" I ask.

"Your mother."

"Mom did this? How? Why?"

"I have no idea. She was gone before I got here. With all the building's power problems today, she was able to get in, but the security guard saw her leaving and he called me immediately," she says.

"But why would she do this to your apartment?"

"Probably to vent her anger. Jeanette always had a bad temper."

"Can you blame her?" My voice is dangerously sharp.

"No. I only blame myself." Aunt Austin stares down at the floor, at the broken glass scattered across the white carpet.

Then she looks up again. She looks at me. "But this is no time for blame. We have to find your mother. Do you know where she is?"

I shake my head, though I suppose my mom has returned to meet Jon. But I won't answer any of my aunt's questions until she has answered all of mine. "What will you do when you find her?" I ask.

"I'll take her back to Grand Gardens. Or somewhere else she'll be safe."

"Why? She doesn't remember anything. She's no threat to them anymore."

"Jeanette's a loose end—an employee who is supposed to be dead—and Keep Corp doesn't like loose ends. That's why I have my best people looking for her. That's why we have to find her before they do."

"Do you know what she discovered about the new keys? We could use that information to protect her. It would give us leverage against Keep Corp."

My aunt's expression doesn't change, and yet it does. The pinch of her forehead, the downturn of her mouth, seems to fix into permanent place.

"*You know*," I say. "What is it?"

She exhales heavily, painfully. "I'm going to tell you, Lora. I'm going to tell you because I trust you. I know you'll understand that these sacrifices are for the greater good. It's about the future of our country," she says.

Then it's all suddenly, horrifically, clear.

"You're working with them!"

"We're collaborating. On a revolutionary new program," she says.

Which makes me think of that tabloid article about Keep Corp transmitting data to radical extremists so they can carry out political assassinations, and what I'm thinking is crazy, but all of this is totally crazy, so I just ask it: "Aunt Austin, are you helping the Citizen Army?"

"*Helping* them? Don't you know me at all?" She seems truly offended.

"Honestly?" I say.

She flinches. "I guess I deserved that. But won't you give me a chance to explain? I love you, and I love Jeanette, and I'm so, so sorry I had to hurt you. Please, you have to let me explain."

After a moment I nod, the barest of nods.

"Thank you, my dear." She sits cautiously on the ravaged couch, and motions for me to sit next to her. When she begins talking again, her voice is clear, and so are her eyes. It's hard to believe she was a mush of tears just minutes before. But this is Aunt Austin's single-minded way.

"You see, Lora, our country has gone from being the most powerful nation in the world to an international laughingstock. Our government is ineffective, our unemployment rate is at a historical high, while our financial markets are dangerously low. So what do we do? To get to the solution, we start at the root of the problem. Can you guess what that is?"

I shake my head.

"Fear," she says, stretching the word so it fills the room. Then she continues. "When innocent people are killed every day, yes, it's fear that's controlling us now. So what would happen if we removed this fear? Imagine a world with no more Citizen Army, no more bombings, no more hijackings, no more murders, no crime at all."

"It's not possible," I say.

"No? But what if we were able to apprehend every perpetrator of every crime, and provide the courts with proof of their guilt."

And then I realize exactly how it's possible.

"The new keys," I say.

"Yes, we've partnered with Keep Corp to create a groundbreaking security program. The new keys have a decryption function that will enable law enforcement to access memory data in order to identify and prosecute criminals."

And then I realize how Not-Darren knew all those things, all those things he shouldn't have known. The medical technicians had downloaded my memory data in order to replace my broken key. So my memories were in Keep Corp's systems.

Keep Corp could access whatever part of my mind they wanted.

I realize and I feel sick.

Meanwhile, my aunt is still speaking: "Eighty percent of our population has a key now, and that number is increasing every year. Once the program is established it will eventually become a deterrent to all crime."

"You can't do this! What about privacy?" I say.

"What's more important, Lora, your privacy or your safety? Do you value privacy over a human life? What about a hundred lives, or a thousand? It's a careful balance between security and privacy, but with so many threats to our citizens, security has to be the priority."

I don't say anything. Because on the one hand, what my aunt says makes sense. But on the other hand, I feel like screaming. I remember the way Not-Darren looked at me, as if he knew everything about me. Because he *did* know everything about me.

Aunt Austin smiles, taking my silence for agreement. "The pilot program will happen right here in Middleton," she says. "If all goes well, we'll take it to the federal government and make it national. Then perhaps other countries will adapt these measures as well. Isn't it exciting?"

"I . . . I don't know," I say.

Her smile melts. "What's worrying you, my dear?"

I tell her that Not-Darren went through the data from my memory key. And not to look for some criminal. To look for my mother.

She frowns. "We have to find Jeanette. We have to find her *now*, before they do."

Then I'm standing. Then I'm shouting. "How can you work with Keep Corp when you don't even trust them? When they're a danger to your own sister?"

"It's not the ideal situation," she says. "But the most important thing is the security program. There can be no scandal until it's in place, in order to prevent public backlash. Think of what might happen then: people would stop getting memory keys or even get their keys removed. There'd be another Vergets epidemic. Society would collapse."

"There are other med-tech companies—"

"Yes, but the most important thing is the security program."

"But, you can't trust—"

"Let's take, for example, Senator Finney. His killer has yet to be arrested. There are no suspects and no leads other than the connection to the Citizen Army. But if there were some way you could identify the murderer, bring him to justice, keep him from hurting any more innocent people, wouldn't you do it?"

All my outrage is suddenly gone.

There is only one possible answer.

"Yes, I would," I say softly, and sit back down on the ravaged couch.

"Oh, Lora, I knew you'd understand." She leans over and slides her arms around me. She smells like roses; she smells like my aunt; the scent is achingly familiar. "If Jeanette had listened, *really* listened, she would have understood too. But you know how stubborn she can be."

"I know." I feel tired. So tired.

"Now I have something to show you." Aunt Austin slips her hand into her jacket and brings out a small plastic bag. She holds her palm out in offering.

I take the bag from her, hold it up, flip it over. The outside is labeled MINT. Inside the bag is a white object the shape and size of a dime. "What is it?" I ask.

"It's her memory key."

"My mother's?" I stare at her.

"Keep Corp arranged its removal without my consent. I only found out afterward. I went to Grand Gardens, saw

Jeanette's condition, and paid one of the doctors to give her key to me. I thought that one day she could have it reinstalled."

"One day?"

"As soon as our security program is in place—it'll be just a few more months." She smiles eagerly. I look at her eager smile. I look at the tiny plastic-wrapped disk in my hand. I think about what this means. To have my mother living close to me again, to have my mother remember me, and to have her be the mother I remember—this is what this means. This is what my aunt is offering.

"Would you like something to drink, my dear? Some iced tea?" Aunt Austin gets up, and I follow, stepping carefully over the shattered glass, moving carefully around a fallen chair, holding on carefully to the little plastic bag with its little white disk.

In the kitchen there are ceramic shards on the countertops and cutlery scattered across the white tile. "Jeanette has always been good at making messes," says my aunt.

"She's not the only one," I mutter, but she doesn't notice, or pretends not to.

"Do you hear that?" She walks to the refrigerator and opens the door. "Thank goodness. The electricity is back on." She reaches for the light switch, flicks a finger, and the room is aglow.

"Now tell me, Lora. How can we find her?"

I gaze down at the silverware on the floor. I think. I think: how does anyone ever know what to do? Sometimes it's obvious and you do it instantly, like when I grabbed Ms. Pearl away from that speeding car. More often, though, you think and think and think and think, and still don't know.

My fist clenches, and inside my clenched fist is my mother's memory key.

"She's leaving tonight," I say. "But there's still time to stop her."

33.

THE SCIENTISTS WHO INVENTED THE H-FILTER ARE NOT FAMOUS. Their names are unfamiliar to the public; there have been no books devoted to their work, no films dramatizing their journey toward innovation. But it is their contribution to medical technology that I have been most grateful to these past few weeks. Because it's their contribution that will eventually help me forget.

And there's so much I want to forget.

I want to forget the day of Tim's arraignment, how pale and scared he was, how pale and scared we all were, when he was finally released after spending two days in jail.

I want to forget Jon Harmon's faked cheerfulness when he called to tell me that he and his family were going away—on vacation, he said—but a vacation with an undisclosed destination and an uncertain return date.

And I want to forget the night I went with Aunt Austin to find my mother.

***

Her aides came to meet us at the train station. Together we waited and waited, and it wasn't until seven o'clock exactly that my aunt began asking questions: "Are you sure she said seven? Are you sure it's tonight? Are you sure she's leaving by *train*?"

Aunt Austin peered at me and I could see in her face how much she wanted to believe I'd been misinformed or scatter-brained. How much she wanted to believe that I had not lied to her. Purposefully. Callously.

Still I stuck to my story, and like everyone else I glanced frequently at the big brass clock on the wall of the Middleton train station. But with each glance I saw my mother.

I saw her waiting in the security line at the airport, calmly smiling at the officer as she handed over her fake passport. I saw her strolling through the terminal, wearing her floppy straw hat, *my* floppy straw hat, and stopping to buy an over-priced bottle of water. I saw her step onto the plane, greet the flight attendant, and walk to her seat, a window seat in the back. I saw the airplane lift up and sail across the darkening sky. And from the ground I watched as the plane got smaller and smaller, a blot, a speck, then nothing at all.

At nine o'clock, Aunt Austin said I might as well go home, and asked me for my mother's key. "I'll hold on to it for safe-keeping," she said, and I gave it back to her without protest. She slid the plastic bag into her jacket pocket.

She didn't notice that in the bag, the tiny disk was broken in two.

She didn't know that hours ago, while I stood in her

kitchen, gazing at the silverware on the floor, I had made my decision. I clenched my fist and inside my clenched fist, my thumb pressed against the disk, pressed it down hard.

I felt it bend and bend and bend.

I felt it snap.

And while my aunt made plans and phone calls, the tears spilled from my eyes. I knew I had to do it—I had to protect my mother's privacy, I couldn't risk letting Keep Corp get access to her memories. Still, I cried. How easily the memory key had broken in two.

Since that night, I haven't noticed any suspicious cars around our house, no silver sedans, no SUVs. Not-Darren has not made a reappearance, nor has Dr. Trent. I imagine it's Aunt Austin who is protecting my dad and me, who is keeping Keep Corp away, but I don't know for certain—we haven't talked since that day at the train station.

Still, I want to call her. I want to warn her about what's coming.

But I know I can't.

Even though I keep waking up in the middle of the night, heart pounding with panic, wondering if I'd been too small-minded to comprehend the greatness of my aunt's vision, wondering if I'd let my mother go at the world's expense.

But when morning comes, I know I did what had to be done. Because a ruthless corporation cannot be trusted with such power. Because history shows what disasters result when governments trespass upon its citizens. Because I experienced firsthand the violation of having someone invade my memories, of having every thought, every feeling, every experience exposed. Whenever I think of Not-Darren groping through my mind, my stomach aches. At least I saved my mom from the same fate.

But I don't mean to sound so tragic.

My mother is alive and free in the world.

So I'll be fine, really. We will all be fine.

And this is how fine I already am: on a beautiful summer day, a perfect beach day, Wendy and I are eating cherry ice pops while stretched on towels stretched on sand, and we are not talking about regret or fear or memory. No, we're discussing her new boyfriend, Travis, a competitive swimmer. "He smells permanently of chlorine," she says. "I kind of like it. Whenever I'm near a swimming pool, I miss him."

"That's disgusting," I say. Then I focus my complete attention on my ice pop. I know what comes next.

"Travis has some cute friends."

"You never give up."

"So you might as well give in." She gazes at me with eyes mournfully wide, lips a squiggle of sadness. "It's been forever since you dated anyone."

"Not even a month."

"That's worse than I thought."

"I still feel bad about Raul."

"Why'd you break up with him then?"

"I liked him, but I didn't *like* him."

She nods. "Then it's good you ended it."

I look at her in surprise. I had expected to be admonished for not giving him a chance, for never giving any guy any chance. How strange to discover I've misjudged my best friend. "Anyway," I say, "I feel bad about Raul because I wasn't sure I liked him, but I went out with him anyway. I'm worse than Greg Lange."

"Who?"

"Remember that guy who asked me out because he had a crush on *you*?"

"Ugh, that guy." She grimaces. "First of all, you're definitely not worse than him. Second of all, you went out with Raul to figure out whether you liked him or not. That's how dating works."

"That's how people get hurt," I say.

"Well, yeah, sometimes. Sometimes not. That's the risk." She pauses, tilting her head. "Are we still talking about Raul?" she asks.

"Who else would we be talking about?"

Wendy gives me a look of pure sympathy, a look that says she knows more than I've told her, maybe more than I've told myself, and sighs. Then scowls. Then complains: "Ugh, stop it!" she shrieks at her brother.

Because there he is, dripping on her feet while he leans over to pick up his towel. "Stop what? Stop this?" Tim says, shaking out his drenched hair, speckling his sister with water.

"You're so immature." She swats him with the stick from her ice pop, then turns back toward me. "Guess I'll go for a swim now. You coming?"

I shake my head. "It's way too cold."

"Wimp!" she shouts as she goes running down to the lake.

Tim sits in her vacated spot and immediately tells me: "No apologizing." This is our joke that isn't really a joke. Because I can't stop apologizing to him. Because he's been fired from his internship, suspended from school, pending the dean's review, and his trial date for trespassing is in two months.

"Just a little apologizing?" I say.

"Not even a little," he says. "Listen, Lora, what I did, I didn't do it for you. I did it because it was the right thing, and I wanted to do the right thing, and I'm glad I did. It sucks I got caught, but it was my fault, it was my choice, and I don't regret anything. So no more apologies, okay?"

"Okay. Nice speech."

"Thanks. I'm practicing. My lawyer said that when Carlos's article is published, I'll get some sort of whistle-blower protection, and then I'll be a national hero."

"Really? She said you'd be a national hero?" I laugh.

"You won't be laughing when the girls start following me around."

"They already follow you around," I say. "Anyway, I wasn't

laughing at you. I was laughing . . . at you. There's sand all over your face."

"Well, get it off me." He grins.

"Hold still." I rub my fingers across his cheek, along his jaw. His skin is warm, and as I brush the sand from his warm skin, he stops grinning. I look at him and he is looking at me with intense gaze and serious mouth. He is looking at me as if he's about to kiss me.

But then he blinks the glint from his eyes. "All gone?" he asks.

"All gone." I remove my hand from his face. I'm taken aback by my own disappointment. After all, I'm the one who decided we should just be friends. Just friends is what I want, isn't it? I think about what Wendy said about dating and hurt and risk.

"Thanks for the grooming," Tim says, and starts talking about this bike trail at the state park, how we should go there while the weather is still good, a whole big group of us, and bring lots of food and drinks, and normally this is a topic I'd love to discuss because it includes all my favorite things—bicycles and food and drinks—but right now I'm not interested in any of it.

"What do you think?" he asks.

"I was wrong," I say.

Then I kiss him. Quickly. On the mouth. Then I lean back and wait for him to tell me this isn't a good idea. That I've missed my chance because he's already met someone new or he doesn't want anything serious or he's tired of my indecision.

That he thinks of me now as just a friend.

"Do that again," he says, grinning.

"No," I say, but then I do it again.

And again and again, until Wendy comes back from her swim.

"Gross. Stop it," she says. Then after we reluctantly stop it, she informs us, matter-of-fact: "It's about time you idiots got together."

Because Wendy knows; she always knows.

Late in the afternoon, after the clouds swallow the sun and the breeze starts biting, we decide we've had enough of the outdoors, sticky and sandy and sleepy as we all are, so Wendy drives us home. When I come into the house, my dad is on the phone. There's something about the gentle tone of his voice, the soft look on his face, that makes me wonder if he's talking to her. Mom.

After he hangs up, I ask who it was.

"Just a colleague." He hesitates before adding: "That woman I was, uh, casually dating, she invited me to a dinner party next Wednesday. I told her I'd go."

"Good." I try to sound like I mean it. "That's good," I say.

"How was the beach?" he asks.

"Fun. The water was cold, though."

"Are you hungry? I'll start dinner."

"I'd like to shower first. If you don't mind," I say.

"Of course I don't mind," he says kindly.

These days, we are very kind with each other, my father and I; we are kind and we are careful. So I carefully do not tell him what I truly think about that dinner party. And I carefully do not tell him that I'd hoped it might be Mom on the phone. It was a foolish hope, anyway, since my mother is not supposed to contact us by phone, fax, email, letter, or telegram; in other words, there can be no contact at all. These are the rules as established by Jon and Carlos.

I understand why. There's too much at stake, at least for now, while Carlos Cruz is finishing his exposé about the security program, and my mother assists from afar, working out an explanation of Tim's complicated diagram. Apparently, it's a schematic of the new line of memory keys.

I understand why. But it still hurts.

That night, I'm alone in the kitchen, cleaning up after dinner, when there's a thunderous knocking on the back door. I can't imagine who it could be. Visitors never use the back door. Except once. Five years ago.

I frown. "Who is it?" I call out.

"A secret admirer," the visitor answers in a sexy voice.

I fling open the door. "Why are you here? Is she all right?"

"She's fine. I'm just here to talk business with your dad," says Carlos Cruz.

"Glad you could make time in your busy schedule of getting other people to do your dirty work for you," I say. I'm still angry about how he got Tim in trouble, though I probably shouldn't be—as Tim said, it was his own decision.

Carlos grins. "Yes, my schedule has been busy lately," he says. "Otherwise I'd have come by sooner to see how you're doing. How are you, Lora Mint?"

"I'm fine, but are you sure it's safe for *you* to be here?"

"I took precautions," he says. "Where's Kenneth?"

"He's in the den. Just down the hall. But, wait, Carlos . . ." My voice softens, and I hate that my voice softens, and I hate that I am about to ask him for something, but it's something I really want to know.

"Yes?" He turns back around.

"Do you, I mean, can I ask you . . . I can't stop wondering why my mom went to her sister's that day. How did she know Austin was involved?"

"Jeanette told us that she'd always imagined that her sister visited her at Grand Gardens, but she thought it was a dream or hallucination or something, since her memory was virtually nonexistent at the time. It wasn't until you showed her some family photos that she realized it actually happened."

"Why didn't she tell anyone?"

"You know how your mom is about her privacy."

I grimace. I *do* know. "And why did she wreck the apartment?"

"She had a vague memory of Austin asking the doctors for her old key, so she went to look for it. She knew it was dangerous, but said it was worth the risk if she could get her memories back."

"My mother said that?" I say.

"Your mother said that," he says.

Then Carlos Cruz goes to talk to my dad. He doesn't stay long. When he leaves I'm still in the kitchen, still washing the dishes, still thinking about what he told me. On the one hand, I'm happy that my mother tried to get her memories back. On the other hand, I feel guilty because I've destroyed her chance of getting her memories back. On another other hand, I know none of this really matters.

Because in the end she left anyway.

What I have to remember is that I'll get my chance to fix things with her; we will get our chance to fix things with each other, after Carlos's article is published. It just feels like such a long time to wait, with more guessing about what will happen than any actual certainty. Though I suppose there can never be much certainty about the future.

And in the meantime what will I do? Distribute flyers for the KCO—that anti–Keep Corp activist group? Be a model library clerk? Hang out with Wendy? Make out with Tim? Move away to school and decide what to major in? Eat some ice cream with my dad?

I close my eyes and try to see her as I last saw her, standing in the department store, arm reaching toward me. Her face is a blur, her arm is a blur, the whole memory is a blur. But I still know she's reaching toward me.

We *will* get our chance to fix things with each other.

And in the meantime I'll just wash these dishes, dry these

dishes, then go across the hall to the den, where Dad is sitting in his armchair, watching the evening news, and when he looks up to ask if it's time for ice cream, I will smile and tell him yes. It's time.

Acknowledgments

For their inspiration and wisdom and invaluable guidance, thanks to Kristen Pettit, Sarah Burnes, and Logan Garrison.

For their help in making this book a book, thanks to Elizabeth Lynch, Veronica Ambrose, and Bethany Reis.

For his super photography skills, thanks to Amir Husak.

For their encouragement and insight, thanks to my first readers, Sara Culver and Alina Romo, and to my teachers, Charles Baxter, Aimee Bender, Maria Fitzgerald, and Julie Schumacher.

For their love and support, thanks to my friends and family, especially Mom, Dad, Karina, and Kristen.